SOMEWHERE IN THE BRONX

PJ ENTWISTLE

SOMEWHERE IN THE BRONX

Copyright © 2020 PJ Entwistle.

All rights reserved. No part of this book may be used or reproduced by any means, graphic, electronic, or mechanical, including photocopying, recording, taping or by any information storage retrieval system without the written permission of the author except in the case of brief quotations embodied in critical articles and reviews.

Certain characters in this work are historical figures, and certain events portrayed did take place. However, this is a work of fiction. All of the other characters, names, and events as well as all places, incidents, organizations, and dialogue in this novel are either the products of the author's imagination or are used fictitiously.

iUniverse books may be ordered through booksellers or by contacting:

iUniverse
1663 Liberty Drive
Bloomington, IN 47403
www.iuniverse.com
1-800-Authors (1-800-288-4677)

Because of the dynamic nature of the Internet, any web addresses or links contained in this book may have changed since publication and may no longer be valid. The views expressed in this work are solely those of the author and do not necessarily reflect the views of the publisher, and the publisher hereby disclaims any responsibility for them.

Any people depicted in stock imagery provided by Getty Images are models, and such images are being used for illustrative purposes only.
Certain stock imagery © Getty Images.

ISBN: 978-1-5320-9640-2 (sc)
ISBN: 978-1-5320-9642-6 (hc)
ISBN: 978-1-5320-9641-9 (e)

Library of Congress Control Number: 2020905626

Print information available on the last page.

iUniverse rev. date: 05/18/2020

Dedicated to Lainie, Allen, and Sandy.
Unconditional love always counts.

SPRING 1968
PART I

Oh, heck.
—Toddy Bethany

CHAPTER 1

Oh, heck. My mama, who really is my grandma, said that when you're under thirty, time moves like a waterfall in slow motion; the water never reaches the river. I guess that is true. I was thirteen and sitting in class hoping that Father or Mother Time would start rocking these minutes so I could get out of there. The huge clock over the blackboard was yelling at me that it was 1:00 p.m. and I had two more hours before this purgatory ended. It didn't help that the class of thirty people, mostly girls, was stone-dead quiet of chitchat, making time seem slow as molasses.

Our favorite teacher, Miss Ciotti, gave us an assignment called "If I Ruled the World, the World Would Be …" So these busy bees of teenage hormones were writing away. I heard the pencils racing down the paper, scratching the desks. But despite this, time seemed to be going nowhere.

I was comforted by the fact that it was spring and in two months I would be fourteen; I had survived my thirteenth year living with my mother, Polly. Everything was okay with us until I'd told her on my thirteenth birthday that I was grown and could do anything I wanted to do.

She'd looked at me with those dark whiteless eyes of hers, which could send chills down your spine, and said, "People who think like that don't live long." I didn't know whether she was threatening me or just musing in general.

I finished my assignment and pretended that I was writing. The open windows brought in the smell of leaves and flowers unfurling for spring. The birds began chirping as if they were inviting me to play hooky from school.

My mind began flying with the birds, and for a second I felt free: free from school, free from the tyranny of adults, especially Polly, and free from the nothingness of being under twenty-one. If only I were grown, I'd be as free as those birds.

The PA system from the principal's office began to scratch, signaling that the principal, Mr. Lieberman, would be talking soon. My heart jumped for joy, hoping beyond hope that this ninety-year-old from the previous century with the Victorian look would set us free like Abraham Lincoln and let us go home. I liked his long nineteenth-century face—it made me touch another time.

Mr. Lieberman said, "Boys and girls, the reverend Dr. Martin Luther King Jr. has been assassinated. Class dismissed. God help us all." He left, then the scratchy sound came on the PA system again.

Miss Ciotti, who was writing on the blackboard, spun around to face us with a frightened look on her face. Her eyes were red because of the soon-to-come tears. A piece of chalk fell from her hand, adding more horror to the silence in the room. "Martin Luther King Jr. dead." These words echoed in my head.

A scream came from the middle of the class, fourth row, fifth seat; it was Viola, the girl who had embarrassed us in hygiene class by announcing that she shampooed. braided, and put a beret on her pubic hair. Thank God the boys and girls were in separate hygiene classes or we would have been a laughingstock.

After that, all the girls gave Viola short shrift, avoiding her like the plague. Viola dabbed at the tears on her face then looked in the direction of Miss Ciotti. "Class dismissed. Homework postponed," said Miss Ciotti tearfully. The class moved to the back of the room to get our coats from the long wall closet.

I was drunk with shock, a fuzzy feeling I got when I occasionally siphoned off my mother's blackberry brandy and replaced it with grape juice. It made me feel grown, like a big, important movie star. Polly didn't care about the drinking—she'd always told me if I took a little nip, it was okay. It was better than joining the knucklehead club with the junkies. She added, "The Bible says a little wine is good for the stomach." But she only wanted me to have alcohol on special occasions when she was around and could supervise.

Polly was pissed off when she'd found out I replaced the brandy with grape juice. "Stop acting like you're grown," she'd say to me. All the while I'd be thinking, *But I am grown. The world just doesn't know it.* Socially I wasn't an adult, but mentally I could hold court with any adult. All I needed was freedom and a good job, and then I'd be right on top of them.

The students spilled from the school exits out into the tree-lined streets like ants looking for crumbs. Not only were school and homework postponed, but fights were too. I was supposed to settle a score with a big bully bitch, but I guess everybody was shell-shocked. When I started walking up Barnes Avenue, a mostly residential street lined with one- and two-family houses, the bully bitch paid me no mind even though we were walking side by side in the throng of people. We marched up the avenue quietly, unusual for junior high school chatterboxes looking to announce themselves to the universe.

The scent of our bodies, sweat laced with raging hormones, mixed with the odor of unfurling leaves and the flowers of spring. Our bodies were adult; our minds, wishing for teddy bears. I wanted Polly. I wanted my mother, just as I had that day when President Kennedy was killed. She was a great person to have during emergencies. If you were choking, she'd save you; if you had a fever over 102, she'd bring it down. The many times she'd saved people from choking and high fevers in our family was the stuff of lore.

A voice from the crowd yelled, "If Martin Luther King were white, you'd be crying like mad." I turned around. It was Viola talking to Corinth, a quiet white girl who was cool. Racism had never been a problem in this area, the Williamsbridge section of the Bronx, especially Williamsbridge Junior High School. The teachers treated all the children the same whether they were white or black.

Viola contorted her face into a plug-ugly look. She wasn't ugly; she just had an ugly mouth, talking about "pussy this" and "pussy that" all the time. Pussy was a great topic for girls my age when the adults weren't around, but who in the devil wanted to hear about it all the time? Yeah, Viola.

Sure, all the girls knew about pussy and about getting your cherry busted. All the girls claimed they hadn't; I hadn't. Everyone wore the virgin pin to prove they hadn't had their cherry busted and were still a virgin. It was a silver or gold circular pin worn on your collar or chest. I had a gold one. But give me a break, there were hundreds of girls in Williamsbridge Junior High

School and in my grade who wore the pin. There must have been someone who'd gotten her cherry busted and was lying about it.

As my body ebbed and flowed with this caravan of teenagers, I thought I felt a drop of blood flow into panties—my red dragon, my period. I wasn't due, but I remembered that with the last assassination, I'd gotten my first period. I was only nine years old then.

The first time my mother and I thought it was a fluke—or menarche, as my mother said in medical terms, something that was a one-shot deal. I was too young. But menarches happen to other people, not me. It was a regular period. My body was an adult with the ability to get pregnant. I only wished the world knew this and treated me like one.

My period came regularly after that, like clockwork. I was scared that the other nine-year-old girls in school would find out about it and I'd be outcast and talked about. When I went to the bathroom, I was afraid that someone would hear me placing the pad in the sanitary napkin bin or, worse yet, that someone would be standing on the toilet in the next bathroom stall and peeping at me. I guess like the old folks say, time heals all wounds. That's true in my case, because now with the girls it was a feather in your cap to have your period—it meant you were grown.

The sky opened, and rain rushed from it furiously as though someone had accidentally dropped a cup of water from the clouds. I pulled off the crinkled white leather coat Polly had bought me and put it over my newly permed head that she'd paid for. She always reminded me of all she had done for me when I got out of bounds. It was like a song—really a broken record; a needle kept spinning over the same lyrics. Whenever I got on her nerves, she'd say, "I try my best to put food on the table and give you the best of everything, so you don't want for anything." Yeah, yeah. Harangue, harangue, Polly. I peeked through an opening in my coat and ran the last two blocks to my apartment complex.

My complex was two buildings whose fronts faced one another, instead of 225th Street, where it rested. The building complex had been built five years ago. In fact, I used to play in the empty lot where the two buildings now sat. East Bronx was full of lots when we moved here in 1959 after my father left. It was only three stories high, but it made it up for this width, having twenty apartments on each floor. It was called Eden Rock, even though anyone rarely used that name. We lived on the first floor. Polly had moved us into this building after she finished nursing school. It was a step up because we'd lived in a basement before.

When I reached the glass doors at the front of the building and walked up the six steps to the first floor where I lived, I passed two black men in the hallway who said, "I can't believe Martin Luther King is dead." Polly often said after the March on Washington, "Martin Luther King won't live long because *they're* going to kill him."

And when President Kennedy was assassinated, she'd said, "Anybody helps the people don't live long; *they* kill them." I never questioned her on who *they* were, but I knew it had to be some evil people; this was some boogeyman that my mother touched, felt, and saw but that I didn't. Polly had very few boogeymen because they were afraid of her. But judging from past experience with Polly, *they* were probably the following: Satan and his army of demons, racist people, the US government, and the Soviet Union, or all of the above.

When I opened the door to the apartment, my eight-year-old brother Kevin was sitting on the floor with his huge green soldier men. He was playing with his chocolate mutt, a two-year-old dog named Buck. They were in the living room, the first room you entered when you opened the door. We lived in a large one-bedroom apartment, but the living room was so big that Polly had divided it with a green curtain with bulls on it to make half of it into a bedroom for Kevin. I had a bedroom near the bathroom, and Polly catted in either room because she worked all the time—twelve-hour shifts. And usually she worked nights while we were sleeping. She didn't mind not having a bedroom. She alternated from bed to bed when we were in school.

Polly was in Kevin's room with the open curtain, vacuuming. She was 203 pounds of pure muscle, not an ounce of fat on her body. She built the muscle from all the patients she lifted as a nurse's aide and a nurse. She didn't even bother to look up and acknowledge me, but above the drone of the vacuum cleaner, she said with the natural edge in her voice, "I told you Martin Luther King wouldn't last long. Anytime anyone is for the people, they're only around for a hot second." I nodded then went into my bedroom, hung up my coat, and put my books away.

When I went back into the living room, Polly had stopped vacuuming.

She was sitting in the dining room, which was a little area she had sliced out of the living room and which was large enough to hold a four-chair dining set. She was eating some huge black grapes.

I could see she had something on her mind. I knew that if she wasn't talking, there was something big going on inside her skull. I went and sat down at the table with her. She handed me a grape. Then I remembered I hadn't washed the dishes the night before, and I knew she was going to motormouth me about it.

She looked at me, and we were eye to eye. It was frightening looking into her eyes, and I wasn't the only member of her family who felt that way. She had stared down one of my cousin's abusive boyfriends, and he had left town after the encounter. Her eyes always warned, *You bite me once, I'll bite you twice.* I could tell by the stare that she was unhappy with me. I waited for the volcano to erupt.

"Don't be sending your brother to the store to get Kotex for you anymore. That's a woman's job," said Polly.

"Amen," said Kevin, who was still on the floor with Buck, playing with his soldier men.

I was beginning to feel surrounded; they were teaming up on me like I was prey. My blood was beginning to boil, and I bit my lip to prevent my cup from running over and spilling something silly from my mouth. I tried to take the anger out of my voice. "I paid Kevin."

"The good book says a man can't live by bread alone. Besides, the kids were picking on him about it," said Polly.

"Amen," said Kevin.

"Why are you two always picking on me, riding me? You two are on me like white on rice," I said. "I didn't feel well. That's the reason I sent him to get the Kotex."

"You'd better get used to it. The whole world is sick, full of aches and pains; just don't be mailing yours to anyone else," said Polly. "So stop copping out and take your medicine like everybody else."

I didn't like the tone of this; they sounded too right and were trying to make me look and feel like a chump. To be wrong wasn't too hip, especially around Kevin and Polly. They had an edge; Kevin and my mother were in the lead, and I was at the bottom. All the blood in my body seemed to have left every part of me and landed between my skull. I felt like my head was going to burst. Kevin had that irritating smug look on his face too, and the chocolate-faced dog had its ears up and was looking at me like I was crazy.

"Since everybody is so righteous in this apartment, why didn't you pick me up from school like you did Kevin? You did it when President Kennedy was shot."

"Didn't you tell me on June 25, 1967, that you were grown and could do anything you wanted because you were thirteen?" Something was in Polly's throat, so she coughed. "Surely a grown person wouldn't want their mother to pick them up?"

"You're always on my back."

"You're on your own back," said Polly.

That was it for me; I huffed and puffed, went into my room, and slammed the door. I switched on the knob of the thirteen-inch black-and-white television that had been with us since year one. Then I sat on the bed, hot at both of them for making me feel like a chump. Those two always acted like they were 100 percent right and I was 100 percent wrong about everything.

Kevin was pigeon-toed. Polly treated him special because of that, along with the fact that our father had left us when Kevin was just six weeks old. When he was one, my mother took him to Joint Disease Hospital. The doctor said he had a damaged muscle in each of his feet, and if he didn't walk funny, he wouldn't walk at all. He gave Kevin braces to wear. Kevin screamed and kicked them off every time he wore them. Polly attempted many times to put the braces on him, but she didn't win this fight because she couldn't work and nurse him 24-7. His disability was our secret; no one else paid attention to his walk as far as I know.

It was too early for the news, but because of the shooting of Dr. King, the talking heads were on the screen. The news flashed on Watts—searing white smoke was billowing all over the place as seams of fire egged it on. Then the camera focused on the people, angry and black; some were slinging things into the flames—Molotov cocktails, bricks—to make it bigger as those whose hands were empty went into stores and stripped the shelves bare.

All this terrified me. Was this the end of the world? Was it Armageddon like the brothers preached at the temple? Was this the end? They hadn't done this when President Kennedy died. But maybe it was better this way: teach these people who were bothering black people that instead of shuffling and singing, we shall overcome—give them a dose of their own medicine.

You give your enemies the fist, not the lip. Yeah, the militants were right. "Burn, baby, burn" was what they said ... but violence was wrong.

President Johnson came on the TV with the same sad face that he'd had when the president was shot and he was sworn in as the new president in 1963. I had been scared shitless that day; I was sure the Soviet Union was going to invade the country. As the theater on TV continued to get hot, my mother came into the room, having completely forgotten the argument and moved on as she always did. She sat next to me on the bed.

"This is so terrible," I said.

"It is—the man tried his best," Polly said. "But that is the way of the world. Like the Bible says, unforeseen circumstances befall us all."

"The thought that something can just come and snatch you up is scary."

"You want to go over to Mama's house with Kevin and spend the night when I go to work this evening?" asked Polly.

"No. I'll be okay, Ma," I said.

Mama lived within walking distance, about a half a mile. We used to live together, but Polly and she didn't get along. I sure couldn't go over to her house; it was bar night tonight, when I dressed in one of Polly's wigs and sneaked out while Kevin was asleep to flirt with the men in the bar. It was fun. It made me feel like an adult instead of a kid.

When my mother went to work at night, I did my best to live the adult life until she came back home the next day. The men in the bar were a little tipsy, and they thought I was eighteen instead of thirteen. The darkness, along with the dark human hair wig, covered up my youth, plus my big tits added some years to me—and I always made sure that they were in the men's eye view. I'd shake my boobs and get the jerks all heated and then tell them I was on my period if they wanted to do the hanky-panky.

I was surprised how handy a period could be if you didn't want to be bothered. Besides, I wasn't going to give some man from a gin mill my cherry and forfeit my virgin pin. It would have to be for somebody I loved. If Polly ever found out about bar night, I'd be in trouble.

"I'll call you tonight," she added as she left the room to go to start dinner. It was a bad idea for her to call, even though she did so all the time. I would have to wait till after I'd spoken to her to leave for bar night. *Oh Lord, why can't I be eighteen already?* I wanted Polly to leave fast and go to work so I'd be in charge.

CHAPTER 2

The hours ticked away slowly for me. Finally, at around 5:00 p.m., Polly started her ritual of getting ready for work after having cooked collard greens, ham, corn bread, and pie. We were eating mighty since she'd graduated from practical nursing school two years ago. Still I hid some fruit because Kevin was a jock. He ate anything like he had a bottomless stomach.

Polly did private duty, which consisted of working with one client who hired her from a nurse's registry. She had wanted to return to the city hospital after she finished nursing school, but there was so much envy on the ward about her graduating and moving up from a nurse's aide to a nurse that she decided to leave. I must say, she really was successful; only two people had graduated from the twelve-month nursing program.

I ate dinner with Kevin and Polly, and when I finished I went back into the bedroom and started watching the black-and-white TV again. The riots were in full swing across the country, but I was in the Bronx, and all of this seemed like it was from a different world. Finally they showed a shot of a senator talking to a group of young black people who had just heard MLK had been assassinated. Whatever he said had a calming effect on them. I wanted to be part of the action of this national event, but not the rioting, by saying something meaningful. But who pays attention to a thirteen-year-old kid?

The riots were the badge of honor of the young. It seemed the people I saw throwing Molotov cocktails were young, militant, and ready to kick ass at the drop of a hat. This beat in my heart to get even, to settle a score for MLK, to settle a score for all people who were oppressed. It was wrong, but my heart had two parts—the warrior and the peacemaker. I was conflicted.

Polly banged into the bedroom, bringing her brand of bedlam in the form of noise. She was outfitted like a soldier getting ready to dress for battle: ironing board under one armpit, the iron in the same arm, and her heavenly white uniform draped over her other arm. She had already taken a bath; I'd heard her running the tub water an hour ago. In what seemed like one fell swoop, she set the ironing board on its legs, plugged in the iron, and dropped her uniform on the board and commenced ironing. I waited for her to start talking, which she always did when she was ironing.

"Your brother Kevin," she said with emphasis, because I had an older brother whose nickname was Butch, whose name she usually said as if it were a bad taste in her mouth. She licked her lips and had an *I got you* look on her face as she ironed a stubborn wrinkle on the collar. "He's gung ho on going to basketball camp this summer."

"Is it a day camp or an overnight one?" I asked, taking my role as her sometime confidante seriously.

"It's a sleepover for two weeks in the Poconos in August."

The room went silent as we contemplated eight-year-old Kevin away from home, away from us for the very first time. I don't remember being away from them any day of the week. Kevin was physically active—he won a trophy for swimming—but nowadays you had to be careful where you sent your kids. Polly kind of trusted my input because she sure wasn't going to get any advice from my father; he didn't give a damn. He'd left when Kevin was six weeks old, Butch was twelve, and I was five. I had seen him only once since that time. Kevin had seen him only once in his lifetime; he didn't even know who he was.

"Kevin knows how to swim. It might be good for him to go away," I said. "Like they say, absence makes the heart grow fonder."

"You might be right, but before I make the decision, I have to check out this place," Polly said, "and let them know in a wise way that if something happens to my baby, their ass is mine."

"Yeah, Ma, that's a good idea—be heard."

Sometimes I felt like a human seesaw when I dealt with Polly; one minute I was a dumb thirteen-year-old, and the next I was a grown person as wise as King Solomon. But that's how adults are with kids. She snatched her uniform off the ironing board, sighed as though her troubles were over, draped the uniform on the television, which was filled with faces of troubles in black and white, and folded the ironing board. Then she headed out of the room with the stuff. Yes, Polly would check out these basketball folks; she always checked out anything or anyplace that had to do with her children.

She'd checked out Kevin's nursery school after she asked him how it was one day and he said, "It was fine—they weren't drunk today." Polly slipped over there and reported to me that the only thing that wasn't drunk in the place were the children and the pictures on the wall. She called the board of education on this wayward bunch; they should be grateful she didn't knock them into the middle of next week, she said. She attended all the Open School Weeks for parents, where they sat in the back of the classroom and watched their children as students, and was there any other time when she was needed at school.

Polly came back into the room full of vigor; she had made up her mind: Kevin was going to basketball camp if everything was okay. I was no longer her confidante. She gazed at me with those eyes that looked like a volcano about to erupt.

"I'm sick of your lazy butt. If you eat tonight, you'd better wash dishes."

"But sometimes I forget."

"Stop copping out."

I zipped my lip. I was too emotionally spent for confrontation. I watched Polly get dressed; it was like a self-coronation. She went into the oak chest, a good piece of secondhand furniture, and pulled out two pairs of leftover pantyhose, each with a run in one leg. Then she took scissors and snipped off each raggedy leg. I watched her pull each good leg up her legs as if this was something new, when I had seen her do it thousand of times to make a new pair of pantyhose. Sometimes I think she invented this. Since my father had split, money was always a problem.

Indeed, this was the least noble act of the coronation. She put on her nurse's uniform, a brilliant white dress, fitting it around her slim waist and muscular body as though it were Excalibur. Now she was a daughter of Hippocrates, ready for battle. She strode to the door mirror, made one twirl to scrutinize the outfit, and gave the proceedings a triumphant face by smiling.

Once she was satisfied that the dress had hit the right professional curves, she went into her jewelry box in the chest and pulled out the curio, the medal of the medical profession—the caduceus. It was a twenty-four-karat gold quarter-inch pin consisting of a staff with two snakes wrapped around it and two angel wings jutting from the top. It was part of her nursing school graduation package. She snapped the pin on her left lapel and started grinning. "I'm good to go now," she said.

She completed the self-coronation by putting on her white nurse's cap with matching white shoes and then draping a royal-blue wool cape over her muscular shoulders. After she kissed Kevin and me good night, she strutted out the door proud as a peacock, befitting of a monarch who has recently been crowned.

Once she left, it seemed she'd taken the energy with her. Kevin started getting drowsy; he played some records and fell asleep. Buck hopped in the bed with him and fell asleep. I started nodding off while I was watching television. After a while my pep came back, and I was restless. I tried looking at the black-and-white television, but all that was coming out of the screen was doom. Riots had started throughout the major cities.

The civil rights leaders were calling for calm; the militants were saying, "Burn, baby, burn"; the world was red-hot—on fire. I had to get these people out of my bedroom. I switched the off button on the TV and then turned on the little silver radio on my nightstand, only to be met with more gloom and doom. I switched its knob to the off position.

I wanted to listen to records, but the record player was in the living room next to Kevin's room. I didn't want to wake him and Buck. I went into the kitchen and washed the dishes, knowing Polly would be saying "amen" to my busting suds. When I finished, I felt odd knowing that I had nothing to do but look at the violent scene on TV. I was bored, and it made my body tense up as it always did.

I went to the end of the long kitchen and opened the window. A damp, chilly breeze hugged my face as the perfumed smell of unfurling flowers sweetened my nose. Some birds were singing in the background. As this scene of spring reared its head, the commercial for cigarettes played in my head like a song. "Spring is for lovers," the actor would say with a cigarette dangling out of his mouth.

The phone rang. I ran to the living room to prevent the ringing from waking up Kevin and Buck. It was Polly's 9:00 p.m. call to see if we were all right. After we hung up, I bent down and pulled the telephone cord out of the phone jack in the wall. If she called back, she'd think the dog knocked it out. This way she wouldn't know I was out, and her call wouldn't wake up Kevin and Buck.

I pushed back the curtain to check on Kevin once more before going to get ready to head out the door. Buck and he were both snoring. A tinge of fear came over me. What would happen if Kevin got hurt or drowned at this camp? Would I be blamed? Would my mother go crazy? Now my role as my mother's confidante seemed too risky. I closed the curtain and went into my room. I started getting dressed, pulling an expensive wig of my mother's out of the drawer, along with her makeup kit. I was not allowed to wear makeup and lipstick because I was too young. The girls at school were not allowed to wear it for the same reasons.

I slapped the pageboy wig on my head and adjusted it. After I dashed some foundation and lipstick on my face, I got my blue miniskirt and a light-blue wool sweater from the closet. I had shrunk it with hot water to make it too tight so my tits would explode in the bar and make me look older. I placed my gold virgin pin beneath my clothes and pinned it to my bra because if it were visible, it would make me look too young in the bar. I really didn't know if the adults or even my mother knew the significance of the pin, but I wasn't taking any chances.

I was going to the Blue Sun Bar tonight. It was only two blocks south, on White Plains Road by the number 2 elevated train. I loved the bar. When you went in, everything was blue and you eventually turned blue—it must have been from the skylight. It had a big jukebox with 1940s, 1950s, and 1960s music. I didn't mind listening to Frank Sinatra and then the Temptations in one on the same side of the album. Someone would put coins in the box and you'd hear Sinatra doing a 1940s song, then Lloyd Price singing a turn from the 1950s, then some protest song or ballad from the 1960s on the same coin like by Bob Dylan or James Brown.

I took one last look at Kevin and Buck, who were still in dreamland, and tiptoed out of the apartment. As I was locking the door, the familiar smell of lavender sweetened my nose. I stopped dead in my tracks and turned around, and there was Mama with an "I got you" look on her face. She was standing with my three-year-old cousin Lisa.

"Where are you going with your ma's wig and rouge on?" Mama asked.

"I was just going to get some fresh air."

"You know what Bible verse John 8: 44 says."

I winced. I knew what the Bible scripture said: "The devil is the father of all lies." Mama was reading me loud and clear. I unlocked the door. Bar night had been adjourned. Once we got inside, Mama headed for the kitchen and got whatever was in the refrigerator—in this case ham and collard greens. Mama and Lisa munched as Mama complained about how the food was cooked poorly, but she still scarfed it down.

"Where are you two coming from?" I asked.

"Alexander's," said Mama.

I knew she was coming from Alexander's Department Store on Fordham Road; I'd seen the little bag she carried with the logo on it. She usually came in when the store opened, which was 10:00 a.m., and left when it closed at 9:30 p.m. After all this shopping, she would come out with one cheap thing, even though she had money she had made from her various ventures—renting out her spare room, babysitting, and sewing. Mama stopped chewing, reached into the Alexander's bag that was resting on the floor, and pulled out a gold brooch with four blue stones in it.

"I bought this. It was on sale."

I took the brooch from her, fingered the stones, and confirmed that it wasn't real gold by looking for a Karat seal on its base.

"No, child, it's not gold. I wouldn't buy gold from Alexander's." Mama had a high-pitched voice, which she blamed on having coughed up her tonsils when she was young, and it woke Kevin, so he stuck his head through the curtain and gave everyone a dirty look. She apologized, and Kevin closed the curtain and went back to bed. I studied Mama's face as she chomped down the food. She had thin lips. She looked like none of her four children—no resemblance whatsoever. She was a prisoner of the one-drop rule: if you have more than an eighth of black blood in your veins, you are in the black race—although she looked white.

She was the color of buttermilk, and she had an aquiline nose that some people would have killed for and pencil-thin lips. The only thing that prevented her from passing for white was her crinkly hair. Her daughters thought she was beautiful, but I couldn't see it—but then beauty is in the eye of the beholder as they say. She didn't have any Negroid features, and she really wasn't looking for any. Sometimes I thought she would have worked for the Confederacy during the US Civil War because she seemed to be opposed to militants, MLK, or anything that would improve the Negro's lot. She wanted the status quo to remain the status quo, and she thought that anything looking to transform it was bad. "Look to God's kingdom, not this world," she would say. Perhaps she was just finished with the world. I don't know, but she seemed to be surrounded by strangeness.

Still, I loved her and didn't pay these flaws any mind, the biggest flaw being her repudiation of the civil rights movement. She had more charm than the law would allow, and her stories were funnier than those of any comedian I knew. Her children had flavors in their skin: my mother was pecan-colored; Uncle Philbin, red, the color of paprika; Carey, nutmeg-colored; and Helen, butterscotch. Unlike her, they were all on board for the civil rights movement.

When Mama and Lisa finished eating, Mama washed the dishes. I was thankful that Mama was a compulsive cleaner; it just made less work for me. She and Lisa were going to spend the night on the sofa in the living room. They undressed in my room and got two cheap nightgowns with fading flowers on them from the chest of drawers. After Lisa fell asleep, Mama came back into the dining area where I sat at the table and sat beside me as I silently lamented about missing bar night, scared to death that Polly was going to find out that I was sneaking out dressed in her wig and lipstick. Maybe I could convince Mama not to tell my mother what she'd seen.

Toddy, with world conditions being the way they are, why don't you come back to the temple?" asked Mama. "Just because your mother is excommunicated doesn't mean that you can't return to the house of God. Look what happened to Martin Luther King."

"I thought you didn't care for him?" I asked.

"No, you got it wrong—it's just I believe Jesus is the only one who can give justice to all of humankind," she said, grabbing a big, juicy grape from the bowl. "I want to see him ride on his chariot with fireballs on Broadway. Every man-made government that has ever been has done just what Ecclesiastes 8:9 says-one man ruleth over another to his own hurt."

We giggled, I guess over the image of a chariot on Broadway. A knot formed in my stomach and traveled to every part of my body until it felt like my entire body was entwined. Why did she want to bring up that Polly had been excommunicated, that her name was announced in every temple as an unrepentant fornicator who had to be expelled, though she had only fornicated once with Mr. Allen? But it was my brother Butch who had gotten the ball rolling. He'd come to the house one day and saw Mr. Allen zipping up Polly's dress. To spare Butch the burden of reporting her, Polly confessed.

I remember the day the committee of brothers came to the house for her to confess. I was hiding in our then basement apartment, sucking everything in as my mother confessed to three brothers dressed in fine suits, while we were strangled by poverty because my mother was in nursing school at the time. The leader of these brothers was Mora. After my mother confessed, he asked her one question to seal her fate: "Would you commit this act again?"

I never knew my mother to lie; she was the most honest person I would ever meet. "I don't know," said Polly. My soul cried because I knew it was over.

"You are excommunicated," said Mora. He threw a Bible scripture in to make the procedure legit. The three horsemen of the apocalypse, those who left doom in the house, left as fast as they had come.

My mother dropped on the bed, wailing like a newborn baby. Inside I was weeping. I went into the room and asked her why she said she didn't know if she would commit fornication again. Why she couldn't have told them that she would never do it again? She stopped wailing and sat up on the bed and said, "I have my integrity. I can't lie."

"Your mother would probably follow you back to the temple if you came," said Mama as she grimaced, hiding her pencil-thin lips until all that was left was an angry line on her face where her lips were. "I don't know why they excommunicated your mother; the brothers could have put her on probation. Maybe I could have treated her more kindly."

"You shouldn't blame yourself, Mama," I said.

But I knew Mama and Butch should blame themselves a little. They had dogged my mother the year she went to nursing school; it was one of the reasons she'd fallen into the arms of Mr. Allen. We were starving at the time, and Butch and Mama laughed at Polly for asking for some eggs.

"Well, I'd like to go to the temple, but if my mother finds out that I was sneaking out of the house, I won't be able to go out," I lied, because the only punishment my mother believed in was corporal punishment or fussing you to death. As she often told me, justice should be swift. Mama had that John 8:44 look on her face again. She grinned.

"If that's what it takes to get you to the temple. But remember, this is the only time I'm not going to tell your mother that you were sneaking out."

"Okay, Mama."

"And as for you, my grandbaby, you want to grow up too fast. Why don't you give childhood a chance? You'll miss it once it's gone."

If she only knew how boring and powerless being a kid was, she'd get off my back. But to me, this was a good deal. We decided on the following Sunday to go. My grandmother told me to let my mother know so she could follow me to the temple. Next time I'd make sure to check to see if she went shopping before I went out to bar night again.

There was a funeral for Martin Luther King, and as I had done when President Kennedy was assassinated, I watched on my black-and-white TV as the heavy hitters graced the screen: Senator Robert Kennedy, the King family, movie stars, and all types of international people. This was a nutty world, always killing. My mother lived through World War II; now I had to live through Vietnam and assassinations. They say every war is the war to end all wars, but really it's just a chapter before the next war.

I started working on my mother about going to the temple. She came in one day, and I asked, "Can you pick up the new dress I paid down on at the Kit Kat Boutique? I need it to go to the temple next Sunday." Her face dropped as if she had been punched in the stomach. Now I felt like two cents because I was doing this to save my behind. I wanted to back out of this deal so bad to remove the crestfallen look from Polly's face.

"Who are you going with?" she asked.

"Mama."

"I'll think I'll tag along with you two."

Hot dog—I'd done it. When my mother left for work, I called Mama and told her Polly had made a commitment to go with us to the temple. She thanked and thanked me for my effort; for a second I felt like a wise twenty-one-year-old. I was on cloud nine—I had done what no other adult in the family could do: make Polly follow me to the temple after she'd been excommunicated. A couple of days before we went, she bought Kevin a three-piece suit and I picked up a blue A-line dress from the store after she had paid the rest of the layaway.

CHAPTER 3

At school, things settled back to normal after we had a memorial service for Martin Luther King. By Wednesday, we had forgotten about the horrors of the assassination in school and went through our regular routine: schoolwork, gossip, and schoolwork. Of course, I never discussed anything about bar night with the kids at school; they would have condemned me. But who knows, they might have been doing the same thing and just fronting that they were virgins and innocent when they really shouldn't be wearing their virgin pins.

By the end of the week, the world and my world had settled; it was as though the assassination had never happened. It was a balmy April night when I figured I'd go to the Blue Sun Bar for my bar night. After my mother left for work, I called Mama to keep tabs on where she was so I would not be caught again. Luckily she was home.

After Polly called, I put on the same outfit I'd had on when I was busted by Mama: a tight blue miniskirt and one of Mother's wigs. And I stuck my virgin pin, as if it were a medal, on the right breast inside my bra. I glanced behind the curtain to Kevin's room and saw that he and Buck were in dreamland. I tiptoed out the door.

The streets were bustling with people enjoying the essence of a balmy April evening. My mind began to clear itself of the world's misery as I took in the beauty of the evening: full moon, cloudless skies, perfumed air, and chirping birds. The sky was flawless enough to get a clear view of the constellation of the stars; the Big Dipper was prominent this night—it was a ladle with a handle created by the guy in the sky. My mother had told me this invisible person was named Jehovah, the Creator of the universe. It was a good thing she was going back to the temple; she was a spiritual person. She just had to be. She had told me that when she was a child she prayed to the devil, but only once. As the ladle shimmered like diamonds, I wondered if this was a symbol of luck to reassure me that I was going to have a great night at the Blue Sun Bar.

I didn't know why Mama and Ma were so strict with me. I had heard they used to be humdingers when they were young. At Aunt Helen's house, I would hide under the kitchen table and listen to all the antics they gotten into. Once they'd found out I was under the table, they'd escort me to the children's room. So what was all the fuss about me spreading my wings and tasting a piece of the adult world?

Once I entered the Blue Sun Bar, the smell of perfume, decades-old beer, and cologne flavored the air. Sinatra was belting out a song called "Only the Lonely" from the jukebox. It finished, then the Temptations brought us into the 1960s with the song "Runaway Child, Running Wild." The bar was crowded, and everyone was either paired with somebody, in a trio, or part of a group.

People seemed happy. Some were giggling, blowing clouds of smoke with their cigars or cigarettes between words. I guess the assassination of Martin Luther King in their minds was gone with the wind. That's why I liked bars—everybody seemed like they were having a good time, and I didn't want to miss a good time. And most of all, it made me feel like I was an adult.

I took a seat at the bar instead of at the tables on the side. The bartender, a big woman with gallons of curls on her head, came up to me and eyed me suspiciously as if she knew I was underage. She hesitated then said, "What are you having?"

Before I could say anything, a deep voice said, "She's having me."

I turned to my right, and in the twilight of the darkness was a tall man of medium build with a moderate-sized afro—I assumed he was middle-aged because only middle-aged people and squares wore conservative afros; the kids and the militants wore the big, out-there afros. He reeked of cologne—not a bad smell, but a little overboard in amount.

"What's your name, pretty thang?" he asked, definitely trying to sound hip.

I was so bedazzled that I almost used my real name, but at the last moment I remembered that I always used the name Sharon at the Blue Sun Bar. Different bars, different names. After I told him my name, he said, "I'm Dick Quick."

I dug my teeth into my lip to keep from laughing. If his name really was Dick Quick, he should have changed it; if it wasn't, it was a bad pick of a name. A ditty played in my head. It was my own personal concert that I'd created: *Dick Quick is sick. See quick Dick. Quick Dick, get Spot. Dick Quick hit Jane. Dick Quick bit Spot.*

He started tugging at his pants. Then he pulled a long white rope from his pocket and shook it like a kid with a new penny. When he figured he had my attention, he began lassoing it like the cowboys on TV before they put the grip on a cow or a bull at a rodeo.

"What are you, a magician or a cowboy?" I asked.

"Neither. I'm the guy who won the national Boy Scouts roping competition."

His voice reminded me of my father's devil-may-care, happy-go-lucky tone; once I'd hear his voice, it seemed like the world was golden. Shame on him for having deserted us, for leaving us high and dry as though we were discarded horses in the desert.

Dick Quick folded and tied the long rope into some sort of configuration and then said, "This is a hitching tie so you can hitch your invisible horse." So, he had a sense of humor—easy to flirt with. And he must be easy to say no to if he were to spring the question for sex. He swung the rope, stopped, and untied the knot.

"I'll show you the Dick Quick special." He tied the rope into a new configuration, making what looked like two little nooses on each end of the rope. He gently grabbed hold of each of my hands and slipped each noose on my index fingers. He pulled the nooses until my index fingers were immobilized. "Welcome to the Dick Quick instant index finger lasso handcuffs," he said with a snicker.

I struggled to remove my index fingers from the two nooses, but they stood motionless as if they were embedded in cement. I felt like a complete chump, so I played it cool. We made such a ruckus that we attracted the attention of the big-haired barmaid.

"Dick Quick, take that lasso off that broad and buy some drinks. This isn't a damn rodeo; it's a bar."

"Okay," said Dick Quick.

After he let go of my index fingers, he paid for drinks for us. I ordered a whiskey sour and he a martini. The big-haired barmaid brought the drinks back in a flash and set them in front of us. I took the stemmed goblet drink like the queen bees on the silver screen: Dorothy Dandridge, Bette Davis, Joan Crawford, and Lena Horne—what the crazy Viola would call "bitches who could make a man itch in his pants." I sipped on the drink like those women of class. I was in my element. Even if I was only thirteen, I felt like I was twenty-one and free as a bird.

As I sipped the whiskey sour and he the martini, the overboard cologne smell became sexy. I wondered if I was turning this geyser on. We started to chitchat. I, almost cooing like a baby, trying to sound sexy, told him that I was in my first year at Hunter College—something not true, but something I desired.

He, in turn, in his happy-go-lucky and matter-of-fact tone, which sounded more and more like my father, told me that he was a medical doctor at a hospital. I found that hard to believe because he had too many *dees* and *dems* in his vocabulary. It didn't matter—after the whiskey sour hit my brain, he was Dr. Quick. He played a couple of records on the jukebox, and we did a slow grind dance. By then the sexy feeling had worn off and I felt nothing.

More people started milling in, and the bar became more crowded. I felt packed like sardines in a can. The music now seemed to be spanking my ears, and the whiskey sour had turned from a happy buzz in the head to its namesake, sour, in my stomach, which made me a bit nauseous.

"Come on, baby, let's split; it's too crowded in here," Quick said.

We unlocked from our dancers' embrace, left the crowded dance area, and went to our seats and got our coats.

Once we got outside, the now chilly evening knocked the buzz from the whiskey sour from my head. The sky was cloudy. Gone were the glad tidings of the Big Dipper and the smiling moon. A couple of raindrops fell reluctantly on my coat as if the sky were trying to hold back a tear.

"The car is across the street," he snapped.

"Dr. Quick, I'm surprised at your demeanor," I said.

Despite Quick's change of voice, I still felt like I was twenty-one years old and going out with the man of my dreams. That powerless thirteen-year-old, controlled by the entire adult world, was now a grown woman. This was a step up, but unfortunately it was all in my mind.

The car was a blue Mustang convertible with the top down. Once we got into the car, there was total silence. It grew like a batch of poison ivy: deafening, irritating, echoing silence until it breathed a sound in my ear—an unpleasant one, a louder, deafening, irritating, echoing silence. A shot of fear crossed me as if I had dreamed of the boogeyman and had awakened up in a cold sweat.

I asked about this silence, this change of mood, but Dick Quick ignored me and sped off into the starless night, driving up White Plains Road under the elevated no. 2 train. He was taking me off somewhere; he probably wanted to have sex. I was finding out that what the womenfolk had talked about as I hid under Aunt Helen's table was true—that men were dogs, and that they would fuck a paper bag if they had a chance.

But Dr. Dick Quick was going to get the shock of his life. When he asked for some hot stuff, I was going to tell him I was on my period—the old Bloody Mary. The Bloody Mary routine always sunk these men's ships; they'd retreat like a dog with a limp tail.

Abruptly, the car went from gliding on level road to driving on hilly slopes with raggedy crests. The slopes were so steep that as you went down, it felt like you were falling from the edge of the earth. This could mean only one thing: that we had crossed the Mount Vernon–Bronx border and were in Mount Vernon, a place I really didn't want to be because I didn't know how to maneuver around the county. The streets, the roads, and the landmarks in the county were like Mars to me—unknown.

"Are we going to Mount Vernon?" I asked.

"Damn right," said Dick Quick.

After he navigated one ragged crest of a hill that made us bump around as if we were on a roller coaster and then a very edgy slope, he stopped the car in front of what appeared to be a park or picnic area. A few long-poled lamps illuminated the area. There were picnic benches and tables resting on soon-to-be blades of grass, but the ground was gray and barren from a wicked winter. I sat not saying a word, waiting for Quick to make his next move.

"Get in the back," he said.

"What for?" I asked.

"Dammit, you know what for," he yelled. "I spent twenty dollars for drinks! I'm no charity."

I knew it was coming. Life is like clockwork; it works on a schedule. I wanted the creep to spell it out: to beg, stoop like a subject, just like a kid has to do when they ask an adult for something, and do whatever else would make him look and feel like a fool. How dare he try to play me for a prostitute? I could get twenty dollars from my mother any old time.

"You dames are something else," he said. "I want to fuck."

"But I can't. I'm on my period."

"That's okay. The bloodier, the better," said Dick Quick.

I was flabbergasted; my insides turned inside out just thinking about having sex on my period. This man was really off the charts—he was sick. I felt my insides shaking from fear of this man, but I bucked up, pulled myself together, and regained my nerve. I knew I had to keep him talking until he saw reason—my way.

"You said you were a Christian. Don't you know Leviticus 12:2 says that menstrual blood is unclean and that the person must be quarantined?"

"I don't do the Old Testament," he said. "I follow the New Testament."

Mama would have had a fit if she found out that he followed only one part of the Bible. She'd say that he was contrary. He dug his hands into my shoulders and told me again to get in the back. He had such a tight grip that it hurt. I pulled my body away from it.

"Get your paws off of me," I said.

He didn't say anything. He reached into his pocket and got out his long rope.

"I guess you're going to lasso me," I said.

He draped the rope, now a noose, around my neck and pulled until I couldn't speak. I began kicking and pulling at the rope with my hands. He pulled the rope until I was pitched into darkness, the second time in my life that this had happened. The first was when I was choking on a piece of ham and Polly dug it out of my mouth. In this darkness I saw Polly's favorite constellation, Orion. I wanted to call Polly's name, but Dick Quick's noose was toying with my soul and I was sure I was about to die. For some reason, he released the noose and returned me to his captive den.

"Now get in the back. I don't care if I have to hang you; I'm going to get my twenty dollars' worth."

I was breathless and gasping for air. I couldn't fight—he was too strong. The only one who could kick his ass was Polly, and she wasn't around. Suddenly I felt small and insignificant, younger than my years, as if I had never been born and was meaningless.

"You win," I said.

"Hot dog," he said.

"But first let me go to the bathroom."

"You take off your shoes first," he said, "and do your business out in the bush." He ordered me as if he were a drill sergeant like the ones I'd seen on TV.

I took my shoes off and dropped them on the car floor. I guess he thought I wouldn't run, but I'd run as soon as I opened the door if I could. He went out the door first, then summoned me and pointed for me to squat a few inches from the car while he guarded me. I pretended to pull down my panties, but I didn't pull them down. I squatted and grunted.

"You'd better hold your nose," I said. "I'm going to do the number two." He turned his back to me quickly, like a wounded animal. Once he did that, I bounced up on my feet and ran off into the darkness. I didn't know where I was going; I only knew that it was pitch-black. My footfalls were slowed by the gravel and the debris that cut and bruised the soles of my feet. At first Quick attempted to run after me, but he was too slow, and it was too dark.

He jumped into his car and started circling the area and calling my name. I welcomed the headlights because it was so dark that I couldn't see my body, let alone the direction out of this mess. But I had to hide from him. I used his headlights for some direction to civilization. This was to no avail because the clouds added another layer of darkness.

Quick finally caught up with me, his car but a couple of inches from my crouched, scared body. I wasn't sure if he could see me. I eased out of the crouch I was in and started running, but the car was coming closer and closer. My heart was beating like a drum in my ears.

"Sharon, where are you?" he screamed. "Bring your ass over here."

I was relieved that he couldn't see me. Then I heard something that sounded like a firecracker, and a small ball of fire whizzed by my head. This dope had a gun and was shooting at me. I tried to move my body faster, away from any more gunshots, but my body was spent; my legs were spindly like a rag doll's, and I was thirsty as if there wasn't a drop of water in my body. My feet started burning in pain, raggedy from being shoeless. I gave my body what seemed like the final push and leaped into the darkness.

As I ran, I heard a second pop, and another fireball passed my ear. I fell to the ground. I was exhausted. I heard the car stop and a door slam. I heard footfalls coming in my direction. A chill as frosty as winter was beneath my skin, and I shivered as if I needed a winter coat. Then somehow the back of my mind made me touch death. I had never been to a funeral because no one had ever died in my family, nor did I know of anyone who was a friend who had died, but I saw the dead people stretched out on TV, especially in Westerns.

"Sharon, where are you?" he said softly. "Let me give you your shoes and take you home."

Hell no, I wanted to say, but I didn't want him to find me. My body was in a crouched position again, resting. As his footfalls neared me, I held my breath so he wouldn't hear my labored breathing. In a short time he was going to catch me because my body had given out. I was exhausted. In my heart I called my mother's name, and then I remembered something Mama had told me: "If you are ever in a jam, call on the name of Jehovah."

I looked at the colorless sky, closed my eyes, and began praying. I made a pact with the celestials that if they would get me out of this jam, I'd walk on the narrow road of righteousness. When I opened my eyes, a full moon appeared, along with the constellation Orion—Polly's constellation—four stars in an almost rectangle housing four stars in its width with two stars on its perimeter acting as a tail. The fool was four feet from me. He looked around for me, and when he couldn't find me, he went back to his car, got in, and sped off. When I was sure he was not in the area, I sat up and saw a road leading to somewhere away from the picnic area that was illuminated by Orion and the smiling moon. My mother and the guy in the sky were taking me home.

As I walked up the road, I searched for my shoes, hoping that Quick had thrown them out the window, but no such luck. I was in a nowhere zone, a picnic area surrounded by what looked like forests abutting each side of the road. It seemed to be an area used only in summer; only the ill-intentioned, like a serial killer, would follow this path on a chilly April night. I trotted up the road with renewed vigor and hoped that angels or something mighty was still watching over me.

I saw a beam of headlights coming down the lone road and the sound of gravel being grinded by the wheels of a car. I scooted to the left side of the road to prevent the person(s) in the car from seeing me, because it might be Dick Quick's return, but it was too late—they honked at me. Then my fear turned to resolve. I had celestial allies; if it was Dick Quick, then just as Jehovah had blinded the Philistines at Jericho, this Quick could be made into easy pickings too.

As the car slowed and came in my direction, I could see that it wasn't Quick but the private cab company car that was headquartered on Laconia Avenue in the Bronx, the Fremont. Eureka! I was going to get a ride home. I had ten dollars in my pocket. The car eased to a stop once it reached me; it was a black Chevrolet with the logo of the Fremont on the car door, along the telephone number FA-111-1111. The driver rolled down the window.

"Do you know where McLean Avenue is?" he asked.

"No, I don't. But I'm lost too," I said. "Can I hitch a ride back to the Bronx? I have money."

"Sure, but I have to pick up another fare and drop him off first."

I was sure that being rescued by this cab company was another sign that the celestials were guarding me.

The driver turned on the light in the car, looked me over, then motioned for me to sit in the front on the passenger's side. I could see he was a small man, even though he was sitting. He was the color of cherrywood, and he had lambswool-textured black hair and a neatly trimmed goatee and mustache. He looked like he was in his midtwenties—my kind of guy, not too old or too young. He quickly turned off the light after he'd gotten an eyeful and made a U-turn to drive back up the road.

"What happened to your shoes?" he asked.

"I'm a flower child, a hippie," I said.

I winced in the darkness. I had made a contract with the celestials to go straight, and here I was lying. He got a cigarette off the dashboard and lit it with the hand that wasn't on the steering wheel.

"What's your name?" he asked.

"Toddy," I replied.

"How old are you?"

I was rather taken aback by the lies I'd just told. Two lies in three sentences wouldn't look good to the celestials; it would show them I wasn't serious about bearing the burden of walking the narrow road to righteousness. The celestials understood that I wasn't perfect and that I could slip on the broad road of unrighteousness for a second, but two lying answers to three questions was wallowing in the mire. Yet I had to let him know I wasn't jailbait so he wouldn't kick me out of the car. I decided to ignore his question rather than lie.

His name was Norman. We finally found McLean Street after he'd looked at his Mount Vernon street map. He beat the sharp slopes of the Mount Vernon hills, and I somewhat enjoyed the ride back to civilization. While we were waiting for the passenger to come out of his house on McLean Street, I had a change of heart and was sure that it would please the celestials if I improved my truth score and reduced my lying score.

"By the way, Norman, I'm not a flower child or hippie," I said.

"What were you doing by the park?"

"I can't mention it."

I looked out the closed window and saw the constellation Orion next to the smiling moon; the tail of the constellation twinkled madly as though wagging its finger at me. Were the celestials warning me that if I lied, I'd be in trouble with them? There. See. I didn't have to lie, but this was hard work. I almost had a perfect score.

He didn't say anything else about it. The passenger finally came, a middle-aged man probably in his fifties who let us know by his ignoring us that he lived in this opulent neighborhood and we were just visiting. Strangely enough, the passenger got off at 241st Street and took the very proletarian no. 2 train.

After the bourgeois man left, I got out of the car to get a Coke to quench the thirst I'd developed after this hellish night. When I came back, Norman turned on the light and began studying me again, as I studied him. His eyes were slanted; he had high cheekbones and full lips that looked like the red candy lips you put over your mouth and eat after you get tired of wearing them. In essence, his lips looked sweet and kissable. He couldn't have been any more than five foot three, a couple of inches taller than I. This was good because at least I'd have a fighting chance if he were to go psycho on me like Dick Quick.

"How old did you say you were?" he asked.

A panic came over me. I didn't know what to do. If I told him I was thirteen, he'd know I was jailbait and he'd drop me like a hot potato. If I lied, the celestials wouldn't like it. How could I juggle this and make it okay for everybody?

"How old do you think I am?" I asked.

"I don't know," he said. "How old are you?"

"I'm sixteen."

A rumble of thunder came out of nowhere. It was followed by a flash of lightning, its tail coming directly near my car window. Perhaps the displeasure of the celestials? The rain began coming down in buckets. Norman closed all the windows automatically, revved the engine, and took me home. We exchanged phone numbers before I left the car.

Back at the apartment, when I got undressed and got ready to put my virgin pin back in its box, I kissed it like a good friend; we had made it through the night and Dick Quick with my cherry intact. I was still eligible to wear this glorious pin.

CHAPTER 4

Even though I'd only had three hours of sleep, I dragged myself to school. I left the house before Polly came home from work so she wouldn't see how terrible I looked. I had a fuchsia noose mark around my neck, which I covered with a turtleneck sweater. My feet felt like hot coals were burning them from the nicks I'd gotten by running barefoot. I'd put some peroxide on them after I'd taken a bath, and greased them. Heck, this adult world could be awful, but still it was more exciting than being a kid.

By midday, my body had returned to normal except for the pain from the nicks on my feet. This was the day I was to go with Polly to meet the director of the basketball camp Kevin wanted to go to—a Mr. Bell. I was bubbly and ready to go when I opened the door to the apartment, went near the kitchen, and saw Polly sitting in the dining area at the table looking crestfallen. I went and sat beside her.

"Ma, what's wrong?"

"Your father has filed for divorce."

No big deal. They had been separated for nine years. What kind of torch were these two carrying? They should have divorced sooner. Why linger? He had made no move to get back to her nor she to him. I just had to jolt my mother out of this melancholia and place her back on her throne. I knew several methods to rattle her nerves and served up the best one.

"Royal was ugly anyway."

"Don't you disrespect you father like that," Polly said. "And he's not ugly."

"Of course he's not ugly," I said, "but he's not my type, and he shouldn't be yours either."

"Speaking of types, some man called here looking for you sounding as old as Methuselah."

My heart did a somersault. I'd forgotten to give Norman a time to call when Polly wasn't around. I looked at the black rotary phone on the table near the fruit bowl as if it were a cancer. I knew Polly was waiting for an answer to her nonquestion. My mind was in a panic, and the farthest thing from it was the celestials.

"He said his name is Norman ... a sure baby-maker name if I know one," said Polly. "What do I have to do, put a chastity belt on you? If you get pregnant like I did, you'll have to stop school."

"He's my tutor."

"Some tutor." Polly threw her head back to start her mimicking performance. She brought her hand up to her ear. "Hello, may I speak to Toddy? Tell her Norman called," she said in an exaggerated male voice.

I didn't take kindly to her mocking my kissable little Gingerbread Man. But she kept me in my place by making the international stink sign by having her nose meet her upper lip. When she made that sign, it was like a signal for war—nothing good would come of it. "Just what does this *Norman* tutor?"

"Algebra."

I knew I'd better leave town after this twist of the truth.

She hired an algebra tutor two months ago, a nice girl who looked like she was joining or already had joined a convent. Everything was fine until I came home for our session late with a torn dress and a bloodied nose after having had a fight with one of my so-called friends. She and I had gone by the Bronx River after having made an appointment to settle our disagreement with fisticuffs.

When I came into the apartment, I was a sight. My brother Butch came in and tried to tutor the tutor about algebra. This was envy, to throw a monkey wrench into something that was working. He had no degree to be telling her what to do. He could have gone to college on a scholarship for his music, but he'd turned it down. The tutor never came back.

"You're lying about the tutor and algebra," said Polly.

It was a statement, and I wasn't going to wait around for her to ask me a question. Three lies in a row wouldn't look good to the celestials; it'd look like I was dogging it. Besides, three strikes and I might be out. I raced into my room, slamming the door and locking it behind me. I had to get away from her questions in order to get away from my lies. Polly tried to open the bedroom door then banged in frustration because it was locked.

"Are you lying about this Methuselah or what?" she screamed. "Open up this damn door."

Okay, I was being Pollied. If she got angry enough, she might come through the door like Superman by taking her 203 pounds of fist-muscle body through the door, or she'd jimmy the lock to open the door discreetly. Whatever. She stopped banging on the door, but she was still fussing. She was not cursing, but words that hit hard were coming from her mouth.

I went to the dresser and pulled out a pair of earplugs. I snapped them in my ears, lay on the bed, and waited for the ill wind to blow over. Earplugs should be issued at birth for anyone born into the Cornwallis-West household; they were a fussy bunch. My uncle Philbin once said my mother is a real motormouth—she just can't stop talking.

Polly didn't want me to date, but after prodding from my aunt Helen, she let me go out on a date with a boy named Ronald. She gave him money for the date, thereby making him feel beholden to her. When he brought me home from the movie, I pushed my face toward his, waiting for a smooch, but he looked at me as if he had been shot out of a cannon and just kissed me on my forehead. I didn't care if Polly was my mother; I had news for her: She'd better leave my Gingerbread Man alone. She'd better back up, Mack, with Norman. You hear that, Polly Cornwallis-West Bethany?

She was afraid that I'd get pregnant and have a baby out of wedlock like she had; she'd had my brother Butch when she was fifteen. When she got pregnant, my grandmother was so embarrassed that she moved from a village full of family to New York to save face. Once my mother had the baby, my grandmother wrote to her relatives that she had adopted a baby boy—a lie that was often repeated within southern families at that time when their unmarried daughters had babies.

My father knew nothing of the pregnancy or the baby. He had joined the air force and was stationed in postwar Germany. After he finished a six-year tour, he came back to the States and was informed by Uncle Carey's wife that he had a son named Ronnie. My father met my mother and Ronnie that Friday, and the following Monday they were married. He reenlisted in the air force to support the family. My mother's warning to me about pregnancy was "Don't be left holding the bag."

I remember my father as the handsome man with the eternal smile; I can't remember him frowning once. Of course, once the marriage went south, there were sporadic intervals of arguing between him and my mother. I never knew what was behind the smile, what it meant. Was it pleasure or amusement? But as I got older, I knew the smile meant nothing. It had no authentic meaning; its purpose was to affect the viewer.

But in a way, I guess I slow divorced my father too; I divorced him by forgetting him. I stretched my forgetting over nine years. All his things slowly disappeared—a piece here, a piece there. The first thing to disappear were his gold and silver medals with the colorful ribbons, issued by the air force, that I used to play with. They left without leaving a trail, as though they had been removed by a magician. Perhaps he took them.

The next thing was the rifle box my father had gotten from the base and transformed into a toy box. He didn't paint it; the stamps and stickers remained from its travels: Germany, 1947; Yugoslavia, 1950; and France, 1952. It stayed around long enough for Kevin to use as a toy box. Kevin never knew its history or that it belonged to his father. The only thing that remained was the lime book issued by the army for US soldiers about how to speak German. The pages were brown from age. Sometimes I would look in it and try to learn the language. I hadn't seen it in a while—maybe it had disappeared, too.

The final caravan of the disappearing act was his photographs. A photograph is really a pictorial history of a point of time. Without photos, time becomes timeless. Those pictures of Dad and Polly sitting at a big round table with other couples at the enlisted men's club did a disappearing act. The only picture that was left was one of him in gown and cap graduating from high school—the proverbial school portrait, smiling as usual, with the cap and gown more prominent than the man. So, I detached from the man as I detached from his things.

I unplugged my left earplug to see if the coast was clear from Polly's ill wind. There was a soft knock on the door and then the words, "Toddy, hon, let's get ready to see this camp director, Mr. Bell." Polly had moved on from Royal Bethany and his divorce papers, Norman and the telephone call, and my twisted truth—and most of all, her bout of melancholia. But this was Polly—life is a fight; get up after every battle, dust yourself off, and get back into the ring. As always, she was completely invigorated by our fuss; it was like a shot of B_{12} vitamins, which we got when we went to the doctor.

CHAPTER 5

We marched to P.S. 21 to meet Mr. Bell; the school was down the block from our apartment complex. As we did so, I sneaked a peek at how Kevin was walking, to see if his crippled feet had improved. He walked stiffly, almost like a monster, as though he were trying to prevent himself from falling over. His feet still angled inward. Polly used to tell him, "Boy, straighten your feet!" as she watched how he struggled to walk, but I hadn't heard that line in years. The last words I'd heard about this foot situation from her was that Kevin was pigeon-toed.

Mr. Bell's office was in the gym because he was also a physical education teacher in addition to being a coach, but he wasn't Kevin's teacher—thus my mother had never met him. The room had about twenty boys between the ages of eight and eleven, shooting hoops. They all started yelling "Crunch" when they saw Kevin. Most of the boys knew us, but the boys who didn't looked at us as if they wanted information about us.

"Crunch, is that your mother and sister?" asked one of the boys.

"Yeah, man," said Kevin as if he were the latest movie star. Crunch—so that was his basketball name. I guessed if I could use the name Sharon for bar night, he could use Crunch for his work.

We went to the back, where the offices were, with my mother leading. Polly knocked on the thick oak door. A tall man with green eyes and the same buttermilk hue as my grandmother opened the door. If this was Mr. Bell, I knew he had a hard road to travel with my mother because he was too light-skinned. Polly didn't like light-skinned men; she thought they were too effeminate. Some of this stemmed from her father's trying to prevent her from marrying my dark-complexioned father. Everyone introduced themselves.

"Crunch, you don't have to hang around while I'm talking with your mother," said Mr. Bell.

"Excuse me, Mr. Bell, this is your office, but that's my son. I'll tell my son when to get lost," said Polly.

Mr. Bell's face turned beet red at the perceived breach. Kevin looked embarrassed and started looking back and forth between our mother and Mr. Bell. My mother waved her hand and said, "Go ahead and play with the other kids in the gym."

After Kevin left, we sat in the small room that was definitely too small for Mr. Bell and my Polly's might. I knew that the conversation between the two would be like a dentist pulling teeth. I had a feeling that my mother was going to give him a Polly tongue-lashing and hit below the belt, as my father used to say when he was subjected to that treatment. After everyone had sat down in this sardine can, Polly and I waited for Mr. Bell to begin his pitch.

"Camp Walla Walla is a basketball camp that is in the Poconos and was founded in 1937. We have swimming, paddleball, board games, glee club, and fishing," said Mr. Bell, "but most of the time we train campers in basketball. In fact, some professional basketball players have been to this camp."

"That's fine, but there's more to life than putting a ball in a basket. I don't want my son to grow up singing 'Put de ball in de basket,'" said Polly. "Do you have some classes to keep him up-to-date with his schoolwork?"

"I understand, sis; I get the hint," whispered Mr. Bell, as if he had a secret he was about to share. "Kevin's such an exceptional talent that I'll let him go to the camp for free."

"Your father's shoes were not under my mother's bed. I am not your sister," said Polly as she wagged her index finger at him. "And how dare you imply that I can't afford to pay my child's tuition to your winky-dink camp."

This time Mr. Bell's face turned as green as his eyes that Polly so detested. He looked a sight getting a tongue-lashing from her. I looked at the black rotary phone that sat on a small table along with some funky-looking sneakers, hoping that the phone would ring like the bell in a prizefight does at the beginning and end of each round. Finally his hue returned to buttermilk.

"How dare you come into my office and insult my camp."

"I'm big, bad, and black enough to do it."

"Listen, Mrs. Bethany, I'm only trying to help. Besides, it would help his feet."

"Leave Kevin's feet out of it. He's pigeon-toed."

The phone rang and saved us. Mr. Bell spoke for a few seconds, then hung up.

"I apologize, Mrs. Bethany; I have a meeting with the principal."

He handed her a fresh brochure for Camp Walla Walla from a stack on the table and told her to let him know by the first week in May, which was the next week, if Kevin was going.

After we had filed out the room, Kevin came up to us looking hopeful, but when he saw the look on Mr. Bell's face, he knew that the teacher had gotten a tongue-lashing, and a shameful look came over his face. It always did when Polly went Polly. Mr. Bell said goodbye to Kevin then went to the other side of the gym.

"Ma, am I going to camp?" Kevin asked.

"I haven't decided yet."

Instead of going home, we got on the no. 2 train at East 225th Street to go to Aunt Helen's house in Harlem. She lived in the projects with her four children: two boys and two girls. One of the boys, Harry, was born on the same day and in the same year as Kevin; they called them "cousin brothers" in the family. I and my brother Ronnie, whose nickname is Butch, had a bad history with these projects. I'd never forget the name of these projects—Stephen Forster. Ronnie had broken his kneecap jumping over benches as he raced in the park in the complex. I had been in a fire in Aunt Helen's apartment and was rescued by her friend.

Kevin was so angry that my mother hadn't given him an answer about going to basketball camp that he completely ignored us on the train once we got off and as we walked up 116th Street to Aunt Helen's house. He sulked and pouted like a spoiled little child; in a way, this was a form of cursing at my mother. She in turn ignored him even though she didn't like the behavior.

But he shouldn't have been too surprised; my mother had some earth-shattering noes that she had executed on her children over the years, for example, her no to my father about letting Butch join the Boy Scouts because he had to salute the flag and it was against her religion but not my father's. (I couldn't join PAL for the same reason.) And then Butch couldn't start his own band because she was afraid he'd join the knucklehead club and become a junkie.

Kevin's bad mood changed once we were in front of Aunt Helen's door and the smell of peach cobbler started seeping out from the cracks. Everything cooked in Kitchen University was good. My aunt Helen opened the door; the gray look on her face meant Mama was there stirring the pot and plucking Helen's nerves. Mama seemed to think this was her job.

Helen and my mother were as different as sun and rain. Helen was tall and athletic, but in a feminine way. My mother was short and squat with muscles that seemed as if they would jump out of her skin if you rubbed her the wrong way. In terms of personality, my mother was the person you brought if you were going to a fight; my aunt, the one you brought if you were going to make peace.

Kevin's cousin brother Harry came out of the room. They were very different in appearance. Harry was very lanky, which made Kevin look short for his age, although he wasn't. They gave one another high fives and went to Harry's room. I followed my mother into Kitchen University after we'd given Aunt Helen our coats to hang up.

Mama was sitting at the kitchen table with the Bible open, reading a scripture to Melaka the Marxist. Melaka was an unlikely friend of my aunt Helen; she'd worn an afro and African clothes before it was chic, and her weirdo ideas were the antithesis to my aunt's mainstream ones. Mama was reading 1 Corinthians 13:1–8, about love. She read in the cadence of a person with a third-grade education, which is what she had; she would have never learned to read if she hadn't read the Bible, but it always sounded like a poem when she read it: "Though I speak with the tongues of men and angels, and have not charity, I am become as sounding brass, or a tinkling cymbal."

When she reached the part "Love never fails," she looked up and said, "How's my daughter and granddaughter?" My mother's face looked like one of those sad masks that people wear on Halloween as she sat down at the kitchen table next to Maleka. I left the kitchen; I was too big to hide under the table if the adults started saying things they didn't want the kids to hear.

But I went to what I considered to be an extension of Kitchen University—the living room, which was right next to it. It was better this way; I could hear everything and would not have to be shooed away when they got to the adult topics After Aunt Helen had put up our coats and was headed to the kitchen, she saw me sitting in the living room and said, "Hon, why don't you come into the kitchen with us?"

"I'm okay. I'm looking at television," I said. "Can I use the phone?"

"No you can't," my mother yelled from Kitchen University. "You might call that old man Norman."

"Polly, it's okay if Toddy has a little boyfriend," said Aunt Helen.

"Not if they commit fornication," said Mama.

"Haven't you ever committed fornication?" asked Aunt Helen.

"None of your business," said Mama.

"All I need is for that child to become pregnant," said Polly. "The last thing I need is a little Toddy Bethany running around the house."

The kitchen went silent after the words *fornication* and *pregnancy* had come up. Aunt Helen was not in our faith. She was separated from her husband and had boyfriends whom Mama believed slept overnight. Mama hammered her over the head with this, but if it weren't for this, it would have been for something else.

"Royal filed for divorce," said Polly.

"I'm sorry, Polly. I don't know what happened to you and Royal," said Helen as she began to spoon the peach cobbler from a dish. "You started off so good."

"Don't feel bad, sis. A penis is just a capitalist tool used to colonize the whole earth," said Maleka.

"No it's not. The Bible says no such thing," said Mama. "God made sex so that it could be enjoyed by people in marriage, and sex beats an aspirin any day."

"I want my husband back," said Polly.

"Well, he doesn't want you," said Mama.

"Mama, don't say that to Polly," said Helen. "Don't listen to her, Polly. She's no prayer book."

Kitchen University was on fire. The students were arguing. This was my cue. Now that things were heating up, I figured I'd head to my aunt's bedroom and call Norman to make a date with my Gingerbread Man. I wanted to know if Polly had let the cat out of the bag on any of the information I wanted kept secret, like if she'd told the Gingerbread Man that I was only thirteen instead of sixteen.

I passed Kevin and Harry in the long hallway as they were huffing and puffing to the kitchen to get either something to eat or something to drink. The males in the family avoided Kitchen University at all costs, preferring the living room or bedroom for eating. I went to Klondike and Minnie May's room, where the extension telephone was. I put on a T-shirt of Klondike's because I was warm.

I sat on the bed and dialed the rotary phone; I knew Norman's telephone number by heart. When he picked up the phone, I heard some classical music playing in the background. I was like, *Oh, wow, he must be really smart to listen to that stuff.* I didn't like it myself; it sounded too much like the music the Hitlerites played on the old newsreels about World War II. But I did like the tune "Here Comes the Bride," which was written by one of those classical music people. Opera was worse; it sounded like someone had been inducted into the castrati singers and lost their balls. But Polly liked all music, especially jazz. If you banged two tin cans together, Polly would call it music.

The Gingerbread Man greeted me in a low baritone voice as if his words were coming from the pit of his gut; this sent bells to my ears and put butterflies in my stomach. He sounded like my father for a second. He sure seemed smart like my father, who'd had one year of college. This Gingerbread Man was getting to be more and more appealing. After we exchanged pleasantries, he gave me a left hook.

"I spoke to your mother, and she told me you were thirteen years old," he said, "and said that she didn't approve of you dating at that age. And I agree with her."

My heart fell to my toes. I wanted to go into the kitchen and tell Polly where to go, to mind her business, and to take a long walk on a short pier— and when she got to the end to keep on walking. My cerebrum was working overtime, and it wasn't taking lessons from the celestials. Finally a creative thought came into my head.

"You see, my mother is mentally ill," I lied. "She went crazy three years ago when I was really thirteen, and she hasn't returned."

"I'm sorry to hear that. But I can't take you out until I see some proof like a birth certificate," he said sadly. "A man can get busted for statutory rape for going with a thirteen-year-old girl. Not so much for someone sixteen."

"Sure, I have a birth certificate."

We made a date to meet on Wednesday night, the time I was sure my mother would be at work. As soon as I hung up the phone, guilt and confusion overwhelmed me. I felt bad about having lied and having disappointed the celestials. And where the hell was I going to get a fake birth certificate? I didn't know any of the type of people who could get me one. On second thought, yes I did. Viola.

She was probably skilled in every vice in the world, along with the pubic hair braiding and putting a beret on it. If something was wicked and bad, Viola would know all about it. I had left my address and telephone number book at home with her name in it; I would have to wait till I got home to call her. I'd hold my nose, close my eyes, and call her to get help so I could keep my Gingerbread Man. I'd make up for all these lies and make the celestials proud; I would marry the Gingerbread Man instead of living a life of fornication.

The bell to the front door rang. I was excited because it could be one of my relatives I hadn't seen in a long time, like my uncle Philbin or, least likely to be at my aunt Helen's house because they didn't see eye to eye, Uncle Carey. According to Kitchen University, Uncle Carey and Aunt Helen had bad blood between them that began in childhood; Helen accused Carey of beating her behind, and he accused her of badmouthing him.

I peeped down the hallway to see who it was; it was Uncle Philbin. He was 6'6" and had to stoop to get into the doorless entrance of Kitchen University. But as was the case for most of the men in the family, Kitchen University was taboo for him unless it was an emergency, so Philbin stuck his head in the entrance and left the rest of his body outside.

"Puny, come on in the kitchen," said Aunt Helen, using his nickname.

"No—I'm not going to get tied up in Kitchen University," he said. "I already graduated from high school."

"You watch your step, Philbin," said Mama.

"Well, look here at old Polly." He snickered. "You know they say that the first sign that you have grown up is when you can move away from your mother. When are you girls going to cut the apron strings from Mrs. Sylvannah Cornwallis-West?"

"You shut up, you old fool," said Polly.

I passed Philbin and his long body in the kitchen entrance and gave his paprika-hued face a smile, really tickled and awed to see him, which was the way I felt about my relatives. I entered the kitchen searching for a spot where I could view the Cornwallis-West theater. He smiled at me, and then a shadow came over his face. He placed his long bony hand on my neck.

"Eh, kiddo, what happened to your neck?" he said. "You look like you've been hanged."

All my lies had had a cumulative effect on my brain, and I struggled like a man in the desert searching for water for a new lie, but there was no oasis in the searing heat of thirst and a want of ideas. Puny moved his long, bony body into the kitchen, and I felt real small standing next to him. My mother got up from the chair, then Mama, then Helen, and then Maleka.

They stood over me like they had discovered either a fortune or a new disease. My mother placed one hand on the noose necklace then the other hand on my head to see if I had a fever. Then she put each hand on the sides of my face and rotated my neck to check for any abnormalities.

"Toddy, were you in a fight?" asked Polly. "Who was it? Did they use a rope? Did you win?"

I nodded yes, relieved that the truth had finally come out after a trail of lies. A little voice told my cerebrum, *See, the truth isn't a bad thing.* Everyone in Kitchen University started asking me questions—the questions circled me like a cacophony of sound, moving so fast that my mind couldn't decipher which person was asking what question. I answered the questions then tallied my score:

Who was it? (Answer: Someone I know—an iffy truth; I had just met Dick Quick). Did they use a rope? (Answer: No—a lie. A big fat noose was used.) Did you win? (Answer: Yes—I'm alive; no lie.) Two truths out of three questions wasn't a bad score. My mother reached into her large red handbag and got out a plastic bottle of saline solution. She poured some of it into the palm of her hands and then rubbed it on the noose necklace.

"At least you won," said Mama. "A Cornwallis-West always wins the fight."

"Mama, it's your side of the family, the Calhouns, who are always raising hell," said Uncle Philbin.

"Puny, stop plucking Mama's nerve," said Helen.

Now with Uncle Philbin on the scene, this must have been too much man for Maleka to handle, so she rose from the table, said goodbye, and left. I followed her to the door to lock it, and then I went to the living room to get whatever news was coming out of Kitchen University on the sneak.

I definitely wanted the focus off of me: fewer questions, fewer lies. I listened as Uncle Philbin played the dozens with Mama, Polly, and Helen, chuckling as they hurled insults and jokes at one another, but when Mama was losing, she threw a chicken wing at Philbin. He laughed like a court jester and left.

Eventually, as the visit wound down, the cousin brothers, Kevin and Harry, got into a fight. My mother and Helen unglued them from their pugilistic embrace. These two were like clockwork; they would fight whenever it was about time for one of them to go home. No one ever knew who started the fight or why they were fighting, but it always started an hour or a half hour before one of them went home.

CHAPTER 6

Kevin was tickled pink when he found out that he was going to the basketball camp, courtesy of Kitchen University. The women—Mama, Aunt Helen, and Polly—had decided that Kevin could go to Walla Walla Basketball Camp if Harry could go too. This way they could watch one another's back, which is what they did when they went outside to play together.

My mother called Mr. Bell on Friday and started talking kissy-poo to him; her words were so sugary sweet that they made me nauseous and caused me to blush in embarrassment. It was so abnormal, so un-Polly-like, after she'd given someone a tongue-lashing. I was in my bedroom, brushing Buck's chocolate hair with my door open, when she dialed up Mr. Bell with that kissy-poo shit. She was in the living room on the black phone, feeding old Bell this crock.

"Mr. Bell, I looked over your brochure, and it has a lot of fine things for the children, but is it possible to add some academics?" asked Polly, who then paused to let Mr. Bell speak. "That's a good idea of yours to have the kids write compositions for each activity and have a math class at least once a week," said Polly.

I was surprised that old Bell hadn't swallowed his tongue over this kissy-poo, sugary, damsel-in-waiting Polly, because I was about to swallow mine. Polly made the pitch to Bell about allowing Harry, the cousin brother, to go to this prestigious Walla Walla Basketball Camp in the wilds of the Poconos.

"Thank you, Mr. Bell. I'll send the check for both boys with Kevin on Monday. Mr. Bell, how is security?" she asked with an edgy warning in her voice. "I want the children to come home in one piece."

She ended the conversation invigorated, without a sign of kissy-poo;

she was Polly Deluxe and ready to knock down anything in her way like a bowling ball. Once she hung up the phone, she said, "High yella with the green eyes, you take care of the boys, or your ass is mine."

I think Mr. Bell had swum through the pabulum enough to know that if the cousin brothers were even thinking about drowning or getting injured, he'd better jump in to take their place, because if something happened, he'd better leave town. I finished brushing Buck, gave him a dog biscuit, and sent him on his merry way.

I was sick of people. I wished Polly would go to camp with Kevin so I could have some peace with my Gingerbread Man. I wasn't making her any coffee tonight before she went to work because she'd messed up everything by telling my Gingerbread Man that I was only thirteen years old. Now I had to go to this damn Viola and ask for a fake birth certificate. Polly was making me lie and causing me to have to deal with people I didn't want to deal with.

Polly bounced into my room with that over-the-top energy that was not tolerable for the weak or sleepy and which seemed to suck all the oxygen out of any space she inhabited. I was lying on my bed without an ounce of energy and didn't want to deal with this dynamo.

"It's official—Kevin's going to camp," said Polly.

"That's good," I said.

"Are you able to make me a cup of coffee for work, or are you too tired?"

"Ma, I'll make the coffee."

I hopped off the bed and tailgated her out of the room. She went into the linen closet by the bathroom and got the ironing board as I headed into the kitchen to make her a cup of coffee so she could work this 7:00 p.m. to 7:00 a.m. private-duty shift at this rich white mama's home. I made her coffee and put two teaspoons in another cup for me, so I could be awake to go to this meeting with Viola we had scheduled for the birth certificate. I hid the cup so Polly wouldn't ask me why I was drinking coffee this late and I'd have to lie again; I sure couldn't tell her I was going out after she left.

After Polly left, I sat in the living room drinking coffee. I captured her energy and felt like a raging bull. The curtain to Kevin's room was open. The excitement about going to camp had tired him out, so he devoted only a little time to play with the newly clean and groomed Buck before he fell asleep. Buck, in turn, looked like an orphan at the front of the bed. He hopped off, took a sip of water from his silver bowl, and rejected Kevin by going to my room.

I followed the dog into my room and pulled back the curtain to reveal the open window. It was an awesome night; there wasn't a cloud in the sky. It was jet-black, and the stars were numerous, twinkling like gemstones. The moon sat full-faced within the layers of stars, looking as if it were smiling and saying, "I told you so." I searched the sky for Orion, the Big Dipper, and the Little Dipper constellations, but they were obscured by the layers and layers of stars that looked like they had been rolled like dice to form clusters of stardust. Perhaps the celestials played jacks with the stars and cosmos using the sun or moon as a ball in the game.

I sat at the window for what seemed like a century and waited for Polly to call. Once I got the call, I started rolling. I closed the window, patted Buck on the head, looked in on a sleeping Kevin, got my things, and left. As I walked up 225th Street to Edenwald Projects with the $20 it would cost for this phony birth certificate, I thought this was too beautiful a night to deal with crazy Viola. The streets were full of people, prisoners from a hard winter paroled into this awesome night, abuzz with chatter and vibrant movement.

Then I remembered what Mama had told me—"Don't be eating in strange people's houses." I had heard strange stories about Viola that I didn't want to talk about or think about—they were so icky. I knew one thing: if I were in the desert, the last thing I would want would be a glass of water from Viola. Indeed she was the queen of strangeness—and it had to be more than just braiding her pubic hair and putting a beret on it. There was something there; I just couldn't put my finger on. Perhaps she had lost her cherry and shouldn't be wearing the virgin pin.

As I waddled through the crowd to Edenwald Projects, I looked to see if Mama was in the vicinity. When I reached the twenty-four-building complex, the lights in the apartment windows looked like stars from afar, though not like the stars made by the celestials. Viola lived on the edge of the complex, which was a good thing; I didn't want to go far into the interior because there were rumors of rapes and all sorts of other bad things.

Viola's apartment was on the first floor, which was another plus for me because I didn't want to be using an elevator; I didn't know whom I would meet up with at 9:00 p.m. The door was lime and dirty. Gobs of used bubble gum pocked the surface, and urine reeked from it like a spilled bottle of ammonia stinging my nose. I held my breath, pinched my nose, and prayed that I would only be in this piss palace for a hot second.

When I pressed the bell, a woman opened the door—definitely her mother, because she looked like her—exposing my nose to more urine and another icky smell that could only be described as shit. To make my nose want to leave town, she smelled of new and stale liquor. She was a light-skinned woman, or what my mother would call "high yella," with blue eyes, or what the racist militants would call "the slits of the slave master," and a crop of red hair that needed some shampoo and grooming. She was wearing an old cheap housecoat with unmentionable stains.

She was blank-faced, and her eyes had an otherworldliness to them as if she were in a drunken mirage. She smiled when I told her that I was looking for Viola, and it removed the masklike look from her face. She invited me in with slurred, drunken speech. The house looked like the aftermath of a bombing, everything strewn on the floor: clothes, a couple of mildewed cloth diapers, food, and many other things.

Viola's mother motioned for me to sit on the sofa, covered with junk from different lives: a man's blue tie wrapped around a man's suit, panties of all shapes and sizes, and a truckload of clothes that looked as if they were bored from resting and not being used. She pushed some of the junk to the side and made a spot for me. She asked me if I wanted anything to eat or drink; of course I declined. She went down a long hallway to fetch Viola. I looked around the living room at this eyesore.

The people downtown, the golden ones with all the money and power, would say these poor people in the projects needed help or that the neighborhood was bad. Mama always said, "The neighborhood don't make the people; the people make the neighborhood." That was true. After all, Aunt Helen lived in the projects, and her apartment didn't look like this. She didn't stink, and she was never drunk. Mama also said, "Stink is of the devil, and those who practice being filthy hang with Satan." I guessed I'd find out how demonized these people were.

Viola came into the room, a replica of her mother, wearing what seemed to be the same cheap housecoat with the same unmentionable stains on it. The only thing that separated them from being twins was that Viola was not drunk or light-skinned. She asked me if I wanted anything to eat or drink. At this point I wanted to say "Hell no," but I respectfully declined.

We waddled through the long hallway, filled with boxes and junk, to get to her room. It was an oasis in the desert—clean and flowery-smelling. It had plants and flowers on two stands, and pictures were on the walls—some framed, some not. Viola motioned for me to sit in a gold rocking chair in front of her dresser with a mirror. On the mirror were twelve large berets with hair wrapped around them. It dawned on me that those were the berets she used to braid her pubic hair. At once the room became taboo to me, and my body got clammy as if bugs were crawling up my arm. I knew I had to get the hell out of there as soon as possible.

"Where's the birth certificate?" I asked.

She reached in the dresser drawer, pulled out the birth certificate, and waved it in my face like a flag. I sensed that she was trying to pluck my nerve. I reached in my pocket, pulled out the $20 bill, and began waving it in her face. I was still in my seat; it felt funny as I waved in an upward direction. She looked at the $20 and laughed.

"Before you can get this birth certificate, you have to do one thing."

"And what's that?" I asked.

She went into the bottom drawer of that dresser and pulled out an ugly doll with a wide mouth and eyes of a color only the devil would know, as Mama would say. She pushed it in my face, and I backed up because it didn't smell too good—like someone's unwashed privates.

"Kiss it," she said.

"What?" I asked.

"Kiss the doll if you want the birth certificate."

Then I remembered the whispers that circulated around school after the Baker girl had committed suicide. They said that she'd gone to Viola's house and that Viola had told her to kiss the doll and she had. If it was the same doll, then the Baker girl must have had a cold and couldn't smell how funky it was. After the Baker girl had kissed it, Viola told her she had rubbed her privates on it and then called the girl a butt-kisser. She also spread it around town, and the prissy girls made a fuss about it. They picked on and teased the Baker girl until she couldn't take it anymore, and she hung herself.

Viola threw the doll in my lap, and I threw it on the floor. She yelled again that if I didn't kiss the doll, I couldn't get the birth certificate. My cerebrum was spinning; I couldn't keep up with my thoughts. I was hungry, tired, and thirsty. And now this funky infidel was making waves. I looked in her face. She had a smug grin on it, like she'd stacked a deck of cards and was winning a hand. *Bitch, you haven't won anything.* She laughed again.

My throat was dry, my stomach growled, and the smell from the doll was blocking my nostrils. I wasn't cool breeze anymore; I was edgy. Her laughter now seemed like a roar from a lion.

I went deaf. Words were coming out of her smug, smart-aleck mouth, and I did what I always did when I didn't want to hear anything and didn't have any earplugs: I invented invisible ones and just blanked out her words to protect my ears and mostly to protect myself.

But it wasn't enough. Seeing her smug face and watching her lips move without sound just made my cup runneth over, as the scriptures say. I got out of the chair, tried to snatch the birth certificate out of her hand, and was stymied when she tucked it in between her titties. I balled my hand into a fist and gave her a prizefighter's punch right in the jaw. She folded fast and fell to the floor like a rag doll. I stood over her and waited for her to get up so I could do it again, but she just lay there like a corpse. My cerebrum told me to get the hell out of that apartment.

I got on my knees, grabbed her wrist, and began to check for a pulse when the door swung open. It was her mother, and she mouthed something, then looked at the floor where her daughter was and let out a scream. "What did you do to my daughter?" I was petrified; my knees started to buckle, and my tongue felt like I had swallowed it. I jumped to my feet and ran out of the bedroom, bolting down the long hallway and flying out the door.

When I got to the street, I was nauseous. I tried gagging, but I had the dry heaves, so all that came up was funky air. I gazed at the sky, searching for some beauty to get away from this sickening feeling, but the night sky had become cloudy, so much so that the moon had disappeared beneath the pink clouds. The other celestials like the stars were gone too; all that was left was a weeping sky. Drops of rain fell slowly on me like reluctant tears.

A chill went down my spine as the sight of Viola's prostrate body came into my cerebrum like a headache. Was she dead? Had I killed her? Would I go to jail? Wells of tears streamed down my checks. If I had killed her, it would hurt my family if I went to jail. Several police cars passed me, and my knees began knocking. I was sure the police were looking for me. I didn't know whether to run or go up to them to confess.

When I got home, I checked on Kevin. Buck had decided to get in the bed with him. I soaked my punching hand in some Epsom salts, because it was sore, as I pondered my life as a murderer. The phone rang; I was sure it was the police connecting me to Viola's dead body. My heart stopped as I saw myself wearing prison stripes for the rest of my life. I picked up the phone to take whatever medicine life was about to deal me. It was Viola. I was relieved from head to toe; I wanted to jump up and down and scream hallelujah.

"You creep, my jaw is swollen," said Viola.

"Serves you right, putting that butt lap doll in my face," I said.

"I ought to beat your ass."

"What's stopping you, bitch?" I asked.

"Okay, you little sawed-off runt, the only way you can get that birth certificate is if you kick my ass."

Before we hung up the phone, we made a date to settle our differences after school on Monday at Bronx Park, a big park that started at Gun Hill Road and ended at East 233rd Street. It had playgrounds and acres of greenery. At the edge of the park was a river that ran the length of the grounds. The park had many uses: picnicking, bike riding, running, fighting, and parking on lovers' lane. I used it for everything except a lovers' lane, but I guessed my Gingerbread Man would help come full circle with his juicy lips.

I got a kick out of fighting tall people. Viola was 5'6", and I was 5'1", but I was thick—thick enough to flip her to the ground and beat her behind like she'd stolen something. This was going to be this cow's date with destiny.

I put on my pajamas and hopped into bed. This Gingerbread Man was causing me a lot of problems—lying and fighting. It wasn't the Gingerbread Man's fault; it was Polly's. If she had let me date out in the open, I wouldn't have to creep around like this. But she'd pitch a fit if she found out that the Gingerbread Man was twenty-eight years old. Maybe Mama could give me some ideas about how to change my mother's mind about dating. I drifted to sleep and dreamed about the Gingerbread Man.

CHAPTER 7

I woke up groggy the next morning. I should have felt good because it was Saturday, but I felt really guilty because I'd broken all the pacts with the celestials that I had made when they saved me from Dick Quick. Lying and fighting topped the list of the breached contract. I was stepping out on so many wrong feet that I couldn't keep up with it.

Kevin was awake and stirring in the kitchen. I heard my mother enter the front door; she always came in with a bang. She'd look around the house to see if we had done our chores, primarily the dishes. Kevin was real kissy-poo since he'd been given permission to go to Camp Walla Walla, so he did my chores and anything else to show he was deserving of this privilege.

My mother came into my room, bringing her energy in and disturbing my grogginess to the point that it just made me more tired. She took off her uniform and put it into the clothes hamper in the bathroom. Then she came back into the room, stretched, and sat in the chair by the bed. For someone who'd just done a twelve-hour shift with a sick person, she looked like new money, but that was Polly—eternal energy.

"Remember, we're going to the temple," said Polly. "You know what to expect."

She slipped on a nightgown then went into Kevin's room to sleep on his bed. He'd gotten up early, so he wasn't in the room. Yes, I knew what to expect when we went to the temple. Polly had been completely shunned, and no one in the congregation could speak to her. That was fine with me because I wouldn't speak to them either.

One of those kids had thrown it up in my face at school one day. A tall boy named Hayes who had more name than brains told me that my mother had been thrown out of the Way religion for fornication. I took his long ass and mopped the street with it. Stinking thing, he should have had better sense than to have put my mother's name in his mouth.

His mother couldn't speak to Polly, so she sent one of her no-account relatives who looked like Hayes to complain. He in turn relayed the information to Mama that I had beaten Hayes's behind. She talked to my mother and me about the situation. I told Mama what had happened, and she went back to the Hayeses and told them.

When the controversy was settled, Polly sat me down and reminded me of the protocol and etiquette of fighting: don't start a fight, and don't hit first. Then she asked me if I understood what she'd said. I told her yes, but I still enjoyed beating Hayes's behind. There were many blah-blahs after that, so I went to my room, put in my earplugs while she fussed, and waited till the ill wind blew over. The first thing I was going to do when we got to the temple on Sunday was look up old Hayes.

After Polly finished telling me about what type of reception we would receive at the temple, I perked up and went to Mama's house. She lived on Paulding Avenue, about a twenty-minute walk from our apartment. It was a residential block that began at 213th Street and ended at 241st Street and had mostly private homes, but Mama lived on the second floor of an elevator-less building, in one of the few apartment buildings on the avenue.

When Mama opened the door, she had a piece of a material in her hand of something she was making on the sewing machine. At one time she had been a seamstress, and she could make a mean dress, coat, slipcovers, or anything that could be made with a sewing machine. I followed her into her bedroom, where the sewing machine was. When we passed the French doors to the bedroom, I saw that a new model sewing machine sat on her sewing machine table. She smiled real proud and grabbed the machine by its grip and said, "Meet Brown Betty." This was her new Singer sewing machine, and it was brown. She'd said she was buying a new model. On her bed was a pattern with material on top that had been cut; the material was bone-colored with yellow plaid stripes down it.

She sat at the machine, ginned it by pressing its foot pedal on the floor, and began working on a piece of the pattern. She took her foot off the pedal and said, "I'm making a spring coat," then pressed the pedal of the machine on the floor to make the machine begin singing its drill song, stitching seams into her new creation. She connected one long piece to another then stopped. She went to the bed to get the rest of the pattern to stitch. Once the machine started singing again, I began to pick her brain.

"Mama, how come my mother doesn't want me to date?"

"She's afraid you'll get pregnant like she did when she was fifteen," said Mama, "but I know better. The last thing you want to do is change diapers. You're too lazy. When you used to babysit Lisa, you never changed a diaper."

I was taken aback by being called lazy by her. If Polly said that, as she sometimes did, I'd get all bent out of shape and yell. Mama was the type of person at whom I didn't get angry when she said something like this to me, but I felt hurt at being called lazy by her.

"Why do you say I'm lazy?" I asked. "I work very hard at the things I do."

"Yes, you work hard at what you like, but what you don't like, you don't bother with."

She pointed to the machine then smiled. "You see me working hard on this Brown Betty and the others I've had … but the only thing I like about the whole shebang is that it makes a dress," said Mama. "I'm lazy like you, and I found out that you have to work as hard at the things you don't like. It'll help you do the things you do like."

She pressed the pedal again and sewed another side to the other. She stopped the machine and took a sip of some lemonade from a glass on the sewing table. I spoke before she started the machine again and asked, "Is that why my ma won't let me date, because I might get pregnant and I'm lazy?"

"Those are just some of the reasons. Let's look at the cause. She believes you're immature and can't be trusted," she said. "I think that incident with Karen gave her that impression."

"But that's been almost five years ago!"

"Polly forgives, but she doesn't forget. It was a bad show for you. I think Karen messed it up for you because she was envious because she didn't have a mother and you did."

I put my head in my hands and shook it from side to side. The doorbell rang. Mama got up from her chair and hurried to answer the door.

Karen was my cousin, Uncle Carey's only child. She was eight when her mother died; I was three years old at the time. When my father and mother separated, she started visiting us when we moved to East Bronx. Everything was cool, but she was boy-crazy.

By the time I was nine, she would come to the house on weekends, when my mother was at work, and bring boys with her. Of course, my mother went ballistic and told Karen not to bring any boys into the house if she was not home. I liked my cousin, but I told her not to bring any boys into the house so as to obey my mother. She brought them anyway, and to protect everybody, I didn't tell Polly.

I thought everything would be all right because Karen had blackmailed Kevin by having him try a cigarette, thereby making him culpable in some collective wrongdoing. By Sunday she'd gone home and left Kevin and me with the trouble.

My mother asked me if there had been any boys in the house, and I lied. Kevin lied too, but after we said our prayers, he fessed up and told everything. My mother looked at me with those black eyes, about to explode, and said, "You're cloaking for Karen, you liar. You're supposed to protect your house, not bring it down." I just sat there numb, praying that this bad scene would go away.

The last weekend Karen came up, my mother told Uncle Carey that she didn't want her in the house when she wasn't present. But Karen ignored my mother's directive and brought a nondescript boy into the house. She and I had it out. I told her she was causing trouble by bringing boys into the house then going home after the weekend and leaving me to catch hell about it on Monday morning.

She ignored me, then sent Kevin and me to the store to get snacks. Karen and the boy stayed in the house. By the time we got back, the nondescript boy was butt naked as my grandmother would say. He was in the front room by the front door, sitting on the sofa and dealing a deck of cards on the coffee table. He wore his nakedness like my father wore his air force medals: proud, bold, and unashamed. He brandished his privates, stretching his legs full mast as though they were medals he'd won on a battlefield as I turned away from looking at them.

I dashed into the room and protested. Karen just snickered and said, "We're playing strip poker; you want to play a hand?"

Kevin started crying and said, "This is bad." He was so overwhelmed that he raced to the bedroom in the back of the apartment. Then we heard the keys in the front door and knew it was Polly. Karen and I hustled the nondescript boy into the closet by the front door.

Polly came in and started for the closet. Karen and I blocked the door by placing our backs to it. My mother looked at us as if we had lost our marbles. She used her muscular body to move us in one fell swoop, in a matter of nanoseconds, and opened the door.

The nondescript Mr. Naked popped out of the closet like a jack-in-the-box, a toy that is shaped like a box and you crank the handle on the side and some wild-looking boy pops out. His eyes looked like he was dodging bullets on a battlefield. He cupped his hands and covered his privates as if they were a sin. I looked in my mother's face and felt faint; she looked like she had lost her marbles. The whites in her eyes were gone. What was left were balls blacker than charcoal.

"I'll be damned," she said. I knew that I was in deep trouble because she rarely cursed—and when she did, it meant warfare. The boy couldn't have been over eighteen. Karen was fifteen, and I was a well-developed ten-year-old with breasts. The boy dropped his jaw as if he were about to faint.

"Young man, who are you here to see?" asked Polly.

"I'm here to see Karen, ma'am," he said.

Polly turned to Karen, wagged her finger, and said, "Where are this boy's clothes?" Karen started gagging as if she was going to throw up, then pointed a shaky finger of her shaky body in the direction of the room. My mother steamrolled into the room. I followed her like a frightened kitten while the two lovers stood trembling by the closet. The nondescript boy's clothes had been thrown over a fading brown recliner that my mother had bought at the thrift shop on her nurse's aide salary.

Polly grabbed the clothes, underwear and all, wrapped them in the boy's pea coat, tied the arms over one another until it looked like a sack, hurled the sack to the front door, and went back to the closet where the two lovers stood quaking with fear. Polly opened the apartment door, threw the boy's clothes out, then threw the boy out the door by using her foot and catapulting his butt—and, alas, she grabbed Karen by the collar and tossed her and her coat out the door. She slammed the door shut, turned to me like one of those huge robots in the cartoons, and gave me a dirty look that I will always remember as the dirtiest look she'd ever given me.

Polly was in battle mode, and as always, she went to the phone to testify to folks. Once she got on the phone, the one hanging on the kitchen wall, she began her testimony with the statement: "Toddy and Karen are running a red-light district in here—a real whorehouse. And that Toddy is cloaking for Karen. She don't give a damn about the house." She bent each relative's ear about how low down Karen and I were, taking particular aim at me, until she got tired or the folks would feign that they had to go to the bathroom and said they would call her back. Maybe Mama was right when she said Polly didn't think much about me after that incident.

It was Lisa at the door, my four-year-old second cousin. She came into the bedroom and gave me a kiss. She stayed with Mama all the time, and my cousin Minnie May paid her; it was an arrangement like the one Mama had made with Polly when Butch was born. She sat beside me and asked, "Where's Kevin?" She loved Kevin; he was like a big brother to her. After I told her he was at the park, she went and got her dolls and started playing in the living room.

Mama was at the sewing machine again, stitching another two pieces of her coat together. I was an open book for her counsel and insight. I inched closer to her by moving the chair nearer to the sewing machine as if I wanted to tell her a secret and resumed this conversation about the incident.

"What gets me is that Kevin always told Ma that it was Karen and I who brought the boys to the house," I said, "when it was Karen 100 percent."

"My poor naive granddaughter. Don't you have any guile?" said Mama. "Kevin wants to get rid of you so he can have his mother to himself."

"So this is what I have to look forward to for the rest of my life, someone trying to move me out of my spot so they can have a wider spot?"

"And for your information, your mother was really mad at you about the Karen incident because you took sides with her."

"I didn't. I was trying to calm things down."

"Toddy, the Bible says that you can't serve two masters; if you do, you'll hate one and love the other," said Mama. "You can't love them both when it comes to good and bad."

"So it was a test and I failed it?"

She nodded with an "I told you so" look on her face. I knew what she meant, and the thought of it made me want to cry, so I raised my hand to my face to shield my eyes. I was thankful when Mama got up from the machine and cut the rest of the pattern on the bed so she wouldn't see that I was about to cry.

I didn't want the responsibility of choosing between Karen and my mother; I loved them both. But whom did I love the most? I didn't want to think about it. Of course it had to be Polly. If not, I'd be crazy. I couldn't answer the question. Mama came back to the machine with a new piece of material to sew on the coat, which now had the sleeves attached to the front.

"You see, Toddy, you're immature because making a decision gives you a headache. You don't want the responsibility when you find out what's what," said Mama. "Once you take responsibility for what you do, then you'll be mature, and Polly and everybody else will know it."

"Aunt Helen believes I'm mature enough to date."

"You're smart with books, but you dumb as fungus when it comes to life. You need a little mother wit," said Mama. "Your auntie wants you to end up like her daughters Klondike and Minnie May."

Minnie May, Klondike, and Karen all had babies without marrying. Klondike and Karen gave their babies up for adoption, and Minnie May kept Lisa but really gave her to Mama. Mama got up and closed the French doors so Lisa wouldn't hear her dishing on her mother, aunt, and grandmother. She sat down again and began rethreading the machine needle.

"Use your head. All the girls in the family are betting that you'll get pregnant," she said, "but if they know what I know, they'll put that money in the bank, because you're too lazy to change diapers and you may be too lazy to get pregnant."

"Mama, but how can you say that about Aunt Helen?"

"I can. All those heifers may be in the oldest profession, Klondike, Karen, and Minnie May."

"What's the oldest profession?"

"Prostitution. Hooking. And don't tell me it's impossible. They don't have high school diplomas or a profession like Butch and your mother. Where they get all this money from?" said Mama. "And Minnie May had the nerve to bring some gangster-face man up here the other day ... saying he's a businessman. Yeah, monkey business. And take Mama's advice: give yourself time to grow up. If not, you'll regret it."

It did sound suspicious. Klondike, Minnie May, and Karen always had long bills and expensive clothes, like mink coats. Butch was the only one of all her grandchildren who had graduated from high school. They were either too young like me or had dropped out like the others. The entire concept of them prostituting made my stomach turn.

"Well, your uncle Philbin says that any woman who takes money from a man is a prostitute ... so I guess all women are like that," she said with a sly look on her face.

"Well, Philbin's no prayer book," I countered.

I left her house with many questions on my mind, questions that I didn't want asked and definitely didn't want answered. The old woman had taken my mind for a spin, and unfortunately it was still spinning. I tried erasing these thoughts from my mind by thinking about my Gingerbread Man. I imagined that I kissed his lips—a deep kiss, a French kiss, until my tongue reached his throat and everything tasted like candy, like licorice. But first I would have to beat Viola like she'd stolen something in order to get the fake birth certificate from her. Maybe she would clean up her act and stop giving people sneak butt attacks with the lap doll she wanted everybody to kiss.

CHAPTER 8

The next day was Sunday. All of us were dressed in our Sunday best to go to the temple. Kevin wore a three-piece suit, fingering the pockets of the vest like he was a gangster in one of those crime flicks. I had on a pastel flowery dress befitting the spring, and Polly had on a beautiful red print dress whose vendor swore it was an authentic Gucci, which might have been true because his store was in the Garment District.

But Polly wasn't her energetic, confident self; instead she looked tired, beaten, and unsure. This is what happened when her mind traveled on a dark road; she was ashamed to go to the temple because she had been excommunicated and would be shunned. I was ashamed and hurt that she was ashamed. I wanted to line up all the suckers who had shunned her and beat their asses like they'd stolen something. But this would defeat the purpose of her trying to be reinstated into the community.

Kevin and I followed the beaten, unsure Polly up East 225th Street to the temple on East 228th Street. She fit the part of the village peasant, humbled with rounded shoulders, and her chin arched in the direction of the ground. All she needed now was a couple of shackles and a master following her with a cat-o'-nine tails.

My mother and grandmother hadn't begun life in the Way faith. They were African Methodist Episcopalian, or else Baptist when they couldn't find any other church in their home of Gaffney, North Carolina. My grandmother had become smitten with the faith when a couple who were missionaries named Dixon knocked on her door preaching what they called "the good news of the kingdom."

Mama said the man's face had been disfigured from burns and that his wife was as sweet as sugar. They came in the house, discussed the Bible with Mama, and invited her to go to a Bible study at somebody's home. She was shocked; it was at the home of the meanest, most racist white man in Gaffney. They went into the front entrance of the house, which was not the custom for black people entering a white person's house in the South; it was usually from the side or back entrance.

When she went into the room where the Bible study was being held, Mama was shocked that white and black people were sitting side by side as equals, rather than segregated, learning the Word of God. The blacks weren't saying "Yes, ma'am" and "Yes, sir" in deference to the whites when they spoke and weren't sitting in a different section from the whites as was the custom in the Jim Crow South. And when the whites called one another "brother" and "sister," this cinched the deal for her; she was sure this was the way God wanted it. She began studying regularly with the Dixons after the first Bible study.

Once she'd begun studying the Bible with the Dixons, Mama became more smitten because the religion believed that only a few people were going to heaven and the rest would live on earth everlastingly if they did God's will. But first the Battle of Armageddon must be fought with Satan thrown in the abyss, and then the righteous and unrighteous would be resurrected to the earth to be educated about God's requirements.

After one thousand years, Satan would be released from the abyss and those who followed him would be destroyed. Of Mama's four children, only one, my mother, had followed her into her new religion. Butch had followed my mother into the faith, and I was on the road. But it was hard for me because it was difficult not to fornicate in this day and age, and I had problems with lying. I was still a virgin, still had my cherry, and didn't want to fornicate, but I would sure like to get a hold of the Gingerbread Man.

It was the last day of April, and spring was in full bloom; it wasn't too warm or too cool. When we reached East 228th Street, the temple, located in the middle of the block, had a lot of people standing in front—they were either going to service or coming from the previous one. They were fellowshipping; this was part of the worship. When we reached the throng of people, they stopped talking then turned to one another and started chatting. They were definitely talking about us, particularly about Polly. Hayes came up to us, feet taller than when I'd waxed his ass for talking about my mother.

"Good morning, Sister Bethany," he said.

"Please don't talk to me, Brother. I've been excommunicated," said Polly.

He knew not to speak to my mother; he was just trying to make her feel bad. The dastard turned and greeted me. I hadn't been baptized then excommunicated, so I could be spoken to. I put my nose in the air and ignored him; my motto was that if you didn't talk to my mother, you didn't talk to me. Polly, Kevin, and I pushed past the people and the oak door. Sister Moorhead, a short Jamaican woman, came up to us and began crying. My mother wiped a tear from her eye when the woman started crying, and the two of them departed from one another, unable to speak. We searched for seats in the back to avoid the condemning eyes. We found one empty row in the back as if it had been waiting for us. Kevin looked like a statue, stiff and sphinxlike, as though he were holding back a well of emotions. We plopped our butts into the cold plastic seats.

When the music began, a signal that services were beginning, the throngs of people in little circles dissolved their arcs and went to the plastic seats. We stood up. Kevin and I were on either side of Polly, who opened a pink songbook.

When we started singing, I looked around for Mama. There was no sign of the grand Sylvannah—my grandmother—who made it her business to be late for all scheduled meetings at the temple each week so she could walk to the front for everyone to see what she was wearing.

The temple was brand new. There was no sign of a cross or any idol. The icons found in other houses of worship were considered to be idols and were not used by the Wayans. This religion believed you are supposed to worship the Father in spirit and truth. The song that we were to sing began to play from the record player.

When I was younger, there was a pianist and a big piano in each temple, but the piano had been replaced with records from the Way's headquarters—I guess because there was a shortage of pianists. The worship area consisted of a hall with two hundred or more chairs in two rows, and a platform with a bone-colored banner imprinted with a scripture hanging above the dais. The scripture was used for the entire year and was in all the temples throughout the world. This year's scripture was taken from Revelation 21:4 KJV, which says, "God will wipe every tear from their eyes." The song was inspired by the Bible book of Isaiah and was called "Lord, Here I Am, Take Me."

> They say God is slow.
> Of a God they do not know.
> They persecute our servants true.
> There is no God, so says the fool,
> Who'll go tell them about Armageddon's war.
> Lord, here I am—take, take me.

The low, soothing tempo of the music and the singing seemed to calm my restlessness, and it helped me overcome the public snubbing. I began remembering the good things about the Way: the ministry school, the magazine study, the conventions at Yankee Stadium, and going door to door preaching to all types of people. Yes, I remembered that, and I missed it. I spied my mother, who looked sated and contented, as though she had put on her nurse's uniform and caduceus pin, things that made her feel and look like she was on the top of the world, not like some prostrate person beaten down from the congregation's shunning. And Kevin, still in a sphinxlike pose, was singing with a smile on his face as if his Crunch side had scored in a basketball game. I felt kind of super myself, as if I had my Gingerbread Man in my arms giving me a big fat kiss.

When we were in the middle of the song, Mama rolled in decked out in her newest creation, that yellow plaid jacket, the one she'd been sewing when I visited her, cloaked on her back like a royal robe. She was followed by Lisa in an almost identical coat. Mama pranced in, swinging her yellow leather pocketbook with one hand and holding Lisa's hand with the other, with her nose in the air, the royal equivalent of turning her nose up at her subjects, who in this case were the singing congregation. She went to my mother and nudged her to follow her to the front seats, which further disrupted the flow of the service. We walked down the aisle like a conga line and sat in some seats right in front of the podium after forcing people on the end to stand up to let us get by.

The public talk, called "Faith without Deeds Is as Lifeless as a Corpse," began. It was to be a one-hour sermon about being a good Christian. The announcer came up to the podium and said, "Brother Richard Quincy, an elder in our congregation, will give the talk 'Faith without Deeds Is as Lifeless as a Corpse.'" A tall man with a blue pinstriped suit, white shirt, and red tie, slightly bald with a moderate afro, some hair forcibly patched over the empty spots to hide his baldness, walked on to the stage. He was handsome in a middle-aged sort of way. My mother handed me a Bible so I could go along with the talk when the brother quoted scriptures.

Brother Quincy adjusted the speaker on the podium to suit his tall frame. "Ladies and gentlemen," he began. His voice sounded familiar, so I put on my thinking cap and stretched my cerebrum to try to place the voice, but my mind went blank. I tried to place his face and voice within different scenes from my life, school, the pizza shop I sometimes hung out in, the movies, and maybe Bronx Park where I played, but I drew a blank.

Once he finished giving the hour-long sermon, I was no closer to placing him somewhere in my life than I'd been the first minute he spoke. Maybe it was better that way; he might have seen me doing something bad, which might make it harder for my mother if she wanted to come back to the congregation.

When he walked off the podium, we finished the last song and prayer, and then Elder Richard Quincy came to where we sat during the break between the two meetings. My mother blushed as though he were my father; she'd gotten the hots for the elder. I guess he had on some cologne that smelled familiar. He spoke to my mother because he was the only one who could; he was an elder, and only elders and family were allowed to speak to the excommunicated in the congregation. He shook my mother's hand, then Kevin's, then mine. His hand felt clammy and gargoyle-like, like maybe Godzilla or King Kong would have that kind of texture of skin or grip, but his touch felt familiar too.

"I'm Brother Richard Quincy. Welcome. So glad you came to the meeting today," he said. "If there is anything I can do to help, feel free to contact me." He waited for some response from my mother, who gave him a too-humble thank-you. Then he smiled, shook all of our hands again, and went to his seat as the second part of the meeting was beginning. After the meeting, Brother Quincy waved and smiled at us as we left. Mama and Lisa trailed behind us as we went out of the oak doors of the temple.

Once we were outside in the spring air, we formed a conga line, Polly leading as we headed to our house to eat, but really to have a yak-it-up. The flowers were abloom anew; they somehow had invented a new scent, a new spirit, to go with the spiritual food we had received at the temple. My mother had returned to her sure-footed, caduceus-wearing Polly, bouncing on the sidewalk as if she ruled the world. Her zest seemed to be contagious; I followed her with new pep—and, lo and behold, Kevin seemed to have been cured of his pigeon toes.

When we got home, my mother heated the collard greens, corn bread, ham, and sweet potatoes until the house smelled like a southern kitchen in North Carolina. We ate, laughing until our insides shook like volcanoes. Everyone seemed to be on a natural high—a pink cloud from Sunday service. Maybe that was part of the celestials' job, to keep people on a natural high.

Our stomachs became bloated from the Sunday eats, and our bodies looked like a replica of Santa Claus with our pot bellies poking out of our clothes. Kevin and Lisa fell asleep on the carpeted floor in Kevin's room. I placed pillows under their heads and covered them with a sheet. After that, Mama and I sat on the sofa, resting our heads on the back end and poking out our stomachs to stretch the bloated muscles. Polly sat in the dining area not too far from the sofa.

"I'm going to ask to be reinstated to the congregation," said Polly.

Mama lifted her head from the back of the sofa, tucking in her stomach as her eyes welled with tears. "Do it, Polly. Come back," said Mama.

"Why should she, after the way they treated her?" I asked.

"Toddy, why don't you forgive and forget? I deserved to be disfellowshipped," said Polly. "I knew what I was getting into."

My mother went into the kitchen, brought back a crystal candy dish with some after-dinner mints in it, gave us some, and went back to the dining area. We munched down on the candies and belched.

"Who is this Brother Richard Quincy? He's handsome," asked Polly.

My grandmother gave her a short biography of the man. He was born in Alabama and had been raised there. He joined the religion when he was twenty, he had divorced because his wife committed adultery (the only thing that could dissolve a marriage in the eyes of the faith other than death), and he was a social worker. After the biography, Mama had a faraway look in her eyes as if she had layers of doubt in her brain. "But there's something I can't put my finger on about the brother."

Yes. And I sure wanted to know where I'd heard his voice before. I'd never been in Alabama. My mother looked like a love-smitten lovebird. I knew this brother could easily take the place of my father. My mother was still young, thirty-six, though that was old in my book.

I belched, too loud for comfort. The good food and good cheer turned sour in my mouth and stomach when I remembered that I had to kick Viola's butt tomorrow. Yeah, what a Christian: go to church on Sunday, go to war on Monday. Hypocrite. Hypocrite. The last type of Christian I wanted to be. We chatted until it became dark, then Mama woke Lisa and they took a cab home.

After they left, I got in bed. The sheets smelled as sweet as those April flowers that had tickled my nose after we left the temple. Polly put on an album: *Song for My Father* by Horace Silver—it was jazz, an instrumental without lyrics, mostly piano. If I could put words to it, what would I say to my father? My mind went blank, and I fell asleep. I dreamed about my father and the white and pink Pontiac he had. The picture in the dream was of Kevin, Ronnie, Mother, and me being driven to the carnival on a hot August day. Oh, what a dream.

SPRING 1968
PART II

Being a kid ain't cool.
—Toddy Bethany

CHAPTER 9

The next morning when I woke up to go to school, the drums of war were banging in my head like a scene from a movie about a gladiator fighting in the arena; this battle cry made me energetic and frightened at the same time. I had to beat Viola's ass to get the birth certificate to go on a date with my Gingerbread Man. It was all too complicated. A cloud of guilt rested on my shoulders because I knew the celestials wouldn't think favorably of my being violent unless my life was in danger or I was a parent chastising my child. I had broken the pact with them many times since they saved me from Dick Quick. Ah, but what the heck? What could I do but what I did? I couldn't back down now; I'd be the laughingstock at school.

My mother left for work on the 7:00 a.m. shift, so I didn't have to bump into her; she would finish the shift at 7:00 p.m. This would be great for me because she would not see me beat up and banged up if this was so. She also wouldn't see me packing my war dress: sneakers, sweatpants, and (just in case I needed them) brass knuckles—one of the crumbs my father had left when he disappeared. I packed my war dress into a tote bag, placing fruit over the top to conceal the contents; all of the items were taboo at school. We had a dress code: no sneakers (except in gym), and only skirts or dresses for girls and pants for boys. It wasn't like anyone checked your bags, but I just didn't want to arouse any suspicion. I needed to lie low because if things got too hot for me at school, they would call Polly. All the teachers knew Polly. The last thing I needed was a charcoal-eyed Polly reading me the law about what I had done or what I should have done.

As I walked to school, I prayed for rain, but I was disappointed when the sun seemed to be thumbing its nose at my desire by shining like it was

August instead of the first of May. When I got to school, my three girls were there, ready to supervise the fight so that none of Viola's friends would jump in and finish me off. I was kind of scared that I had lost my nerve, that I really had no stomach to fight now. If this was so, there was a possibility that I could get beaten up.

The three girls who were in my corner were my maids-in-waiting for the battle. I guess I called them that because it reminded me of medieval times when there were knights and ladies. My three backups were Rene Wilkins, a tall, red-skinned, freckle-faced girl with red crinkly hair; Marion Logan, a medium-height dark-skinned girl with crinkly long hair; and Virginia Baily, a short, light-skinned girl with blonde crinkly hair. These were my bodyguards to keep the fight honest so no Viola sympathizers would jump me if I was beating her ass. They all had fathers and they owned houses—a step above me. I didn't resent them, but I sometimes felt that I wasn't worthy of their friendship.

Viola in turn had three maids-in-waiting for the battle, and they were the school lowlifes: Rachel Zack, a tall, light-skinned girl who was afraid of baths and a bar of soap, so much so that the kids told the assistant principal in grade school that she smelled so bad that they couldn't concentrate in class; Beth Fenster, of medium height, who people said would have sex at the drop of a hat even though she wore her virgin pin as if she were as pure as the first snow; and Mary Barker, tall, peach-colored, with black hair, who acted as if a bottle of liquor wasn't safe in New York State.

When I was in the second-period class with all the principals in my war party, still praying for rain from the shiny skies, I wrote a kite in my notebook to Rene Wilkins to try to stop this fight. It read: "Ask Viola if she would take $40 for the birth certificate and we can call it a day. Make love, not war, as they say nowadays."

I tore the letter out of my notebook, folded it into a kite, and printed Rene Wilkins's name on it, and when the teacher turned to write on the board—in this case, the most disliked Miss Lederen—I propelled the kite to the first row by pressing the folds on it and throwing it in the direction of where my maid-in-waiting sat. Peaches Milk picked it up and gave it to Rene Wilkins.

I waited with bated breath for the reply from this lengthy process; Rene would have to write to one or more of Viola's maids-in-waiting, who in turn would have to write and wait for an answer back, and then it would be sent to Rene, who in turn would send the answer back to me. As I waited for the process to run its course, I wondered if this go-between bullshit went on during the First World War, the Second World War, and the Vietnam War. I was a history buff and liked to see newsreels about all the wars.

After what seemed like hours, Miss Lederen turned her back and started writing on the board again. A kite flew in my direction and landed right on my notebook. It was big and fat, more like an airplane than a kite, if you could call it that. I opened it and saw it had three letters inside. The first one was from Rene Wilkins, and it read: "They said no; see the attached. Rene."

Disappointed, I balled up the letter and put it on my desk. The second letter read: "Viola said no, and she said she's dying to get to Bethany's ass. Rachel." The third letter was from my Goliath-in-waiting Viola: "I want Bethany's ass like I want a million dollars. I'm gonna beat her ass till I'm satisfied."

My wait for peace was over; the war was to begin. I felt my father's brass knuckles in my bra; they were taboo for fighting by the girls, but if push came to shove, I'd use them on Viola like a razor.

The lunch bell rang, and I headed to the cafeteria. In the hallway a couple of girls asked me if I was fighting Viola. I guess the word was out. It had probably come from Viola's big mouth that she couldn't keep shut.

My maids-in-waiting were seated at a table with their meals when I entered the cafeteria; they waved to let me know where they were seated. I got on the chow line and filled my tray with french fries, a hamburger, and a thick piece of chocolate layer cake. Just as I was about to leave, someone whispered in my ear, "Bitch, your ass is mine." I turned around and saw it was my personal Satan—Viola.

"We'll see about that, Miss Skunk," I said. I quickly walked up to the cashier, paid, and then went to where my maids-in-waiting were seated.

They sat looking erudite and carefree, their faces hidden behind pairs of pilot glasses. If you wore those glasses, you were hip. But it was a phony pose because if they had an unexpected blast of reality, they'd fold like a cheap camera. Their attitude made me feel cool. I sat beside them without a care in the world—like I had it all together. It was as phony as their poses.

"Remember, Bethany, we can't fight Stink Cakes for you," said Rene Wilkins.

"Yeah, Bethany. And what are you doing going to the projects? You know only lowlifes live there," said Virginia Baily.

"The only time you're supposed to see the projects is when you see them on television, not in person," said Marion Logan.

"Yeah, you know how it is," I said, "sometimes you have to cross over to the other side."

I stabbed a fork into a french fry. I wanted to say that not all people who lived in the projects were bad like Stink Cakes, that my aunt Helen lived in the projects, that my uncle Carey once had and now he owned a house, but I didn't say anything.

After lunch, my mind continued to be outside of class, but this was always the case. It wasn't that I didn't have the ability—I scored high on achievement and aptitude tests. It was that my brain was rarely in school except when the course was something I really liked. Besides, it wasn't cool to sit in a chair for eight hours.

By the time the bell rang to end the school day, it seemed that the entire school knew about Viola's and my war. I went into the girls' bathroom and changed into my sweat suit and sneakers. When I and my maids-in-waiting went outside, Viola was waiting in a pink sweat suit with her maids-in-waiting. They looked mean. And then I remembered they were from the projects, too; they seemed to have a poor, stinky look to them with unkempt hair and wrinkled clothes—like I used to look like before my mother went to nursing school. To me, just to look at them felt like the sound of chalk screeching on the blackboard. I think they knew their diminished social status because they followed behind us like lowly dogs as we walked to Bronx Park.

When we reached the main roads, White Plains Road and Gun Hill Road, a great crowd had followed us to see the carnival we were about to perform. We were the new television show, better than *Bewitched* or *Batman*. All of us crossed the boulevard that connects White Plains Road and Gun Hill Road as if we were marching in a parade.

Once we reached Bronx Park, the war parties settled on a slope of a hill, then both sets of maids-in-waiting stood at the side of their respective charge. The leader of each group would set and maintain the tone of the fight. In my corner was Rene Wilkins, and in Viola's was Rachel Zack. Viola and I stood about two feet apart as we gazed at one another with contempt.

My face contorted into a mean girl look as demonic as hers. I looked up at the sky, flawless and blue, looking like candy, good enough to eat. The celestials could see me, and I'm sure they didn't like what they saw. I the hypocrite. Me the hypocrite.

"Bethany, get the show on the road," said Rene Wilkins.

"Weeks, this is no kissy-feely," said Rachael Zack to Viola.

The crowd started tut-tutting its discontent. I'd seen instances in other fights when some of the crowd turned on the combatants, so I stepped closer to Viola to let the mob know I meant business. Her ass smelled like a cacophony of the odors in her house; my nose began to water from the stink. I rubbed my nose, then she caught my jaw with a fist. I wobbled and started falling backward, but I steadied my feet before I fell and was able to hoist my body up.

Once I was steady, I socked her in the mouth, and then we grabbed hold of one another and started wrestling. She started biting my shoulder, and I started pulling her hair, while at the same time I had wrapped my right leg around her left leg, trying to bring her to the ground so I could manage her size because she was taller than I. But the Bethany trip that I'd used many times on these humongous amazon women to cut them down to size wasn't working because she had locked her knee so it wouldn't bend; it was like wrapping my leg around a log.

Then she really hit below the belt—she bit my left nipple. It was the worst pain I had ever experienced. I bent my knee and pushed it into her stomach, and she catapulted off me. I screamed, "This bitch has gone titty city on me."

"What do you expect? All's fair in love and war," said my maid-in-waiting Virginia Baily.

The crowd began grumbling. I looked at the people, and they looked like a crowd who had gone to a bad movie and were ready to throw tomatoes, or tar and feather the fighters, or run the actors out of town. This was not too good; the natives were getting restless.

"Somebody is going to finish this fight and win," screamed a blond boy, "or I'm going to come in and do both."

I hung my head low, and then Viola and I took the cue and started fighting like cats and dogs again. I gave up on the trip method and just started fighting and dragging Viola in the direction of the river. I didn't know if she was aware that I was dragging her in that direction, but she was flailing away at me as we held on to one another's bodies as if they were anchors. In a matter of seconds, I pulled her down the hill, flailing at her as she was at me, onto the paved road, and down the narrow embankment. Once we were at the river, I took my foot and kicked her into the water.

She tumbled into the murky, deep Bronx River, creating a splash as she screamed. Her pink sweat suit, brown from the dirty river, clung to her body like a sea diver's suit, making her look like a pink penguin. She waddled in the waist-deep water, cursing at her predicament.

The crowd began cheering and clapping. One of Viola's maids-in-waiting got a branch and started to fish her out of the shallow river. Then another handed me the birth certificate, and I felt like I had graduated from the school of hard knocks. My maid-in-waiting Rene Wilkins slapped me on the back and said, "Right on, Bethany."

Polly wasn't home when I reached the apartment. I was glad of this because I didn't want her to see the blood on my shirt and know I had been in a fight. The whole process left me feeling like a class-A hypocrite; I'd gone to church on Sunday, and here I was Attila the Hun on Monday. I looked at my face in the mirror; there were a couple of scratches here and there, but nothing to write home to Mother about.

The next day in school I found out, much to my surprise and dismay, that I had become a school celebrity. This was bad news because the publicity could get into the hands of the adults and there could be backlash. The folks even made a ditty about me and went about the day singing it when they could: "Toddy went rat-a-tat-tat and got an itch to throw the witch/bitch into the river. Hardee-ho, hardee-ho, that Viola witch/bitch had to go."

The *witch* word, they used inside of school so they wouldn't get into trouble; the *bitch*, outside of school where they could get away with it. Despite this, the only thing I thought about after all the hubbub was my Gingerbread Man. When Wednesday finally came, butterflies filled my stomach and goose bumps pocked my skin; I was overly thrilled.

CHAPTER 10

After my mother went to work and she called me, I quickly called the cab station where the Gingerbread Man worked, asked for his cab number, which was 56, and told them to tell him it was Miss Bethany, sounding as sexy and adult as I could on the phone.

When the Gingerbread Man called me back, he told me he was in front of my building on the pay phone, sounding very male with his baritone voice. I went out to meet him in a red velour jumpsuit and a black leather jacket. I had stuffed the very official-looking birth certificate in my pocket. And I have to admit that Viola had done a good job, all the way down to the state seal at the bottom.

Once I got into the car, the Gingerbread Man said, "Hello, beautiful." My heart became full. This was the first time in a long time that any man had told me I was beautiful. My father used to do it all the time when he lived with us, but it somehow seemed more worthwhile when a man unrelated to me said it. The women in the family always said I was pretty —maybe once in a while beautiful—but it always seemed they were forcing it as if it were awful-tasting medicine.

I pulled the birth certificate out of my pocket and handed it to him. He was playing classical music on the car radio, and images of World War II played in my cerebrum like a migraine headache. He smelled as if he had just bathed, his black lambswool-looking hair freshly groomed, as was his goatee. In my opinion he looked good enough to eat. He was fly, the girls would say at school.

"So you were born June 29, 1951. You have a birthday coming up," he said.

"When is your birthday? I remember you told me you were twenty-eight," I said.

"I was born May eighth."

Well, I'll be a son of a gun. He was born the same day as the cousin brothers. I told him about them, and he seemed to find it fascinating, like everyone else did, that both were born on the same day. He revved the engine, and we hit the road.

As we rode up 228th Street to pick up a fare, he pointed to a big house that looked like a mansion. It was red and had two Greek columns on either side; it must have been three stories. In the moonlight and on this starry night, it looked more ostentatious than it was.

"That's where I used to live ten years ago," he said.

He stopped three doors down from the house. The fare—a woman with a sleeping baby in one of those hand carriers—got in the back. She was going to Manhattan, 125th Street. She could have been going to Mars; I didn't care. I liked to ride around in cars ever since I'd taken the first ride in my father's pink and white Pontiac. Once we dropped the fare off at 125th Street, Norman bought us some fish and chips. We ate it in the car with the never-ending classical music that was playing on the car radio.

"You like classical music?" he asked.

"No, it sounds like Hitler music," I said.

"You just don't understand it—it has a lot of history to it that has nothing to do with Hitler," he said. "Would you like me to take you to Lincoln Center? There's a classical concert playing there next week."

"Yes, of course."

I wanted to bite my tongue for having made fun of something he loved, but the truth had slipped out; it almost always did when I was with him. Perhaps being around him would keep me on the straight and narrow road of always telling the truth. It certainly seemed that way. He put down the plate of chips and turned to an opera station, of all things. It sounded like the singers had lost their balls. As the singer belted out the aria, the sound made me want to go hide under a rock.

"I guess you don't think much of opera either," he said.

"No."

"You don't have to tell me what it reminds you of."

We laughed. Once we'd finished eating, he picked up a couple more fares. After he finished dropping off the fares and the car was empty, he parked a couple of blocks from my house. I was sure he was going to kiss me. I was looking forward to it.

"It's midnight. Don't you have to go to school this morning?" he asked.

"Yes, I do."

He started the engine, drove up to the front of my apartment building, and parked. I waited and hoped for a kiss, and when I figured I wasn't going to get one, I kissed him right on his juicy lips and hurried out the door. He stuck his head out the window.

"You sucker-punched me," he said.

"You asked for it," I said.

Sure, I went to sleep and school the next day, but the only thing that stayed in my head was the Gingerbread Man: his clean, soapy smell, his neatly trimmed goatee, his thick candy lips, and that baritone voice that sent chills up my spine and made my toes curl. I was on a pink cloud and enjoying every minute of it. This was love; it just had to be.

CHAPTER 11

But Polly didn't see it that way. When I came home from school, she was waiting for me in full battle regalia: taut muscles ready to explode in every part of her body, black eyes that had swallowed the whites, a grimace that could make the dead shiver, and an angry look on her face. She waited patiently for me to hang up my coat and put away my books before she started haranguing me. I sat at the dining room table like one of the instructors at Kitchen University and waited for the trial to begin.

"Mr. Weiner called and said you threw a girl into the Bronx River."

"She started the fight first," I said.

"You've been getting in a lot of fights lately," said Polly. "First that noose-looking scar around your neck, and now this. Why don't you try praying?"

Mr. Weiner was the guidance counselor at school, and when he called, it was always bad news. A tear trickled down my face. I had been caught. The empress had lost her clothes. My mother was now sitting right in front of me at the dining room table, watching and deciphering every inch of my face. Uncle Philbin always said she was psychic and could read people's thoughts; I knew she could read mine. He also said she was a jinx.

"Let me tell you one thing, Toddy Bethany: I'm going to get back into the congregation," said Polly. "I've asked to be reinstated to the community. The brothers will be here Saturday."

"That's good, Ma."

"Huh. Now that we're coming back into the fold," said Polly, "I don't want you bringing reproach upon the organization's name with your bad behavior."

Polly had said a mouthful. The last thing I wanted to do was give the celestials bad publicity; it would be adding insult to injury. I had enough to contend with, with my nonstop lying. I didn't want some nonbeliever to be going around saying, "The Wayans are this, the Wayans are that." My heart folded over from the weight of the responsibility I held for making the celestials shine.

"Look, I tried to move you on up by going to nursing school," Polly said, sighing, "but if you want to wallow in the mire—phooey, you even outdo Adam and Eve in badness."

At that, I huffed out of the dining area, went to my room, closed the door, and got my earplugs from the dresser drawer. Polly got one last word in before I plugged my ears.

"Got the nerve to throw somebody in the Bronx River?" she yelled. "What are you, a mermaid?"

I lay in my bed and waited for at least ten minutes for Polly's ill wind to blow over. Then I got brave and pulled out one of the earplugs and was met by the voice of Dinah Washington singing "I'm Mad about the Boy." This was a sign that Polly had forgotten about all the razzmatazz at the Bronx River. In a couple of hours, she'd get ready for work—put on her uniform, polish and put on her caduceus pin, and strut out the door.

The next day we were all in Mr. Weiner's office talking about the incident: Viola and her mother, and my mother and I. Viola's mother was half drunk, and Polly had decided to show off her status by wearing her uniform to the meeting with Mr. Weiner. True, she'd gone to work the night before, but she still could have changed. This was definitely a power play. Polly knew how to play footsie with the powers that be.

Mr. Weiner favored her too because she came across as a hardworking, interested parent. I could tell by the smile that came on his face every time Polly spoke and the blank look that came on his face when Viola's mother spoke. After these adults had had their tête-à-tête, it was decided that Viola and I should pay for our transgressions; the punishment was a half hour after school in the cafeteria for six weeks, which would take us to June 6.

Of course we said nothing about the birth certificate and Viola's funky lap doll. This was a kids' oath of silence; an adult's life was an adult's life, and a kid's life was a kid's life, and as kids, especially teenagers, we would not tolerate rats. I put all my troubles in an invisible paper bag and threw it in a part of my brain called Garbage.

By Friday, the only thing on my mind was my next encounter with the Gingerbread Man. When I went to sleep on Thursday, I smelled his freshly scrubbed body, tasted his candy lips that I had just gotten a dab of, and heard that baritone voice that males of a certain age had—a sound that had not been in my house for a long time, since my father had left.

CHAPTER 12

It felt like I was sitting on pins and needles on Friday waiting for the date. Thank goodness Polly went to work, or I probably would have ended up in an insane asylum, unable to go on my date. The Gingerbread Man called me after Polly had gone to work. I had on a new black dress with white polka dots; it was a minidress that had pantalettes with frill that dropped below the hem.

When I got in the car, I could sense something was off-kilter. Once the light was on, I knew I was looking at a different Gingerbread Man. He had a gray hue to his face, his hair looked as if it hadn't been brushed for days, his beard and goatee were scraggly, and worst of all, he had a bad odor about him.

"I'm kind of in a blue funk today," he said.

"What's wrong?"

He reached into the glove compartment and got out a glassine envelope. He opened it, scooped up its contents with the back of a matchbook, and sniffed the white contents into his nose. Oh my God. My Gingerbread man was in the Knucklehead Club. I knew what this was; I had seen these glassine envelopes on the news when they arrested people for selling dope.

"I've been getting these headaches again. I started getting them when I was in Vietnam," he said.

He handed me the glassine envelope, and I smacked it out of his hand. The white powder splayed on the dashboard. He licked his finger, reached up to the dashboard, scooped the remnants of the powder onto his wet finger, and began licking and sniffing it. He kept scooping the powder from the dashboard and licking and sniffing the powder until it was gone.

He looked at me and probably saw the shock and disgust in my face. He in turn sighed and had the most sorrowful look on his face. He rested his head on the back of the seat and closed his eyes. The dispatcher radio beneath the dashboard was making scratching sounds; he jerked his head up and picked up the receiver. "East 222nd Street going to Manhattan, five dollars," said a voice from the radio. Norman started driving; thank God, we could get away from this scene. He began sniffing, making those funny sounds with his nostrils without blowing anything out.

"I started getting these headaches in Vietnam after me and my buddy went on recognizance and they blew out his brains," he said. "It splattered in my face."

"I'm sorry to hear about it," I said. "How long were you in Vietnam?"

"Four years."

I thought, *Okay, tell me about it sometime. But why did you pass the knucklehead powder to me?* When we reached East 222nd Street, he cut off the engine and glided down the hill until he stopped at a stately stone house only two doors from where Rene Wilkins lived. He honked the horn, and a large woman came from between some trees in front of the building. It was dark, but I could tell from her silhouette that she was a handsome woman because she was shapely and her hair fell on her shoulders. Once inside the car, she talked in what the Caribbean called the King's English—a Jamaican accent with a British lilt.

We rode down the West Side Highway and then FDR Drive to Mulberry Street. As we drove, the lighted windows of the skyscrapers looked like stars on this cloudy night. For a second, I thought I saw my and my family's constellations—the Big Dipper, the Little Dipper, and Orion—but it was all a mirage. I looked from the corner of my eye at the Gingerbread Man's movements, and they seemed slow and awkward as if he were an old man.

He gripped and moved the steering wheel like it was a beast of burden. We dropped the handsome woman in front of a brownstone on Mulberry Street. He made a U-turn and went back up the block. He drove until we reached a pizza shop with a neon sign with a large pizza on it and parked across the street from it.

"Toddy, you want some pizza?"

"Sure. I'll have what you're having."

After he got out of the car and ran up the hill to the pizza shop, I felt tired, used, and old—the way I felt when I had the flu. The nerve of him snorting that knucklehead powder and offering me some. If Polly got wind of this, she would have a fit. I could just hear her now: "*No* time for knuckleheads and bums."

He brought back two pizzas and two Cokes. I wasn't really hungry, but my stomach seemed to be exploding with acid because it growled. We ate, and I had gotten down to half the pizza when the radio started making scratching sounds again. Norman picked up the receiver, but there was no answer, so he hung it back up.

"I guess you don't think much of me using smack," he said.

"I wouldn't care if you snorted talcum powder," I said. "By the way, where is your fancy-pants opera and classical music tonight?"

He turned on the radio and Jim Morrison and the Doors showed up, belting out lyrics that sounded as if they were talking to me: "Don't you love her madly? Wanna be her daddy? Don't you love her as she's walking out the door?"

For reasons unknown to me, I wanted to hide under a rock and cry. Instead, I drew a picture in my head of an ugly Gingerbread Man—a new one. His lips became oversized coffee coolers blowing over a cheap cup of java as he nodded and drooled from his precious smack. Instead of the Gingerbread Man, his new name was "king of the knuckleheads."

The radio started scratching again. Norman picked up the receiver and took a call. He hung up and started the car again. He smelled musky, and it turned my stomach.

"Where you headed?" I asked.

"Mount Vernon."

"Drop me off once you get to the Bronx," I said.

He had to go through the Bronx before he got to Mount Vernon. I had to get out of there, away from him and his smack. As he drove back up West Side Highway, I got angrier and angrier at him. I had thought he was smart like my father, but he wasn't. He was dumber than dumb; he was a knucklehead.

Once we made it to my block, I told him he didn't have to drive me to my apartment building; I didn't think he was worthy to come in front of it. It's like Mama's always said: bad associations spoil useful habits—her favorite quote from the Bible. I guess I was like Polly, unlucky in love. First I meet Dick Quick and he almost takes my neck off, and the next thing I know I'm in love with the king of junkies, a bona fide knucklehead. I didn't even say goodbye to the knucklehead; I just opened the door and slammed it once I got out.

When I entered my apartment, Buck met me at the door; he wagged his tail and jumped up on me. I opened the curtain to Kevin's room and saw he was asleep. He slept hard because he played hard: basketball, swimming, track, and whatever else could stretch his body to the limit. I needed something to knock me out so I wouldn't think.

It was Saturday. I overslept. I really didn't want to get out of bed. I was entombed under the top sheet and blanket, listening to the sounds in the apartment. I heard when my mother came in from work, when she got undressed, and when she and Kevin were talking.

Chirping birds and a gush of spring air from a cracked window resurrected me from my linen tomb. I opened my coffin and sat on my bed. I felt like I had felt after my noosing from Dick Quick, like a fallen angel. Polly came into the room and saw me sitting in the lotus position on the bed.

"Girl, you look like you've been chased by the devil," said Polly.

"Bad nightmares."

"Remember, I have a meeting with the elders today to get reinstated."

"If they ask you if you would commit fornication again," I said, "be sure to say no."

"No. I'm not lying," said Polly. "I really don't know if I would ever commit fornication again. I can't predict the future."

I unfolded my kimono and got off the bed. I was infected by Polly's energy; it had erased my fog. I sighed. She had told the brothers the last time that she didn't know if she would commit fornication again, and they excommunicated her. But Mama had told me that Polly would tell the truth no matter the consequences—so much so that when Polly was growing up, the family kept secrets from her so she wouldn't tell the neighbors.

Kevin was calling her from his room, and she raced out of my room as if she were his servant.

CHAPTER 13

We all got dressed and looked at the Saturday morning shows on television. When the brothers came, I got nervous. There were three of them: Brother Richard Quincy, Thomas Cristlo, and David Myers, all dressed in their Sunday best of suits and ties. They had hard, judicial looks on their faces as if they could send someone to the electric chair at a drop of a hat, but they managed to give Kevin and me a smile when they were in the living room.

My mother directed them into Kevin's room. The curtain that divided his room from the living room was open, and my mother had placed three folding chairs for the brothers in a circle, and a chair across from the circle for her, as if they were in court—I guess appropriate for the judicial proceedings. I said something cordial, left them to their business, and went to my room. I left the door to my room wide open and put a chair in front of it so no spring wind would slam it shut what with all the windows being open. I had to watch and hear what they were going to do with Polly about this excommunication.

There was a silence in the house that I had never heard before. It was surreal, as though I were in the center of lifelessness. Brother Quincy, the head elder, began praying, and I closed my eyes and lowered my head to participate. The prayer was so low that I couldn't hear it. Then the prayer ended with an "amen" from Brother Richard Quincy, unnerving me with the familiarity of his voice and my inability to remember where I had heard it.

"Sister, you called us because you want to be reinstated in the congregation," said Brother Quincy. "Have you prayed to Jehovah for forgiveness?"

"Yes I have, Brother," said Polly.

"Have you committed fornication since that time?"

"No."

"Will you commit fornication again?"

I wanted to grab Polly by the neck and manipulate it like she was a marionette and I ventriloquist until "no" slid from her tongue.

"I don't know," she said, "because I can't predict the future, but I'll pray to Jehovah for strength."

I rested my head on the door, closed my eyes, and grimaced. I was proud that my mother stuck to her guns and didn't lie, but I was afraid of the consequence: that she might not be reinstated into the congregation. She had told the truth, but she could become a truth fool, a person foolhardy about what they say. Mama always said my mother talked too much, but who was she to say?

"Let's turn to Bible Verse Acts 3:19," said a brother whose voice I couldn't identify.

"Please read it, Sister Bethany," said Brother Quincy.

"Repent therefore and turn around so as to get your sins blotted out that seasons of refreshing may come from the person of Jehovah."

"It is with great pleasure that we reinstate you to the congregation," said Brother Quincy.

My mother began sobbing. Tears fell down my face as I wondered why she was crying. Okay, I got it: tears of joy. The brother said a final prayer, which I couldn't hear. When he finished, I moved the chair back by the bed, where it had been originally. I heard the key enter the cylinder of the apartment door. It was Kevin, which gave me a cue to enter the living room so as not to arouse suspicion that I had been listening in on the proceedings.

Kevin and I came into the living room about the same time. The brothers were standing over my mother, who was still wiping tears from her face with a white handkerchief, and were about to make their way out of the apartment. This didn't seem to faze Kevin, who was spinning a basketball on the tip of his finger, which I'd seen him do hundreds of times before.

"Hey, man, you driving that basketball crazy," said Brother Quincy. "What's your handle on the hardwood?"

"They call me Crunch on the hardwood," said Kevin.

"I got a handle myself," said Brother Quincy, "but it's not on the hardwood."

This was some sort of man speak, a language I guessed men reserve for conversations between men in the presence of women. Polly looked over at Kevin, I guessed watching to see if he was going to cross the line of disrespect with an adult, which was a no-no to her.

Brother Quincy reached into his pocket and pulled out a long rope. "My handle is Ricky Quick, and my hardwood was the Boy Scouts, army, and circus," he said. Brother Quincy moved closer to Kevin and placed a small noose on both of Kevin's index fingers, forming index cuffs. Kevin struggled to get out of the cuffs, but to no avail. Kevin laughed at the futility. In one fell swoop, Quincy removed the cuffs from Kevin's index fingers.

I remembered the night of Dick Quick and grabbed hold of my neck as I had when he put the noose around it. Then my cerebrum screamed: *Oh my God! Brother Quincy is Dick Quick.* The blood rushed to my head, and my knees felt as if they were going to buckle; I quickly locked them. I felt a hand on my shoulder and got so spooked that my entire body flinched, but from the corner of my eye I saw it was Polly.

"What's wrong, Toddy? You look like you've seen a ghost."

"I'm fine. I just have a little headache."

Dick what's-his-name, Brother Whatchamacallit, was dangling the rope by his side. I moved closer, and I smelled that sickening cologne that had almost strangled me along with his noose on that almost fateful night in his car. He had a devilish look on his face. I thought, *I've got news for you, Dick, Ricky, brother: You get noosey around Kevin or any of my folks, I'll do a Polly and mop your behind all over the Bronx.*

Brother Quincy placed the rope back in his pocket. Everyone said farewell, and away they went. I slipped into my room, lay down, and closed my eyes. My cerebrum told me I was in a dilemma. What would I do with the Gingerbread Man—a knucklehead to boot? What about Dick Quick? He was one of the powers that be in the congregation. There's nothing in the Bible that tells you, you can strangle a thirteen-year-old girl. Was he leading a double life, or had he stopped and repented? I fell to sleep with a big fat headache.

I woke up around 8:00 p.m. Polly didn't have to work and was in the kitchen cooking tonight's and tomorrow's dinners. When I walked into the kitchen, she was singing a temple song: "From house to house, from door to door, we go to praise his name." She was also basting a ham. She turned to me and smiled.

"Hello, sleepyhead ... too much excitement for you," said Polly, "knowing your mother has been reinstated at the temple."

"Congratulations, Ma. You deserve it."

She put some food on the plates for me and Kevin. Kevin took his food to his room, and Polly and I sat in the dining area.

"What do you think of Brother Quincy?" Polly asked.

"Okay, I guess."

"He's cute, isn't he?" she asked. "Kind of reminds you of your father, doesn't he?"

I looked at her from the corner of my eye. She had the same gleam in her eye as when she and my father were living the good life and fights, and arguments were rare birds, the same look I had before I found out the Gingerbread Man was a knucklehead. She waited patiently for my answer, which I was sure she wanted to be a yes.

"In a way," I said.

"The thing that really impressed me is the way he bonded with Kevin."

She went on and on about the Dickster, my hanging judge, listing his attributes like they were items on a menu—so much so that the descriptions seemed like a cannibalism initiation. She blushed as if she were a schoolgirl fanning her estrogen for her first crush. After I got sick and tired of being sick and tired of this lovelorn song, I slipped into my room.

Between the knucklehead and the Dickster, my life had become an algebra equation, and I needed a tutor. The only one who I could think of who was smart enough and could give me some insight into this mess, particularly with the Gingerbread Man, was Rene Wilkins, my sometimes classmate. She was in the gifted students' program at our school, and most of her classes were not with the regular students. She was wise for her age. I called Wilkins and made an appointment to meet at her house after detention on Monday. I fell asleep confident that the knucklehead and Dickster problem could be solved.

The next morning a bunch of birds were resting on the windowsill outside the window, chirping and personally serenading me. My mother was singing a religious song, which came through loud and clear because my door was open. Once I sat up on the bed, Kevin popped out of the bathroom, freshly showered, with a towel wrapped around his torso. He stuck his tongue out at me once our eyes met.

"Buga," he said.

"Joe Rock Head," I said.

Kevin was gone in a flash; despite his feet, he always moved quickly and with a certain grace. Polly was singing and cooking at the same time, and the smell of bacon tickled my nose. I knew she was happier than happy because she was going to be reinstated into the congregation and the whole world would know that Polly Cornwallis-West Bethany was back in the religious fold today.

We were dressed for this event in the colors of spring. Polly had on a pale pink suit the color of a carnation; Kevin, a pale blue suit with white shirt and red tie; and I, a pale yellow suit the color of a daffodil. Once dressed, we packed our pride in our hearts and went into a May day that only the celestials could have created: a clear sky, warm but not hot, and birds chirping like songstresses. Kevin and I followed Polly down the street because her fast pace prevented us from walking side by side with her. Kevin almost caught up with her, but I lagged behind both of them. She put the brakes on her feet when we reached East 229th Street, where the temple was. Polly had slowed down so much that we were now a row instead of a column on the sidewalk.

The services hadn't started, and there were little clusters of people chitchatting in front of the building. Once they saw us, they gave us a smile; they must have heard that my mother had been reinstated to the congregation and were just waiting for it to be made official so they could speak to Polly and give her love for coming back into the fold.

When we entered the temple, people in chitchat groups stopped talking and smiled at us. And lo and behold, Mama had made it on time, probably the first time in decades. She and Lisa were sitting in the back row, grinning from ear to ear when they saw us. Mama beckoned us to come to the back by waving her hand, and we went over to where they were seated. Mama had saved us seats by placing objects on them. Mama kissed my mother before she sat down, which was unusual because she wasn't a kissy-poo kind of person. Really none of the Cornwallis-Wests were. I didn't know much about the Bethanys because they weren't around.

"I got the seats back here so you can see the people's reaction when they announce that you've been reinstated."

"Oh, Mama," said Polly.

"Look who's here, Polly," said Lisa, pointing to the row in front of us.

It was my brother Butch and his wife. He winked at my mother and then at Kevin and me.

"Don't you folks remember me?" he asked.

The mic started scratching, and the people in the congregation took their seats. Brother Quincy got on the stage and announced what song we should sing. After we finished, a brother named James Unger was introduced as the speaker for the talk: forgiveness. He was tall, blond, and white, from a congregation in Mississippi named Harness.

Brother Unger adjusted the podium to fit his height. His voice was low as if he was talking from the bottom of his stomach; the tone was soft and earnest. As he got into the discourse, my eyes became misty thinking about my ex–Gingerbread Man, Norman. I shouldn't have been angry at him for who he is: a knucklehead sniffing knucklehead powder. I should have forgiven him for his transgressions, and I thought I should forgive the Dickster too. Mama gave my gut a soft poke with her elbow.

"Stop sleeping," she whispered. "Start looking up the scriptures the brother is reading."

I decided to look up all the scriptures the brother quoted so I wouldn't fall asleep. After the lecture and a song, we studied *The Magazine*, a magazine with questions on the bottom of the page and paragraphs that had the answers. I used to love this because the brother on the platform asked a question and then people raised their hands to answer it. I didn't feel too good about speaking in front of strangers now; it didn't seem too cool.

When we finished *The Magazine*, Brother Quincy came up to the podium and smiled, and for a second I forgot that he was the Dickster, the one who had tried to snuff out my life because I wouldn't give him my cherry.

"It is our pleasure to announce the reinstatement of Sister Polly Bethany," he said.

The hall thundered with applause. Once people were done expressing their delight at Polly's reinstatement into the congregation, Brother Quincy—or the Dickster—said the prayer. When I closed my eyes, I could hear my mother sobbing. Once the prayer was finished, members of the congregation who had known her for years and had been prevented from speaking to her came up and hugged her. Sister Moorhead, a short Jamaican sister, gave my mother a bear hug then unlocked the embrace and said, "Polly, don't do that no more and get excommunicated."

Polly nodded at Sister Moorhead, completely humbled her body, and moved like a rag doll, without muscle or strength, as other people came to show love to her. I was relieved when our trio of Kevin, Polly, and me were pushed out, or we clawed our way out, by this throng of well-wishers and goody-two-shoes folks; besides, too many spankings or too many hugs can make you an eternal rag doll—in essence, a wimp.

Mama, Lisa, Butch, and his wife, Suki, were waiting outside for us. Butch had gotten his car, a Dodge Dart, on loan from the company where he worked. Nestlé Tea Company seemed to give him everything as a sales associate. My brother was bright; he had recommended his friends for this position, but they weren't able to take it after a week. You had to ride around to different stores and take orders, have the gift of gab, and wear a suit. Butch was good at all these things.

When we all piled into the car, it was a tight fit. Lisa sat on Mama's lap, Kevin sat on Polly's lap, and I was squashed in the front with the married lovebirds. Those two made me nervous. We hadn't gone to their wedding—or should I say funeral—because my mother was too ashamed; she'd been excommunicated at the time, and the entire wedding party, except family members and in-laws, was forbidden from speaking to her.

I noticed that the lovebirds were kind of goofy. When someone talked to Butch, Suki would grab hold of him like she was protecting a pot of gold, and old Butch would act like a little boy who had lost his water. Actually, what Suki was protecting was a crazy guy who had claimed he was still a virgin when he married her and said he was so because he couldn't fornicate or else he would be excommunicated like Polly. Whatever; these birds gave me the creeps. I just hoped the Gingerbread Man and I wouldn't end up like those two if we got married, one grabbing the other like he's a pot of gold and the other acting as if he'd just pissed in his pants. I said phooey on that.

We were in front of the building in no time. All of us got out of the car so Butch could park, except Suki. She eyed all of us suspiciously when they pulled off and rode to the next block to park. Mama sighed once they were safe from her words.

"Butch could have done better than this," said Mama. "Suki is too dark and materialistic-minded."

"Mama, Butch isn't a vanilla cone," said Polly. "That's the same thing you and Daddy said when I married Royal."

Yes. In Polly's and my book, the blacker the berry, the sweeter the juice. When the light-skinned boys started coming around me and wagging their tails, I always hung out the unwelcome sign; if they were lighter than my Gingerbread Man, they had to back up, Mack. I guess the dark-skinned ones reminded me of my father.

But Mama's case for the materialism was more important than skin tone. I had heard via Kitchen University that Suki was a snob and was putting Butch into enormous debt. True, they both worked, but why get underwater in debt? I remembered a conversation my father and Polly had—it was really an argument about debt.

"Royal, what are we going to do with these bills?" asked Polly.

"I don't have any bills. Miss Bloomingdale's on a master sergeant's salary," said Royal. "Those are your bills."

All my mother's dreams were in Bloomingdale's department store; she went there and bought me dresses on sale. She didn't have a high school diploma at that time, so she did menial work in factories part time. I guess you could say she had Cadillac dreams on a bicycle income.

Once we were in the apartment, my mother started heating Sunday's dinner. The goofy couple came in. Butch was carrying his second heart, the saxophone, in a mahogany case. I guessed there was going to be a jazz jam after we ate, and most likely a fight; there were just too many Bethanys and Cornwallis-Wests under one roof. After we ate and folks were sitting wherever with their stomachs sticking out, Butch got out his second heart to play us a jig.

My mother put on a record of John Coltrane the saxophonist so Butch could play along to the music. Of course there were other noteworthy saxophonists or instrumentals that she could have used, but she sanitized her collection whenever a musician was busted for drugs by throwing out his records and washing down the shelf where they had sat in the cabinet. I also noticed that she had gotten rid of all the female singers once my father left, whether or not they used drugs. It seemed that she didn't want any chanteuses in her home.

The first song on the record was the "Laura" theme from the movie of the same name. It was a soulful, mournful piece, and Butch did it justice, as he always did. The sound that came from his shiny saxophone sounded like a woman moaning in grief over her lover. I thought of the Gingerbread Man and how it seemed our relationship had hit a blank wall; I wanted to let go of this bad feeling. Then Coltrane did me a favor and went to another song, playing "Summertime" at a fast tempo that sounded like people singing and dancing at a picnic. Butch transitioned from slow to fast tempo without a glitch or a miss.

After we had eaten the heavy southern food, which consisted of ham, macaroni pie, string beans, and corn bread, it nearly put us to sleep, but we were invigorated by the replaying of "Summertime" and Butch's saxophone. Mama jumped from the love seat where she was sitting in the living room and began swinging her hips and waving her hands in dance.

"This is Charleston music from the 1920s," said Mama.

We all giggled at Mama doing the Charleston dance, all except Suki. She sat with her nose in the air like a poor little girl who had gotten lost. Butch was rocking back and forth as he played the saxophone—a dance for musicians, I guess, who moved to the beat of the music in their heads. His eyes were closed, but I could see he was rolling them back and forth because his eyelids quivered.

His head swayed in ecstasy as he blew into his saxophone, playing the notes we heard and the notes in his head; perhaps the latter were different from the ones we heard. He was on his own mountaintop, perhaps with the celestials. Pretty soon everyone—Ma, Kevin, Lisa, a reluctant Suki, and I—were on the floor dancing to the beat of "Summertime."

"Summertime" came and went, and once it was over, we were spent and fell back into our seats. I looked around at my relatives: Kevin, my pigeon-toed brother; Butch, definitely goofy in mind; Polly, always or most of the time a ball of fire; little Lisa, abandoned by her mother; Mama, a woman who looked nothing like her children and appeared white; and the newest addition, the in-law Suki, neck so long and nose so high up in the air, it reminded you of an ostrich. Who the heck were these people, and who the heck was I? What had I gotten myself into?

The hullaballoo went on until it wore out its welcome. Butch finally got around to talking man speak to Kevin. He tickled Kevin by balling his hand into a fist and rubbing it against Kevin's stomach. Kevin giggled in delight. Butch did that a couple of times then removed his hand.

"Eh, man, how are you on the hardwood?" asked Butch.

"Ma's sending me to basketball camp," said Kevin.

Butch's mouth twisted to the side, his whole happy-go-lucky look completely spooked off his face. He looked at my mother, who was nearby seated in a chair opposite to him, still happy from being reinstated to the congregation. "Well, it's good you're going; maybe it will help your bad feet." He said, "Try not to hate your mother too much for not doing enough for your crippled feet."

"Watch your mouth, nigga," said Polly, "before you lose your tongue."

Kevin stared at Butch blank-faced, keeping to his script of never letting anyone know what he was thinking. The apartment grew silent, a tone so horrifying that it brought with it its own noise, its own music. It seemed as though an invisible musician with an invisible instrument was calling the shots on sound in this apartment. Sukie stayed Butch's arm by grabbing the cuff of his sleeve. The album had stopped, and the sound of the needle brushing against the record sounded like a cat scratching inside its litter box.

"I'm telling the truth," said Butch. "You neglected his feet, and he's gonna hate you for it."

Polly pushed past Suki and got in Butch's face. I closed my eyes, sure that Polly was going to beat the hell out of him. Her specialty was bullying grown men who liked to push women around.

"Get your music box, your wench," said Polly, "and take you disrespectful butt out of my house."

"I'm not scared of you," said Butch.

"Don't press your luck, Buster," said Polly. "It's later than you think."

"Butch, why did you spoil it?" asked Mama.

Butch complied. In one fell swoop he put his saxophone back in its case, gathered his wife and things, and left. I was rather surprised that Polly didn't mop his behind on the floor; maybe she was getting old and mellowing out. All the men in the family were terrified of getting their butts beat by Polly, except Uncle Philbin. Her forte was people her size or bigger; she didn't care for hitting anything smaller than her or any little children.

Butch had started the fight. Maybe he was jealous that Kevin was going to basketball camp and he himself had never gotten to go. But what had I expected? Too many Cornwallis-Wests and Bethanys spoiled the broth.

CHAPTER 14

The first thing I thought about when I woke up Monday was how I hated Mondays, and the second thing was how I was going to straighten out the Gingerbread Man about this drug thing. Without the drugs, he was my Gingerbread Man; with them, he was the ultimate knucklehead.

This Monday was particularly bad because I began the detention for fighting Viola and throwing her in the Bronx River. At 3:00 p.m., I went into the cafeteria with the other miscreants and sat silently for half an hour, looking at the wall and smelling the lunch that had been eaten that day. As I sat looking at the wall, I wondered if I learned anything sitting in the cafeteria. But the time wasn't so torturous because I thought about my Gingerbread Man and how we were going to get married after we straightened out this drug business and I got a little older. We would make a much better couple than old Butch and Suki. We definitely wouldn't want to cling to one another every time someone said a word to our beloved.

The bell rang, signaling that the detention was over. We detained students hurried out of the cafeteria like a bunch of lost ants. I waved to Viola, and she waved back to me; it was like we were letting bygones be bygones.

I made a date with Rene Wilkins to discuss my Gingerbread Man. She was in the gifted student class, so she was smart; I was in the next rank below her in a one class. The educational system ranked us in descending order, with a one being more proficient than a two. We obtained the ranking via standardized tests in reading and math. I was supposed to be smart. As Mr. Weiner, my guidance counselor, had told my mother when she came to school for the fight: "Toddy could really be excellent if she applied herself." Sorry, guys, it was hard for my brain to register sitting eight hours a day.

Rene Wilkins lived on East 222nd Street, a ritzy block between Bronxwood and Paulding Avenues, the entire block sloped like the side of a hill. The houses were huge and detached with big front yards and large backyards. To top it off, some of the houses were stone like Rene's. Sometimes when I went over to her house I felt I didn't belong there because she had a mother and a father, they had a big private house, and they all seemed to be living a storybook life. Rene's mother, Mrs. Wilkins, was a nurse like my mother, but she was a registered nurse, a step above my mother's licensed practical nurse certification. But my mother told me that in a couple of years she was going back to school to become a registered nurse.

And Rene's father had been in the service too, like my father was, but he was an officer, unlike my father, who was an enlisted man. Somehow it always seemed that Rene was a step above me. She really was, and that felt funny. I didn't know whether I was envious or just felt that we were not the same.

When I reached Rene's house, I navigated through the big gateless front yard, trying not to crush the grass, until I reached the stone steps; it always seemed as if I was going to the Museum of Natural History when I came to her house. I pressed the bell to the front door, which seemed to chime like the church bells on Sunday. Mrs. Wilkins opened the door, a tall, brown-skinned woman about my mother's age who was as aloof as a corpse; I guess adults called that cool. She was the only person whom I'd ever met who could smile without moving a muscle in her face. Polly knew Mrs. Wilkins via the informal and formal nursing grapevine, but Polly wasn't as cool as a cucumber; she was a knot of emotion tied into a knot of emotion. But at work she was as cool as a cucumber.

I entered the museum-sized house, where every room in it was bigger than my entire apartment. We'd lived in a house when our father was with us; it was at Mitchell Air Force Base. I can't remember anything about it because we moved back to the city when I was three.

Mrs. Wilkins took me to the basement, where Rene sat at a big pool table that looked as if it had been in a scene in a movie. She gave me her mother's sphinx smile, and I went and sat down next to her. Mrs. Wilkins went upstairs and came back down carrying a small tray of half sandwiches and a pitcher of lemonade, which she set on the pool table. Rene and I dug in and took a half sandwich each. Once Mrs. Wilkins went back upstairs, we got down to business.

"What's up, Bethany?" asked Rene.

Without giving Norman's name, I told her his story, saying that I liked him but he was using drugs. In a way, I felt ashamed to tell her that my man—my Gingerbread Man—was using drugs. As I told her the story, the only thing that moved on her face were her eyeballs, which she circled to and fro.

"That man is too old for you," she said. "My grandma says an old man gives you worms."

"Yes, I heard my grandma say that too."

"The drug business is bad. My cousin started sniffing airplane glue, then he went to beer and cigarettes, next liquor, next marijuana, then heroin," she said. "Then when he got a real habit, he started stealing from Aunt Suzie until she went crazy and died. Now he's a junkie on the corner, begging for change for a dope fix."

I was sorry that I had told Rene my Gingerbread Man's age; it was just another negative for her to assess. She poured each of us a glass of lemonade, and we gulped down the drinks. A belch escaped from Rene's mouth, and a shadow darkened her light freckled face as though she had done something really bad. The most cool Rene apologized.

"But my Gingerbread Man isn't like that," I said. "He's no bum. He has a job."

"Maybe not yet, but he's headed in that direction. And besides, I heard their dick don't get hard because it's drugged up too." She belched again then apologized. "And another thing—if and when he gets off that stuff, he's going to want to take out his gun and bust your cherry."

"Gun? What's this gun business?"

"My cousin told me that's what they called dicks when he was in basic training. They'd run around with their rifles singing, 'This is my rifle,' and they'd point to their dicks and say, 'This is my gun. The rifle's for killing; the dick's for fun,'" she said. "And remember, once your cherry is busted, it's busted for life; you can't grow it back like a fingernail."

I touched my virgin pin at the top of my blouse and started circling it with my finger. I was kind of pissed off that she was stating or implying that my Gingerbread Man was headed for the life of a lowlife. I know Polly had told me that the last thing a dope addict would do was have sex.

"But you make up your own mind," she said. "It's a free country."

Mrs. Wilkins banged down the steps, interrupting our talk. Once she reached the pool table, she cracked her frozen smile again. "Rene, it's time for your ballet lesson," she said. Rene's mother picked up the empty tray, placed the empty glasses and almost empty pitcher of lemonade on the tray, and banged back up the basement steps. I gathered up my things, my book bag and coat, and as Rene and I were walking over to the steps, she whispered, "I can't go on these after-school fights with you anymore. We're getting too old for this."

"Yeah, we could have been arrested with this Viola stuff," I said.

"Precisely."

I didn't even bother to ask her advice on the Dickster because I could never tell her about bar night; it would make me look like a whore, going into a bar at my age and getting men to buy me drinks, then teasing them when they asked me for sex. Rene Wilkins couldn't handle it; she was too young. True, we were the same age, but my mind was older and wiser than hers.

I left the Wilkins's house half sure and half unsure about the Gingerbread Man situation; I was sure that I was going to see him again and unsure if that was the right thing. I shook my head in confusion and thought maybe that all of this was above my head, that maybe this adult life was too much for me.

When I got home, there was a big moving van in front of the building's entrance. Two burly men were lugging a set of mahogany end tables that seemed familiar, and another two were pulling a leather sofa on a long dolly that seemed even more familiar.

A tall black man in a gray suit was talking to the two movers. It was Butch; he was moving next door to us. *Wait till Polly hears this!* I thought. I went over to where Butch was, and he smirked.

"Hi, neighbor," he said.

"Do Ma and Mama know you're moving in?" I asked.

"No, I'm going to surprise them."

This was not a good thing. The thought of the goofy couple Suki and Butch as neighbors made my skin crawl. Now Butch would be on my back about doing the right thing like Mama and Ma were. Now when I sneaked out at night, I had another person who could potentially catch me in the act. I politely excused myself and raced into the house to tell Polly the news.

She was in the kitchen frying fish. I put down my books, went to the closet, and hung up my coat, then gave her the news about our new "neighbors" by yelling the information once I had closed the closet. By the time I reached the kitchen, she was giggling like a little kid.

"Well, he was really sneaky-deaky," Polly said. "He didn't tell anybody the news."

"Yeah. But of all places, why did he have to move here?"

"Your brother can move anywhere he pleases," she said. "Besides, you don't have to worry about him wearing out his welcome with us. Suki has him on a tight leash."

That was true. I couldn't imagine those two dropping over for a cup of sugar or coffee unannounced. Butch and Polly weren't like mother and son. I'd come to the conclusion that it was true what I'd heard Aunt Helen say in a session of Kitchen University: that Butch treated my mother like his sister and Mama like his mother because Polly had him at fifteen and Mama really raised him until my father and mother got married, when Butch was seven.

Polly placed a piece of fish on a plate and handed it to me. I wasn't too hungry, so I wrapped the plate in aluminum foil and left it on top of the stove. When she finished cooking, she couldn't wait to get on the phone to give the latest news to the folks that Butch was moving into our complex.

As I lay in bed mulling over my Gingerbread Man problem, Polly got on the phone and yakked it up about our new "neighbors." My bedroom door was open as she dialed the family. First she called Aunt Helen and said, "Yeah, that good-for-nothing Butch had the nerve to sneak in and move into the complex."

After she finished bending Aunt Helen's ear, she called Mama.

"Those two are something else," said Polly. "Butch and Suki could have told you they were moving over here."

Families are the ties that bind, but it would take me decades to understand what made my family tick—even then I would only get the tip of the iceberg of knowledge. But they sure couldn't live with or without one another—kind of like the situation with my Gingerbread Man and me right now.

After Polly finished bending everyone's ear on the phone, the doorbell rang. It was Suki and Butch, looking tired. When they came in, my mother welcomed them as if the argument she and Butch had had on Sunday had never happened. I could see Butch was hungry because he was sniffing the fish smell and trying to hold it in his nostrils.

"We don't want to stay long," he said. "We haven't unpacked our stuff, and we're kind of hungry."

"Yeah, Toddy told me you moved into the other building," Polly said. "I've got some whiting and collard greens, if you're interested."

They were very interested. They sat down and ate fish like they had just finished combat in World War II, Suki forgetting about protecting Butch and grabbing the cuff of his shirt and Butch acting as if he were part of the world instead of in some secret club with Suki. It was like the odd couple had returned to earth.

My mother fried some more fish, and everyone polished that off. When the couple had eaten enough, they got up to leave, and Suki resumed her protective gestures. Butch acted like a little cat again.

"Ma, we haven't unpacked our pots and pans yet," said Butch.

Polly packed up some pots, some utensils, a frozen steak, and a bag of kidney beans and sent them on their merry way. I guessed if those two could be a couple, my Gingerbread Man and I could be one too; those two goofies had a bad case of love.

My mother and father had made a good couple; he was happy-go-lucky and always had a smile on his face, whereas she was the more edgy of the two. Despite this, they were a good fit and seemed to complement one another—until their marriage went south. The Gingerbread Man reminded me of my father sans drugs. Daddy drank alcohol moderately.

After my mother went to work, I called the Gingerbread Man at his home at around 8:00 p.m. He sounded sad until I told him that I would go with him to Lincoln Center to the classical music concert. He said he'd pick me up at 8:00 p.m. on Wednesday.

Once I hung up the phone, I got butterflies in my stomach as I did the math in my head. My mother was going to work on Wednesday, and she usually called me around 9:00 p.m. to check on us. How was I going to work this out, going out with Norman, answering her call at 9:00 p.m., and keeping everything hunky-dory? And the biggest question of all: What did one wear to a concert?

I remember the lime evening gown I'd worn to a piano recital at Carnegie Hall when I was three. Butch and I were being tutored in music by a man we called Professor Mills. He taught us how to play the piano, and the class got a gig at Carnegie Hall. I played "Robin in the Cherry Tree" and had to be escorted off the stage for trying to do a thousand curtsies. My mother and father were really proud of Butch and me that night.

After school and the cafeteria detention, I went to a store to buy something for this concert. Maybe I could find a gown like the one I'd worn at the recital at Carnegie Hall. I went to a clothing shop on White Plains Road and East 226th Street. It sold formal clothes like gowns and wedding dresses.

When I walked in, the sour-faced Mr. Glok was sewing the hem of a gown draped on a mannequin. He always looked at everyone as though he wanted to chew them up and spit them out. I often wondered how he could stay in business with that attitude. But one day he had his sleeves rolled up, and I saw the numbers from the concentration camp tattooed on his arm. He didn't try to hide them but wore them like a badge of honor. It was like, *Hey, world, look what you've done to me*. I guess it was like having been a black slave during the 1800s and saying to the world, *Hey, look what you've done to me*.

Mr. Glok looked away from his work and tried to squeeze a smile onto his stone face, but it was like seeing a terrible actor make a fool of himself onstage. He might have smiled and felt like smiling a long time ago, before the war, before the concentration camp, but those days were long gone.

"What would you like?" he asked.

"I'm going to a classical concert in one of the finest halls in the world," I said. "What evening gown would you recommend?"

He placed the pin in the mannequin, pushed the fake person aside, and came to where I stood. He looked me up and down, definitely sizing me up, then went down an aisle where formal dresses hung on racks. He brought back three dresses. One was the color of a daffodil; the second, white as snow; and the third, lime—the exact color of the dress I'd worn to Carnegie Hall so long ago when I tried to wow the universe to death with my never-ending curtsies. I didn't care how it looked on me; the color was the charm. It was like Carnegie Hall revisited with curtsies. I'd make the Gingerbread Man proud of me as my father had been that night.

"If I buy this, could you have the alterations done by tomorrow afternoon?" I asked after I'd chosen the lime dress. "The concert is tomorrow night."

"Of course. There is not much to do," he said. "Try it on in the back."

I went into the fitting room and tried on the gown. It wrapped around my behind like a leather glove, and the bodice made my breasts look like the sculpture *Venus de Milo*, unlike my Carnegie Hall gig, where I was flat-chested and without a womanly shape. But still I felt as if I were at Carnegie Hall. If I could have given Mr. Glok a million dollars for this dress, I would have; I was going into my mad money to pay for it, an emergency fund I had under my bed in a shoebox.

I twirled around in front of the mirror in the fitting booth and marveled at how womanly I looked. This would knock out the Gingerbread Man and hopefully knock the knucklehead powder out of his hand. It was this dress against the powdery substance that was killing my baby, my Gingerbread Man, and I was going into the ring to give it the knockout punch with this dress.

After I got exhausted looking at my beauty, I went to Mr. Glok, who was still doing alterations on the dress on the mannequin. When he saw me, he pushed the mannequin aside, walked to where I stood, and looked at the gown. He stretched a tape measure in his hand and wrapped it around my chest, then my waist. He removed it then wrapped it around his hand.

"A seam needs to be opened in the chest and the waist," he said. "If not, you'll bust out of the dress if you breathe."

"Okay, but can you still have it for tomorrow?" I asked.

He nodded yes. If the dress were to fail in front of my Gingerbread Man, I would just crawl under a rock. Mr. Glok placed a pin around the hem to shorten the length.

"That'll be two inches on the hem," he said. "The entire cost is fifty dollars, but I'll charge you forty-five dollars."

"Thanks," I said. I knew he'd given me a discount because he favored Polly. All the vendors did; they thought of her as honest and industrious, from the people at the pizza store to the workers at the Chinese restaurant.

Of course they were all men; maybe they thought she was a looker. But she held her head high no matter how good or bad the circumstances were.

I went back into the fitting room, observed my eye candy one more time, and took off the dress in a flash. I imagined dancing with my Gingerbread Man in this dress, but what would I dance to, a waltz to go with the classical music, or a square dance like we did in physical education class with country music blasting in the background? Whatever.

I came down from the clouds, put on my other dress, and left the store. As I walked up White Plains Road to my apartment, I wondered what my Gingerbread Man would be wearing tomorrow. Polly and Mama always told me that it really didn't matter what a man wore—he still looked like he belonged—but a woman had to look her best. I always wondered why this was so.

I walked past the stores, which had displays for summer: the delicatessen with the stinky cheese had a wheel cut in the shape of a boy with shorts on; the pizza shop had put faux grass in its front window with clay figurines of children playing; and all the other stores shone with the pastel colors of summer.

Polly said when she moved from North Carolina to New York City, she met people from all over the world. Mama said that NYC was like the United Nations of the misbegotten, it had so many different people. My civics lessons ended when I reached my block, East 225th Street. I hustled up the long block to my apartment complex. The familiar tan Dodge Dart was parked at the curb with Butch sitting inside in his brown gabardine suit, a good fit for spring with its light wool texture. Suki was nowhere in sight.

Butch seemed to have everything: he was tall and handsome, and he had a high school diploma, a good job, a wife he loved, an apartment, and musical talent, all at the age of twenty-one. How in the heck was I going to match that? In seven years I'd be twenty-one; how could I beat his shine?

But just what was Butch doing sitting in the car—waiting for Suki, or spying on me? Suki came barreling down the long path from the building to the curb. She gave me a quick wave and got in the car. They pulled off. Maybe they were going to Bible study.

The next day in school, I was confident that I had most of the bases covered for my date with the Gingerbread Man. Despite Rene Wilkins's warnings, I had accepted the invitation to go to the concert. I had the gown, and it was a knockout—but how could I account for the time? He was going to pick me up at 8:00 p.m., and Polly normally called us at 9:00 p.m.

When I went to the cafeteria at the end of the day to do my detention, the problem weighed in my head about the time issue. I couldn't call Rene Wilkins and ask for pointers; she didn't agree with my seeing the Gingerbread Man. I pretended to be doing homework in the cafeteria by bending my head down and scratching on a piece of paper as if I were writing something profound as I searched for answers about the time problem.

Strangely enough, on this day the half-hour detention went fast. It always felt like hours to me. I bolted out of the cafeteria, past the mean-looking monitor, and that was when my brainstorm came to me about what to do with this time problem. I'd bribe Kevin with $20 to say I was in bed sick; that sleepyhead would stay up for $20. He was a sponge for material things. Besides, his birthday was at the end of the week; he'd suck up anything coming his way. But I'd better be careful: Kevin was like my mother, a stickler for the truth. But I guessed he would finesse it for $20. After all, a lie was just a creative truth.

When I went to Mr. Glok to pick up my gown, his mood seemed even sourer than it usually was, but once I tried on the dress, his face glowed like a new penny. It was a perfect fit, and he looked me and the gown up and down till he was satisfied. He placed the gown in a box, and I was gone. I'd tell Polly anything about the dress; she'd be thrilled that I had the culture to buy the gown. Just in case she asked me, I'd tell her that I was going to a concert at school.

I was relieved when I heard the sound of Duke Ellington playing "The A Train" when I got to the apartment door. If a big band like Duke Ellington's or Count Basie's was playing, then Polly was upbeat. If it was a balladeer like Frank Sinatra or Nat King Cole, she was trying to drown her sorrowful torch. The two songs that made me want to cry when she played them were Nat King Cole's "Mona Lisa" and Frank Sinatra's "Only the Lonely." I guess they could make a corpse cry.

Polly was in the kitchen percolating and circulating. She was mopping the kitchen floor with one hand, popping her fingers in time to the music with the other, and humming the tune to "The A Train" as it played. She looked at me with a girlish grin.

"Guess who's coming to dinner this Sunday after services at the temple?"

"Who?" I asked.

"Brother Richard Quincy."

I felt like I was going to swallow my tongue. The Dickster was coming to our house to eat, perhaps bringing three nooses for Polly, Kevin, and me. This was some no-good dick shit. She finished the last spot on the floor that needed to be mopped then placed the mop in the bucket.

She steamrolled into Kevin's room, where the record player was, and put on a Johnny Mathis album, passing my big boxed gown without so much as a word about the contents. I took the box and books to my room and put the box in my closet, well aware that the biggest fear of my entire life had come true: I was going to be having Sunday dinner with Satan.

When I returned, Polly was singing the song "Chances Are" along with Johnny Mathis from his album. She sat at the dining table spicing the two chuck steaks on a plate she was going to cook for dinner. I sat at the sofa a distance from her, close enough for us to see each other's faces but not the emotions.

"Ma, this might not be a good idea," I said, "getting touchy-feely with an elder."

"Toddy, don't feel left out," she said. "Whatever happens, you kids are still number one in my book."

"Yes, I know that." I remembered she quit a suitor because Kevin had asked him for a piece of gum and Mr. Allen, the suitor, told him he didn't have any. Kevin, who was three at the time, reached into his pocket and pulled out a piece of gum. That was the end of Mr. Allen.

"But, Ma, what if you make a mistake and curse in front of him?"

"Don't be silly, Toddy."

Polly finished spicing the steaks, picked up the plate, went into the kitchen, and broiled them in the oven. Johnny Mathis was on a new song, and my mind wasn't listening to it even though he was one of my favorites; it was on the Dickster and what to do with this problem.

I was sitting in the living room when Kevin came in, dressed in his basketball team's suit of gold and blue and spinning his basketball on the tip of his index finger. He went to his room, leaving the curtain open, and placed the basketball on the floor near his bed and Buck. Buck began rolling the ball back and forth.

"Guess who's coming to dinner this Sunday?" yelled Polly from the kitchen. "Brother Quincy."

"Wow. The man with the rope," said Kevin. "Ma, why is he coming here?"

"Because I invited him."

He sat beside me on the sofa, dropped his jaw, scratched his head, hopped off the sofa, bolted out of the apartment door, and slammed it.

"What's eating him?" asked Polly.

"Beats me," I said.

But it was good that he didn't like this Dickster business, whatever the reason. I had an ally in my "get rid of the Dickster" movement. There was the women's movement, the black power movement, and the civil rights movement, and there had to be a Dump the Dickster movement. Kevin came back into the apartment and apologized for having slammed the door.

When Polly was finished cooking, I began my faux illness, telling her I had a headache and didn't feel like eating. She pressed her hand to my forehead and then placed it on my chin. "You don't feel warm," she said. "I'll take your temperature." As long as I wasn't feverish, bleeding, or not breathing, I was okay, so Polly left for work at 5:00 p.m. As soon as she closed the door, I made the pitch to Kevin. He was in his room brushing Buck's hair with one of those metal dog brushes. He seemed disinterested at first, but when I whipped out the twenty-dollar bill, he became enthusiastic.

"Yeah, but I'm not lying for you," he said.

"I'm not telling you to lie for me," I said. "Just finesse it and tell her I'm still not feeling well and am unavailable when she calls."

After he took the money, I took a bath and washed and scrubbed my body until I was as clean as I thought the Gingerbread Man wanted me to be. It was as if I'd never had a bad odor come from my body ever. I put on my gown and it shined; I twirled around in front of the door mirror and felt like I had felt that night so long ago when I was at Carnegie Hall.

I went into my mother's makeup drawer, got some pale peach lipstick, and put just a dab on my lips. I twisted my hair into a French roll. I was ready to get the show on the road. When I came out of the room, Kevin looked at me and did a double take.

"Wow," he said, "you look like a princess."

"Just like I did when I went to Carnegie Hall."

He looked at me like I was crazy. He hadn't even been born when Butch and I played at Carnegie Hall. It's like we lived in separate worlds, we were so far apart in age: I five years older than Kevin, and Butch seven years older than I and twelve years older than Kevin. One of my mother's friends joked to her, "You must have been on a long honeymoon after each birth."

Kevin touched one of the frills on the dress—I guess to see if it was real. He looked kind of sandy-eyed, and it dawned on me that he was a heavy sleeper; the last thing I wanted him to do was miss Polly's call.

"You look like you're going to pass out," I said. "How you going to stay awake?"

"I'll drink coffee."

"Well, don't overdose on it."

I strutted out the door like I was a piece of new money. I had a shawl over my shoulders—a white wool one that I'd knitted. There was a chill in the air, but the night was beautiful; it was clear, and it looked as if every star in the universe was out that night. There was a half-moon with an orange hue that gave it a smoldering look. As I walked down the path in front of the building to the street, I saw Butch and Suki going into the building, he dressed in a suit and she in a dress covered with a trench coat. I held my breath and waited for them to go into the adjacent building. Thank goodness they didn't see me. The first words out of Butch's mouth would have been "Where you going in that get-up?" followed by a thousand words that would sound like "blah, blah, blah" when they reached my ears.

There was a red El Dorado Cadillac parked in front of the building, and my Gingerbread Man was standing by the headlights, resting his behind on the hood of the car. The streetlights made a round path around his body, and I could see he was dressed in black Levi's and a black shirt—what he always wore. I wanted to run and hide under a rock because he wasn't dressed in tux and tails as I had imagined he would be to go to a concert at Lincoln Center. Was I overdressed, or was he underdressed? Whatever. This was bad news;

I felt like a live fool. When I reached him, he gave me a big hug then kissed me on the cheek.

"Hello, beautiful."

"Do you think I overdressed for this?" I asked.

"No, this is New York; anything goes," he said. "You look like a queen." He bowed to his waist. "Milady, I am your faithful serf."

"Rise, my serf," I said.

He opened the passenger's side of the car and bowed again. I was tickled pink; whatever uneasiness I had went away when he called me beautiful again. I felt like I had felt the night when I gave the recital at Carnegie Hall—as if I were the object of everyone's affection, especially my father's.

Traffic wasn't great going down to Lincoln Center. We hit the highway, and I ignored the gridlock and amazed myself with how the skyscrapers with their lights on looked like a miniature version of the celestials. This reminded me that I hadn't prayed to the celestials in a while, ever since I'd had to deal with Norman's knucklehead problem.

I usually asked for their direction with tough problems; even though they didn't answer me back, they always seemed to guide my feet in a sensible direction. Years before, Kevin, my mother, and I avoided a cabstand we usually entered and went to a store next to it. Seconds later, a cab drove into the stand, injuring and killing the people inside. It could have been us—the celestials saved us. And the fire at Aunt Helen's, when I was shielded from the effects of the smoke and saved by her neighbor. Maybe I was afraid they'd direct me away from Norman.

We got off the highway at Thirty-Fourth Street and Ninth Avenue, far away from Lincoln Center, to park the car in a garage on Sixty-Sixth Street. We were under the bedazzled starry night. I was excited that I was going out with a real man. When we left the parking garage and he held my hand, then put his arm around my waist, it was like I'd had a thousand of those Carnegie Hall nights. The smell of his manliness and cologne mixing with the testosterone made me want to faint.

When we reached the end of the block, the Gingerbread Man left me in the middle of the sidewalk and went to the edge of the curb to hail a cab. One stopped. When he saw Norman's face, the cabbie said, "I don't go to Harlem." Before Norman could say we weren't going to Harlem, the cab whisked away a couple of feet and picked up a less elegant white couple dressed in rags. Norman made two more attempts to hail a cab and got the same results. Seeing that the odds were against us in getting a cab, we headed up Thirty-Fourth Street to catch the subway to Lincoln Center, where we wouldn't be denied.

"Damn people," Norman said, "they think all colored people live in Harlem."

But I guess we knew what the cab drivers were really saying: it wasn't Harlem that was the problem; it was us. I guess Rene Wilkins would say, "These damn Hondos are a mess. These racists are always popping up when you want to have some fun." Norman and I began speed walking up the block to the subway, past the throngs of people flexing their muscles. We got on the northbound no. 1 train in the subway at Thirty-Fourth Street and Seventh Avenue. It too was crowded, but not crowded enough for the passengers to ogle my evening gown. Some looked at it like I was out of place, and others gave me admiring smiles as if I were the belle of the ball. I blushed under the spotlight.

As Norman and I stood holding the pole in the middle of the car with our fellow travelers, my dress and I were all but forgotten by the crowd once we pulled into the station at Forty-Second Street. A throng of people got out of the train, only to be replaced by another group of people. The throng that came in looked no different from the one that had just left, except one person who stood out from the crowd.

He was a tall blond in his twenties, in a full-dress army uniform. It was tan from head to toe. I knew my uniforms; after all, my father had been in the air force for thirteen years. Despite the pomp and status, this man seemed a bit nervous, moving his head from side to side as if someone was following him. The throng of people fanned him to the pole where Norman and I were standing. Norman tapped him on the shoulder, and when the man turned and faced him, Norman smiled at the uniformed man, who eyed Norman suspiciously as if he were the people who were following him.

"Hey, man, I served in Vietnam," said Norman.

"Where?" asked the man. "I was in Da Nang."

"I was in the Mekong Delta theater of war."

The uniformed man smiled. A boo came from the crowd. I turned. It was two longhairs, probably hippies because they had no shoes on. One of the flower children said, "You imperialist baby killers!" to Norman and the soldier. What the man said stumped Norman and the uniformed man, whose name was Sergeant Swift, but they ignored him and exchanged telephone numbers before we got off the train at Sixty-Sixth Street. Poor Norman—he had it bad: a knucklehead, a black man surrounded by Hondos, and in a theater of war that was tearing the country apart.

I had never been to Lincoln Center, but that was true of most famous sites in the city. It was a few yards from the subway and was not long like the skyscrapers that loomed toward the heavens. Instead its width seemed to stretch to infinity. It reminded me of the pictures I'd seen of the antiquity of the Colosseum in Rome, and it was much bigger than Carnegie Hall. Norman guided me through the awesome columns leading to the inside, holding my hand gently as if I were a child. I felt out of place in this colossus.

"Have you been here before?" I asked.

"Yes," he said. "Don't be bedazzled by the size."

He must have known I felt out of place, like I didn't belong, as I had when I bumped into a rich person on Park Avenue or met up with one of those Hondos who either said "nigger" out loud or with their faces or eyes. But now I didn't have to prove myself; this mass of people circulating through the long, carpeted corridors weren't here to see me at a Carnegie Hall recital, but someone else.

When we went into the hall, we sat in the orchestra section. The lights were on, even though they were dim. We sat in the middle of the row. I looked around at the people and rubbed the velvet plushness of the upholstered seat. I was relieved when I saw a couple of women in evening dresses.

The lights in the seating area went off, and a large spotlight focused on a closed purple curtain. Then the curtain started to rise slowly, like a coquettish woman raising her dress on a leg to seduce someone. Finally, the curtain was finished with the flirt and the stage was fully exposed. It was entirely lit with bright lights. The orchestra consisted of about thirty people or so. A tall man, the conductor, with hair the color of a snowflake, began waving his baton, and the musicians responded to his command like puppets.

Norman and I were holding hands; I squeezed his at the excitement. All the instruments were playing in harmony. The musicians swayed their heads like Butch did when he played the saxophone, as if they were in a different world and hearing different notes from what they were playing for us. It was then that I believed that musicians could see sound.

The conductor pointed his wand at the violin section, and they sounded as if they were a lover begging for forgiveness. Then the great shock of snowflake-colored hair bounced and the conductor pointed to the horns. Their honks sounded like horses racing. He pivoted again and pointed to the piano, which dominated all the instruments even though it was outnumbered. The piano sounded like the narrator of the orchestra. Then the conductor waved his baton again, and everyone was together and harmonious. It sounded like the history of humankind from Genesis to Revelation; it was the Bible.

Just when the music started getting good, I had to go to the bathroom; if I didn't find a restroom quick, it would be curtains. I whispered in Norman's ear that I had to go to the restroom. He in turn asked me if I knew where it was. I wanted to laugh because Mama always said a woman could spot a restroom a mile away.

I navigated through the row of people, trying not to be too disruptive. I hurried quickly down the corridor because I didn't really want to miss too much of the concert. And presto, like a bloodhound, I was in front of the bathroom in the mezzanine. As usual there was a long line in front of the women's restroom and none in front of the men's, both of which were adjacent to one another. My bladder couldn't calm down while I waited on line for my shot at a toilet. People were coming out of the women's bathroom looking as if they had pulled an eight-hour shift at work.

As I waited, hopping on one foot and then the other to keep my bladder under control, a familiar whiff of perfume passed my nostrils; then it remained steady until the entire smell was up my nose. I looked up and there was Polly leering over me with a "What are you doing here?" look. Beneath her gaze she was holding the handles of a wheelchair with a pale, sickly woman seated in it, her skin so wrinkly that it looked like scales on a fish. The woman was wearing a pearl and diamond necklace and a dark dress. You could see that she was rich by the pronounced way she held herself—*I am the queen of the world*. But her eyes were as kind and inviting as a soft bed.

My mother wiped the "What are you doing here?" look off her face and replaced it with the professional woman in the white uniform with the caduceus. She looked at me in a detached and cold manner.

"Mrs. Kellogg, this is my daughter Toddy."

The wrinkly woman smiled, forcing the wrinkles to smile too. She looked at my gown, darting her eyes up and down as Mr. Glok had done the first time I put on the dress at his shop. She extended her hand, and I extended mine.

"Pleased to meet you, ma'am," I said.

"Pleased to meet you too," she said. "Your mother must be proud of you—very few young people are interested in classical music."

"Yes, I am," said Polly.

The orderly working with Polly came out of the no-line men's bathroom. It was a guy named Mack whom I had met at the nursing registry where they assigned the nurses the cases to work on. He grabbed the handles of the wheelchair and began wheeling the dowager to her seat. My mother gave me one last whiteless-eye look, which I decoded as "I'll tend to you later" or "Your ass is mine." I knew I was in deep quicksand once we both got home.

When I returned to my seat, the concert was almost done. I grabbed hold of my Gingerbread Man's hand and watched the ending with intrigue. I was surprised that I found classical music somewhat enjoyable, but maybe it was because of Norman, my Gingerbread Man.

Norman and I flowed with the crowd once the concert ended, until we got outside. Even though it was so crowded that an inch of footstep felt like a mile because the crowd was gridlocked, I checked for any sign of Polly; all she needed was to see me with "a baby maker," as she called my suitors and potential suitors. I felt somewhat confident that lightning wouldn't strike twice with Polly, but I couldn't be too sure.

When we made it out to the starry night without seeing Polly, I relaxed a little and began enjoying the Gingerbread Man. I felt a rush go through my body as I realized that we were completely alone and I was holding my one and only Gingerbread Man's hand. As we walked to the train station, he pulled me closer so we wouldn't be separated by the throngs of people.

"How did you like the concert?" he asked.

"It was beautiful." I smiled. "What was it?"

"Beethoven."

I felt very cultured and rich when he said that, I guess as much as the dowager Ms. Kellogg. I felt I belonged in her scene with the high and mighty, and I was grown as the adults because I was on the town with my Gingerbread Man, who was handsome and cultured. And at this moment he was all mine.

Norman took me to a restaurant once we got off the train. I was glad because my stomach was beginning to growl and I had a bitter taste in my mouth. It wasn't fast food, but still it was nothing fancy. It was more like a family restaurant, the kind they had where I lived. It seated no more than fifty people and had the homey smells of spaghetti and cheese like it was from someone's home instead of a restaurant. Soft violin music came from a record player, which we couldn't see, sounding like the orchestra at Lincoln Center.

We sat in the middle of the dining area at a table for two. A waiter marched in, dressed in black pants, white shirt, and black tie. We both ordered spaghetti and meatballs. As we waited for our order, I looked at Norman from the corner of my eye so he wouldn't know I was staring at him. His cherrywood-colored skin looked like it had been shined by the celestials, his thick lips as inviting as a piece of candy. His fresh haircut and trimmed goatee made him look clean-cut, as if he'd never touched the knucklehead powder. He sure didn't look like the disheveled knucklehead high on smack like on our previous meetings.

Our eyes locked and he smiled, his white teeth making his mouth more sensual. Whatever testosterone-laden hormone he was sending to me was making my head spin. We just had to make small talk; I didn't want him to see my tail wagging like I was some kind of dog. Mama, Ma, and the folks at Kitchen University always said, "Don't be too easy with a man, especially if you like him."

"You were in the army?" I asked.

"Yeah, sure," he said.

He sounded sad. I should have known better; I hadn't served like the soldier on the train. My uncles, my mother's uncles, and her father were in World War II and saw combat; they never discussed their stint in the service. It was as if they had never been in the military. My father, on the other hand, went into the service during the postwar period of World War II. He never saw combat.

"I really don't want to talk about it," he said. "It was really a bad scene."

Now I felt like two cents. He looked down at the table as if he was in deep thought and then raised his head. He looked up at me with his sad Gingerbread Man eyes and gave me a half smile. I touched his hand to try to cheer him up. When he gave me a wide, toothy smile, I quickly removed my hand.

"I want to apologize for handing you that envelope with the smack in it," he whispered. "I was kind of high."

I didn't know what to say. If he was taking me out on the town just to say he was sorry, it was of no use to me. I wanted him to take me out because he liked me, not because he felt guilty for being a knucklehead. The waiter came with two large plates of steaming spaghetti, carrying them on his shoulders as he strutted like a matador, and placed them on the table. Once the waiter left, Norman reached over and touched my hand.

"Look, I won't do that stuff in front of you anymore."

"Why do it at all?" I asked.

That smile, which just moments ago had bedazzled me, turned south and morphed into a frown. I had taken the pacifier from the baby, and he was going mad; the knucklehead powder was winning the war. He quickly gave me a wide, frozen smile, then he picked up the fork and dug into his plate of spaghetti as if giving me the cue to eat and end this sick conversation.

As we ate the meal, sometimes between bites we gave small bits of information about ourselves. He had been studying classical piano at a conservatory before he was drafted. That was all the army information I could get out of him. I told him about Butch and his saxophone. He asked me what I was going to do when I left high school, and my mind went blank. I told him I didn't know—which was true.

After we ate, we got the car and drove to the Bronx below a sexy moon and equally sexy stars. I daydreamed that we were on our wedding night and I was about to give him my virginity as I fingered my virgin pin that was hidden under my gown, pinned to my bra. When he dropped me off in front of my house, I waited for a deep-throated swooning kiss, but he just pecked me on the forehead with his lips closed as if I were a little child. I quickly licked the outside of his lips with my tongue, ran out of the car, and started giggling.

"You gave me another sucker punch," he yelled.

"Yes, my faithful serf, I did."

As I walked up the path to my building, I graded the quality of this date as a half-empty and half-full glass of water. It was a half-empty glass because he was determined to be a knucklehead and use smack, and it was half full because otherwise our first date was fantastic.

Buck greeted me at the door, wagging his tail and jumping up on me. I patted his chocolate mane until he was satisfied and went about his merry way. The curtain was open to Kevin's room; he was zoned out, sleeping like a baby. I wondered what he had told Polly when she called, but it didn't matter—she was hot on my trail; she'd seen me at Lincoln Center. But I had news for her—I was leaving early, so I wouldn't have to deal with her haranguing in the morning. I knew she had an earful to give me.

I woke up an hour earlier to avoid Polly—or should I say to avoid being cornered by her for a tongue-lashing. I wasn't going to be easy prey for her so early in the morning, so I rushed out the door and down the road in front of the building, but I ran smack-dab in the middle of Suki, Butch, and Polly. It seemed they were locked in some sort of conversion; I hoped it was not about me. If I was on their minds, it wasn't a good thing. They saw me, and I couldn't help but notice the smirk on Polly's face.

"Cluck-cluck," she said. "Run, chicken, run."

Mr. and Mrs. Goofy and Polly laughed as I sped past them and gave them a quick hello. I didn't care that Polly had called me a chicken; I'd rather be a thousand chickens than hear her haranguing. Yes, her Polly-wants-a-cracker haranguing so early in the morning was enough to make a person sick.

By the time I got to school, my thoughts were strangling me: Norman and his knuckleheadedness; Polly keeping me in her stubborn pregnancy-prevention jail and presenting problems; and the Dickster—these three were causing me fever. Being a kid was bad enough, but now these problems were making me into a nothing, something below a teenager, a toddler perhaps. When would I be twenty-one so I could deal with all these problems and be on my own?

These thoughts kept me from being bored, which was what I always felt in school. Whoever thought up a system where you had to sit around eight hours a day and read and write was nuts—another jail. Being a kid can drive you nuts; you're always doing things an adult tells you to do but never the things you want to do. I bumped into Rene Wilkins at the end of the day when I was going to detention. She looked cool in an orange A-line dress with four navy-colored stripes circling the top. As always, she looked perfect; she was a brainiac, so what did I expect?

"Bethany, you look terrible," she said. "That old man give you worms yet?"

"No, I just have a lot on my mind."

The last thing my Gingerbread Man had on his mind was sexing me; he was in love with the knucklehead powder. She offered to take me to pizza after detention because she was staying over to do work for her special classes, but I declined. I was going to have a battle royal or perhaps meet my Waterloo like Napoleon Bonaparte had with old Polly.

CHAPTER 15

When I got home, Polly was in battle regalia. Her was hair in a bun on top of her head with a pearl barrette holding it; she was wearing some ugly housecoat with green flowers that looked like they were from outer space; and don't forget those dark eyes. She sat at the table eating grapes. The curtain to Kevin's room was open, which signaled there was going to be a battle royal and he wanted to watch, because he usually liked to keep it closed after he came home from school. He sat on the floor playing with Buck and his basketball.

"Honey child, where were you last night?" asked Polly.

"I was with you, picking cotton, honey child."

"You don't know how to pour piss out of a boot," she said, "leaving your brother in the house by himself."

"He knows how to take care of himself," I said. "What am I, the maid?"

She loved to go back to her southern hillbilly roots when she wanted to make a point, but she blanched at those roots when she was "up north," as the southerners would say. Polly bounced out of the chair and started clunking against the parquet floor with what the family used to call wooden shoes as they laughed at her; they were clogs that had become very fashionable last year. It gave her 203-pound frame more pizzazz for this tongue-lashing she was about to give me. She began splaying her arms and hands as she talked.

"And worse yet," she said, "you tried to get your brother to lie for you."

"No I didn't," I said. "I just told him to tell you I was unavailable."

"You're just determined to go through life not taking responsibility for anything and not apologizing," she said.

"I didn't do anything."

"I've been trying to get you to apologize since you were two," she said, "and I'm still waiting. You're a triple-A copout."

Here we go again. She'd told me all the time that when I was two I did something and she asked me to apologize, and I said every word in the dictionary except *sorry*.

"Let's not go down memory lane now," I said. "I wouldn't have to sneak around if you let me stay out late every once in a while."

"You're too immature. Charity begins at home," she said. "When you begin acting like an adult and fulfill your responsibilities in this house, you might get a shot."

"Dammit—Rene Wilkins's mother lets her stay out late sometimes."

"Don't you curse at me," she said. "Remember what the Bible says: 'Honor your mother and father so all may go well with you.'"

"And the Bible also says, 'Parents, don't be irritating your children.'"

I went to Bible study. I knew how to biblically spar with the best of them. Polly slapped me with a scripture, and I slapped back. But it seemed kind of profane to use the celestials' sacred book to settle a common verbal brawl.

"What's next, Toddy? Another naked boy in the closet?"

"You're like an elephant—you never forget."

"Like I said, you're not mature enough to have a late night," she said. "You don't even know how to wash a dish most of the time."

"Amen," said Kevin.

"My cup runneth over with both of you chumps," I said.

I huffed and puffed myself into my room and slammed the door. Polly went to the closed door and started her haranguing again. Her voice sounded as if she were using a bullhorn to get it across.

"When I was your age, I had respect for my mother's house and my mother."

I went into my dresser drawer and got my earplugs. I thanked the celestials for the human who invented them. I put the earplugs in, sealing them tightly so Polly's ill wind wouldn't penetrate them. I lay on the bed until the ill wind had blown over.

I couldn't fight Polly. She was king and queen wrapped into one 203-pound human fist. All I could do was sneak around and hope that I didn't get caught. The only thing that could topple Polly from her throne and have her release me from this birth control penitentiary was Mama and

Aunt Helen. They seemed to have some control over her. I sure didn't. It's funny how one minute an adult can treat you like you're grown and then the next say you're too young to do this or that. Boy, they get away with murder.

I figured I might have a chance to get Mama and Aunt Helen to help me at the cousin brothers' birthday party on Saturday. After all, Mama had said she was not against me having a boyfriend and other privileges; she just told me what my mother believed about my immaturity. Helen would blame all the troubles I had with my mother on Cousin Karen. She didn't like her because she didn't like her father Uncle Carey—mixed-up family and mixed-up world.

I unsealed the earplugs to see if the coast was clear of Polly's haranguing. It was, but then there was an urgent knock on the door. I knew it was Polly's knock. If the door hadn't been locked, she would have walked in. I unlocked it to see Polly with a professional look on her face, the one she had when she put on her nursing gear.

"Mrs. Kellogg is in the hospital," she said. "I have to leave now and won't be back till Saturday."

I nodded. I was glad she was going so I wouldn't get any more tongue-lashing, but I also wanted my mother home with me. One night I could stand without Polly, but two I didn't like. I kind of missed her haranguing me to get out of bed in the morning to go to school.

"Mama and Lisa can come over Friday night to stay with y'all," she said, "or you can go over to their place and stay with them."

Polly left the room then came back in and started dressing for work. I wondered how I could want Polly to stay home and go at the same time. She gave Kevin and me a peck on the face before she left. She rarely kissed us before she went to work. She smiled at me after she'd pecked my cheek. "You know, you looked good in that evening gown last night," she said. "It was the spitting image of the dress that you wore at Carnegie Hall."

"What's this Carnegie Hall business again?" yelled Kevin from the other side of the curtain.

"Another life I don't have time to tell you about now," said Polly. "I'll tell you about it some other time."

When Polly left, Kevin prodded me about Carnegie Hall as I sat in a folding chair in his room. He brushed Buck's hair as I motormouthed about the performance. He sat intently and began yawning.

"So this guy was into music?" Kevin asked.

"What guy?" I asked.

"Ma's husband," he said. "Royal whatshisname."

"You mean your father."

"I don't know the man," said Kevin.

That was true—he had only met him once, and at the time he'd asked my mother, "Who was that man?" Kevin looked just like Daddy, Butch looked like the Cornwallis-Wests, and I looked like a Bethany and a Cornwallis-West. You could never tell how Kevin felt about anything, whether it was his pigeon toes or his father. The only glimpse you got of his inner thoughts was when he was angry. If he felt emptiness, he filled it with basketball. Butch filled the emptiness with his saxophone and religion, and I—I guess I was filling whatever internal hole I had with the Gingerbread Man.

I hated my father, but I loved him too. I hated him not for anything he'd done to me—I'd gotten got the best of his fatherhood—but for what he'd done to my brothers. When I was born, he wanted me and was in love with my mother, so I was part of a happy future, whereas Butch was an accident of teenage love and Kevin was the end-of-marriage baby. How could this be so, that you could hate someone and love them at the same time? Beats me.

After a while the story got boring to Kevin, so he fell asleep. Buck crawled into Kevin's bed and fell asleep next to him. I called the Gingerbread Man but hung up when he said hello because he sounded like he was on the knucklehead powder. Who would win the war to capture Norman, the knucklehead powder or me?

Polly called in the morning to see how Kevin and I were doing and to remind me to go to school since she wasn't there. As soon as I finished talking to her, I decided not to go to school. I needed my rest because too much was going on: the Gingerbread Man, trying to get paroled from Polly's birth control jail, and the forget-me-not Dickster eating off Mama's plate this coming Sunday.

While Kevin was in the house, I made motions like I was going to school by piling my books on the kitchen table: the algebra book, which I detested; my social studies textbook, which I loved; and an English book, which I loved. Well, two out of three wasn't bad. As soon as he went out the door, I went back into my room. Buck followed me to hang out; he sat in front of the black-and-white TV. I turned it on and then got in bed. Some anchorman was announcing who'd won the presidential primary the previous night.

I knew everyone in social studies class had to do an assignment for Miss Ciotti in June about the California primary—that meant we had to stay up late. She'd made a deal with administration that we could come in an hour later. Sounded good to me. Maybe I wouldn't come in at all.

I slept like a baby. I sat the alarm for 2:00 p.m. so I could pull myself together before Kevin came home and keep up the ruse that I had been to school. The Gingerbread Man was in every second of my dream, and the scene was about us getting married at the temple after he'd been baptized. Butch would be able to marry us since he was male and baptized in the faith. Uncle Philbin or Uncle Carey could take the place of my dad and walk me down the aisle. I knew that after the ceremony, my mother would pull the Gingerbread Man aside and say: "If one hair on her head is missing, your ass is mine, you knuckleheaded shrimp, you."

The alarm went off after that, and I jumped out of bed and got dressed. By the time Kevin got home, I was stirring about in the kitchen like I had just gotten in and was looking for something to eat. He came in and peeked into the kitchen.

"You know, Ma's right," he said. "You don't know how to pour piss out of a boot."

"What do you mean?"

"You're so feeble-minded that you left the schoolbooks in the same spot they were in this morning," he said. "If you wanted to cover up that you didn't go to school, you sure didn't do a good job."

"Are you going to tell Ma?"

"No. I don't waste my breath on lost causes."

The jig was up, so I went to my room. He yelled from the living room that we were going over to Mama's house to spend the night because Polly had said so. That was good, because it was getting kind of dull around the house without Polly. Besides, I could put the bite on Mama about getting on Polly to let me have a late night. I needed all the help I could get.

We packed clothes for the next day, so we wouldn't have to come back home to dress for the cousin brothers' party. Kevin did the unthinkable by bringing Buck with him, knowing Mama would have a fit. We stopped at Chicken Delight, a fast-food restaurant, to buy something to supplement the food that Mama would give us. Her idea of a meal was palm-sized portions and one serving. Thus, you were either not too hungry or half satisfied.

It wasn't that Mama didn't have the money to buy food; it's just she didn't believe in gluttony. She made exceptions for Butch when he lived with her, and Lisa because she was still growing. She told me she detested seeing people pig out when they weren't hungry—just eating for sport, she said.

When we got to Mama's apartment and she opened the door, she frowned at the sight of Kevin with Buck at his heels. "What is this? I'm not running a zoo," she said. Kevin squeezed out a fart in protest, which he always did when she got on his nerves, then he stormed past Mama and went inside the apartment, completely ignoring her. She went in behind him. I tailed her and closed the door behind me. When we reached the living room, Mama said, "You've got the nerve to bring this mutt into my house?" She added, "I should throw you and that mongrel out."

"I told him not to bring Buck over here," I said.

"He's impudent," she said. "I told your ma she should stop spoiling him. You've got to lay down the law to these men-children."

Kevin sucked his teeth then rolled his eyes, letting Mama know that he couldn't care less about what she thought. Lisa came into the foyer, where we were still bundled down with our bags. She was in her pajamas, rubbing her eyes and yawning. Once she focused, she smiled.

"Kevin and Toddy," said Lisa. She gave me a hug, then went to Kevin.

"None of this hug stuff," said Kevin.

"Okay, Kevin," said Lisa.

"You take yourself and that mutt into the side room," said Mama.

Kevin and Buck trotted off to the side room by the door with Lisa trotting behind them. Mama seemed to be bent out of shape. She was more the happy-go-lucky type than this whining old woman. She was much more dynamic than that. I followed her into her bedroom and sat down at the sewing machine table. She sat on the bed not far from where I was seated. Her face was lined with worry.

"I'm so sick and tired of those cousin brothers," said Mama. "If Helen and Polly don't start putting fire to Harry and Kevin's behinds, they're going to be a menace to society."

"Yes, those cousin brothers can be something else."

"The Bible says 'spare the rod and spoil the child,'" she said, "and it also says a fool and his money will part."

"It sure does."

"Well, Mama cut a fool today. A man and a woman dressed real nice came up to me and said, 'Miss, we found ten thousand dollars, but we can only spend it if we play it against somebody's bank account,'" Mama said. "The man went in his pocket and pulled out a roll of bills. My mouth began to water, so he says, 'After we play it against someone's bank account, we can split the ten thousand dollars up evenly.' They went with me to the bank, and I pulled out every dime in my account I had—five hundred dollars. We went outside, and I handed him the five hundred dollars. The man and woman's feet started moving like car wheels, and they sped off. I told Polly about it, and she said, they must've seen me coming."

Five hundred dollars! That was like end-of-the-world money, gangster money—enough money for about five months' rent for our apartment. Mama had released her burden, so she grunted, and then she flashed her usual happy-go-lucky smile on her face.

"Child, Mama done spilled her guts about being a fool," she said. "Now what's on your mind?"

I spilled my guts and told her what an ogre my mother was for not letting me have a late night out like the rest of my friends. I whined that Polly was treating me like a criminal in jail, except there were no bars—just restrictions. Mama nodded. Finally, after a long, whiny pitch, I began to question her.

"Do you think I'm immature?"

"You're mature in some ways and immature in others," she said, "but that's normal for most people."

I was getting somewhere. Now all I had to do was ask her to stand with me against Polly's tyranny. If she and Helen stood for me, I'd have a shot at getting a late night. I didn't know how to ask her to stand for me. She looked at me, and a smile formed on her pencil-thin lips.

"Yes, I'll stand for you. If Polly has the nerve to go out with Brother Quincy and then ask me to cook Sunday dinner for a man who I think is off his rocker," Mama said, "then what's good for the goose is good for the gander."

Just then something sounding like a crash came from the foyer, where Kevin, Lisa, and Buck were. We raced into the foyer, and there was Buck sitting on top of Mama's china closet, where all her valuable silver and china was, with one of Lisa's doll hats resting on his head.

"See, I told you not to put that girl stuff on him," said Kevin.

"Get that beast off my china closet!" said Mama.

Kevin snapped his fingers and Buck jumped off.

After that we finished the evening by eating palm-sized servings of roast beef, sweet potatoes, collard greens, and fruit cocktail, washed down with a six-ounce glass of lemonade. Kevin supplemented the meal with the food from Chicken Delight. I wasn't really hungry, but I was giddy from the thought that I was going to beat Polly at her own game—abuse of power—by letting Aunt Helen and Mama take a swipe at her; they were more her equals than I, so she would listen.

But when I lay down to go to sleep, the Dickster, the man who had tried to end my life over some sex, ticked in my head like a broken stopwatch. The Dickster was a fungus that seemed to be growing in my family's life. Now he was eating Sunday dinner at Mama's house with us. What would be next, pajama parties at our house? What if Polly and he got married? Would I have to sleep with a neck brace around my neck so he wouldn't strangle me?

For one split second before I entered dreamland, I daydreamed about when my Gingerbread Man and I were at the concert and I was the belle of the concert hall with that replica of my Carnegie Hall recital dress and he was my knight in shining armor. All this made me feel tingly inside. The only thing missing was the thick, juicy candy lips of my Gingerbread Man kissing me like there was no tomorrow. But they seemed to be always missing; the knucklehead powder held him captive, so he gave me pecks on the cheek instead of real kisses. It just had to be the smack. The Dickster had given me a better kiss than Norman had.

I awoke the next morning to the voices of Mama and Kevin arguing over a quarter. She accused him of leaving the bar of bathroom soap in water to linger until it was soggy and melting; it was standard procedure for her to charge a quarter for that. If you stayed around Mama long enough, you would end up owing her something. I guess she was starting another $500 war chest to replace the dough she had been swindled out of. "Just give me the twenty-five cents," said Mama, "and stop sassing me."

"No," said Kevin.

Polly said that those two were just alike—stingy—and they even had those pencil-thin mouths to prove it. I knew they were bona fide Cornwallis-Wests; they loved to argue. I eased past them in the foyer on my way to the bathroom to take a bath. Lisa was sitting on the floor, watching them argue. I bet she was hoping Kevin won this round. Kevin was her tin leg god, as Mama liked to say. As I took a bath, I was angry that I hadn't brought my own bar of soap, because I knew Mama was going to charge me a quarter for melting hers.

Sure enough, when I got dressed Mama came in the room with a sheepish grin and asked for the quarter. I complied. After all, I wasn't a fusser like the Cornwallis-Wests; I was a Bethany, and I liked peace and quiet like my father did.

As we walked up the street to the train station, Kevin and Mama continued to bark at one another about the quarter. Lisa watched the two as though it were a drama on television, while Buck walked slowly next to Kevin as he held him by the leash until the dog stopped to do his business. Kevin and Mama's bitching was giving me a headache. Despite this, it was a day with a cloudless sky—a sky so blue that you felt like you were walking on it because it seemed to be everywhere. The event, the assassination of Martin Luther King, seemed to have happened years ago, but it was only a little over a month ago.

The tears, the wailing, and the rioting that had taken place the week he died seemed now to be in the history books for ages. It felt like something I had read about, not something I had experienced. I didn't know whether to be glad or sad about this feeling. How could I or anyone so quickly forget about a man who had tried to help the world?

I got some rest from the two barkers when Kevin dropped Buck off at the house. The rest of us waited in the street. When Kevin came back, Mama and he continued the barking. Once we got on the train, they still wouldn't let up. I was embarrassed. I sat across from them and pretended not to know the two.

As I ignored them, I began plotting in my head about what I would do when Helen and Mama confronted Polly about this birth control prison she had sentenced me to. What would I say if Polly said I was immature? I would say what Mama had said: "I'm immature in some things and mature in others, like the rest of the world." If Polly slapped me in the face about the naked boy who had popped out of the closet, I would remind her that it was Karen's boy in the buff.

We bounced off the train at 116th Street and Lenox Avenue in Manhattan, which seemed like a carnival to me; it was always awake and had so many people, who seemed to be mostly kooks. When we got into the street, there was a man in a gray suit with a dog-eared Bible, yelling at the world: "When your chickens come home to roost, don't be yelling boo-hoo-hoo. 'Cause God's gonna spank you."

A couple of feet from him was a man with an afro and an orange and red dashiki, screaming: "Revolution now. Down with the pigs. Burn, baby, burn—now and forever." He was a black militant like Melaka. We lived in the age of black militants and white revolutionaries like the Black Panthers and the Weathermen. I wondered if Melaka was going to be at the cousin brothers' birthday party.

We zigzagged through the clump of people on Lenox Avenue until we made it to 114th Street. Then Mama said, "I don't know why your ma let Kevin have a birthday party; you know the Way don't believe in that."

"I know, but she arranged the party before she was reinstated in the congregation," I said.

We were in the faith now and back to this again: no holidays except the memorial of Jesus Christ's death. I didn't mind; I was used to not celebrating the holidays. I had tried celebrating Christmas once but felt like a fool. Sometimes it felt real bad being different when everyone else was celebrating the holidays and I was not. One time I even sneaked to celebrate Halloween and went out trick-or-treating in a costume. Polly found out, but she didn't even give me a tongue-lashing.

When we got to Aunt Helen's apartment, a big blue and silver sign was on the front door that read: Happy Birthday, Cousin Brothers. The apartment was already full of cousins. Karen, Minnie May, and Klondike were strutting around the apartment like bored divas. They gave me a cool hello. They were all older than I, so they treated me like a shrimp. Old hags. Someday I'd be their age. The house smelled like food, as it always did. The cousin brothers met up and forgot about the whole world and began laughing and giggling. We went in the kitchen where Helen was standing over the stove, stirring a pot of something. She turned and smiled at us: Mama, Lisa, and me.

"Guess what," she said. "I'm going to work at Child Support."

"Helen, that's good," said Mama.

I congratulated her too. She'd wanted to leave working the elevator at Bellevue Hospital from day one; she was terrified of working with sick people because she was scared of catching a germ. She was so afraid of germs that when she was outside eating potato chips, she used a paper towel to separate her unwashed hand from the chips.

"Hon, don't worry," she said to me. "We'll straighten Polly out about letting you have a late night like the other children."

"Thanks a lot," I said.

Then my blood turned to ice until I was shaking inside like Jell-O. Anything could happen with these Cornwallis-Wests under one roof. They liked to argue, and to take Polly on wouldn't be easy. She was the general of these Cornwallis-Wests fussers. Polly could outfuss all of them put together. Klondike came into the kitchen with her blank, light-skinned face. What got me about these cool, nonchalant people was that they acted and looked emotionless, like robots; they weren't human, even though they swore they were. Klondike looked at me like I was a piece of dust.

"Come out here in the living room," she said, "and help us with this party."

I nodded like a little puppy. "Okay."

I was the youngest girl in the family. Uncle Carey had just gotten remarried to a woman twenty years his senior. They had a baby boy and would eventually have more children (girls), but for now I was a private among the female cousins. Klondike put me outside the kitchen entrance by the wall. Nearby there was a long hallway that led to the bathroom and three bedrooms. She told me to watch the little rascals when they went down the hall to the bathroom and under no circumstances let them go into the bedrooms.

This was good for me. I wasn't breaking a sweat, and I could hear what was going on in Kitchen University. I peeked into the kitchen to see what was going on. Mama had gotten comfortable and was nibbling on something, and Helen was at the stove stirring what was in the pots. Once Mama finished chewing, she began what Aunt Helen called "barking the Bible."

"The birthday party business is pagan," said Mama. "No true Christian should practice paganism."

"Here we go again," said Helen. "We're having fun, and you're killjoying it."

"It's the truth," Mama said. "The only recorded birthday party in the Bible was when Salome asked for John the Baptist's head for her birthday. And King Herod chopped it off and gave it to her on a platter."

"Don't worry, Mama, there're not going to be any beheadings at this birthday party," said Helen.

Yuk. Of all the stories I'd read at Bible study, this one made my skin crawl. Here was a man preaching, and some nondescript asks for his top. The kids started leaving the living room and bouncing down the hallways. Klondike stuck her head out of the living room entrance and said to me, "Put some elbow grease into your job!" She pointed her finger at two boys bouncing down the hallway. "Follow those two. They look like mischief!"

I followed the two little rascals down the hallway, and sure enough, they entered Harry's room and started jumping up and down on his bed. I quickly escorted them back to the party area. When I sat back in my chair, I heard my Polly's voice in the kitchen, and I was glad she was there because I had missed her.

"Mrs. Kellogg died," said Polly.

"I'm sorry to hear that," said Aunt Helen.

This was bad. Polly kind of took it personally when one of her patients died. They were like family. After all, she had worked in Mrs. Kellogg's house for over a year. This was a bad time to deal with Polly because she was kind of in mourning too.

"Eat something, Polly," said Mama.

I heard the clanging of the plate as she began eating. I waited with bated breath for Helen and Mama to stand for me. I heard someone belch in the kitchen.

"Excuse me," said Polly.

"Polly, don't you think it's time to start letting Toddy go out and start dating like the other girls her age?" asked Helen.

"Yeah, Polly—let the child off your leash," said Mama. "Let her have a late night like her other friends."

"Huh. I'm not letting her get in trouble," said Polly. "You don't know ... that Toddy is sneaky. If I let her stay out one night she'll be plotting how to stay out every night."

I thought, *You're darn right I would be. Life's all about getting an inch and growing it into a mile.*

"Polly, she's no sneakier than you were at that age," said Mama.

"That's something coming from a woman who slept with half of Vasselburge."

I' heard the whispers about all the alleged hanky-panky Mama had engaged in back in North Carolina and before she became involved with the Way religion. There were rumors that she had married her blood uncle, my maternal grandfather; she claims that he was her step-uncle. It seemed every man had gotten a turn, to the point that the widow Pike had told Mama to leave her son alone because she was a married woman. She didn't, so Widow Pike went to the root doctor and got some herbs to cast a spell. They said Mama was rocking and rolling with pain in her back after Widow Pike's fix. But a rumor isn't truth; it is either a lie or perhaps truth decorated with viciousness.

"Whatever I did is between me and God," said Mama, "and let me tell you to your face before you poke out from behind: the Bible says to honor your mother and father so all will go well with you. It also says don't bear false witness—that means don't go by rumors—and it also says don't judge so ye won't be judged. Besides, you shouldn't talk. What you did with Strap Lias would prevent you from entering an atheist's church."

After that, not a sound came from the kitchen; it was like a soundproof room—sound didn't come in or go out. My father often said my mother could hit below the belt with her mouth. He was right; sometimes garbage came out of her mouth and it stunk up the whole place. But Mama was no slouch when it came to a terrible mouth.

"You leave Strap Lias out of it," said Polly.

"Yeah, Mama, why did you have to bring up Strap Lias?" said Helen.

"Don't pay Polly any mind; you know she says anything when she gets mad. She doesn't mean it."

"You two are picking on me about my daughter while all I'm doing is trying to prevent her from having a baby out of wedlock as I did."

"What are you trying to say, that my daughters are lowlifes because they had babies?" asked Helen.

"No. But if the shoe fits, wear it," said Polly.

"You're a lowlife for messing with Strap Lias," said Aunt Helen.

Both of them broke and took turns barking at my mother, dredging up all the sewage from the past, reminding Polly that she'd once been sent home from school for stinking when she was ten. This was enough. I wanted them to stand with me, not crucify my mother, I got out of the chair and raced into the kitchen.

All of them were standing and barking at one another. It sounded like an off-key symphony whose melody no one could identify. Mama and Helen were using their index fingers like knives, stabbing the daggers repeatedly an inch away from Polly's face to make their points. Polly responded in kind, knifing her index finger like a sword, but her other hand was curled into a tight fist as if she were going to whack one of them.

Polly was outgunned. I stepped between her and the two barkers. They smelled like the spoils of war, the adrenaline before the kill. It acted like a contagion on me. I curled one of my hands into a fist as it rested at my side. I loved all of them, but I loved my Polly first, and if push came to shove I'd whack them if they were a threat to her.

"Leave my mother alone," I said.

Mama and Helen dropped their faux daggers and looked at me as if I had slapped them in the face.

"Turncoat," said Helen. "Didn't you ask us to stand for you?"

"I'm not a turncoat," I said. "I just don't want you to drag my mother through the mud to make a point."

"Don't you heifers call my daughter a turncoat," said Polly.

My mother was going cow, using words from the farm they'd had in North Carolina. I closed my mouth; I knew the pecking order in the family, and I was at the bottom, a newborn chick. I didn't want to fray any feathers in the family, so I zipped my lip. But I inched closer to Polly, protecting her just in case this posse of two made a grab for her. All three of them continued barking; it sounded like a broken record.

"What's happened to Kitchen University? Have the inmates taken over the scholars?" someone yelled from the kitchen entrance. It was Uncle Philbin, the head of his long and lean body hanging in the kitchen while the other part was hanging out of it, keeping with the tradition of the men in the family, who considered Kitchen University taboo.

"You girls sound like rabble," said Uncle Philbin. "What's happened to all the scholarship in Kitchen University?"

All four of us fell into the kitchen chairs, exhausted like prizefighters in the twelfth round.

"Puny, don't be sneaking up on us like that," said Helen.

"Okay. But what's with all this racket?"

Helen and then Mama told him about my situation between gasps of air. My mother also told him her side of the story. Then Polly summed up her entire feelings about letting me have a late night. "I don't want her to grow up too fast and get into trouble like I did."

"Well, you can't keep old Toddy locked up in the house like she's a piece in a museum," said Uncle Philbin.

This didn't sit well with Polly, so she gave him a tongue-lashing by reminding him that they had different fathers and then calling him a bastard. This was old news and an old technique. When Polly was on the warpath, she would lob anything dirty at you if she was arguing with you. Philbin was no slouch; even though he wasn't a blood Cornwallis-West, he was one in spirit, and thus he was expert at arguing. He dropped his hat into the ring and started barking too. If you folded over words that people said to you, you didn't need to be around the Cornwallis-Wests, because to them fussing was a blood sport.

They argued for what seemed like hours until their mouths turned dry and thirsty and their stomachs growled from hunger. Once they finished and got chummy again, which was always the case, I knew my needs, desires, and wants had been lost in the fog of war. My needs were now kid-sized and meant nothing to these adults. My problem had been discussed, barked about like dogs by them, but now it had been laid to rest.

The party began thinning when parents picked up their children. The bash was officially closed when Kevin and Harry began fighting as they always did when it was time to go home. Philbin was going to drop us off in his car. As we waited in front of Helen's building, I popped the question to Polly.

"Ma, can I have a late night out?"

"I don't know," said Polly.

I knew her answer meant I had no chance; if the crowd of Cornwallis-Wests couldn't sway her to my side, it was useless—it was like pouring water on a duck's back as Polly liked to say. I felt hopeless and pissed off at the same time; it ran through my veins like ammonia poisoning my soul. I was glad it was dark so no one could see the expression on my face.

Philbin pulled up in his green station wagon. As soon as we got in the car, Kevin and Lisa fell asleep. Mama, Polly, and Philbin started chitchatting about back home in North Carolina. Sometimes I painted pleasant pictures in my head about the state that had birthed them. My brain made images of blue-green grass on acres and acres of land with few people but lots of chickens, cows, and horses. But tonight there were no visions of such things in my head as they recalled their home. I was beside myself with anger; I wanted my late night.

My eyes became glued to the stars and the moon as Philbin went up the West Side Highway. It was a night without clouds, with a full moon and stars filling the darkness, shimmering as if they were making new life second by second. I thought about the celestials, something I had not done for quite a while. The thought of them and their reverence had been replaced by my Gingerbread Man, much to my dismay.

"What's up, kiddo?" asked Philbin. "Why you so quiet back there?"

"Just thinking," I said.

"You sound like you're ready to step into the ring," he said.

No. I'm not like you Cornwallis-Wests, fussing my way through life; I'm a Bethany: quiet, intelligent, and mild-mannered. My mother piggybacked on what Philbin said, but I ignored her, so much so that her words blended into the sound of the wind passing us as the cars went by and honked their horns—the usual hustle and bustle of NYC, moderate compared to other nights on the West Side Highway.

Philbin first dropped off Polly, Kevin, and me, and then Mama and Lisa. We bid our farewells in tired and spent tones. Since Polly's patient had died, she'd be home for a couple a days, and eventually her nursing registry would give her another patient. As a result of this, she opened the sofa in the living room and bedded down there.

Everyone fell asleep except for me once we went to bed; the others snored like thunder. I lingered in the darkness and listened to the chirping of the sparrows that had built a nest in a loose brick inches from my window. When they first came to the outside of my window days ago, I watched the two sparrows gather leaves and branches to build their little hut. Once they finished, they started chirping at one another as if they were fussing, and then one flew off in a huff. It came back in a couple of hours, refreshed, and nested with the other sparrow, who was sleeping. I guess they were as free as birds, as they say—free to roam, unlike a kid.

I started sweating at my brow, and that was followed by a splitting headache. I was nowhere; everything had failed for me. But I had news for Polly—she had better give me an answer, a good one, by tomorrow night or else I'd be out of there Monday morning. I would be running as far away as I could from her and the fussy Cornwallis-Wests—and as fast as possible. I would begin a new life without them, one where I could have the freedom to be my own person. At that declaration, I fell asleep, determined that I would have it my way.

I awoke Sunday morning determined to test Polly like she always tested me when I wanted to have fun. If she answered yes and let me have a late night, then everything would be hunky-dory; if she didn't give me an answer, I'd be out of there. Ditto if she answered no. And to top it off, I wasn't going to ask Polly again; if she didn't bring it up, I wouldn't remind her and would take it as a no.

Polly was in the kitchen singing something or other and cooking. The smell of bacon and eggs oozing through the closed door reminded me that there was a Dickster problem. Dick Quick, Brother Richard Quincy, Rick Quick, and whatever other aliases he used for his evil works, was having dinner with us at Mama's house. I would be on high alert just in case he whipped out a rope and lassoed me or my family like he had done to me in Mount Vernon.

First and foremost, we had to get some spiritual food at the temple; the magazine study and Bible lecture would give me a different outlook on life for a while. I took a bath, put on a housecoat, and went into the kitchen to partake of some real food. Polly was in an old, cheap housedress, glowing like a flower recently bloomed. I sat down in the dining area and waited to be served my breakfast.

"Have you forgotten, Toddy?" asked Polly. "Brother Quincy will be eating dinner with us at Mama's house."

"No," I said. "What's Mama cooking?"

"Beef or something or other."

I wasn't really concerned about the palm-sized meal Mama was going to serve everyone, but a chill came over me that my mother, the smartest woman in the universe as far as I was concerned, could be bamboozled by this Dickster. That she didn't she through this demon surprised me because she saw through everyone else's shit, including mine. But I guess love is blind, as they say.

We dressed in our Sunday best: Kevin wore a tan cotton suit with a yellow shirt and a yellow and tan tie; Polly, a black and white A-line quarter-sleeve dress to soften her thick figure; and I, a bone-colored two-piece suit with black patent leather shoes. I looked and felt well-heeled, being dressed up and walking next to people who were well-dressed. Polly gave us her final seal of approval by looking at us and smiling.

"Pretty feathers make a pretty bird," said Polly.

When we got to the temple, the Dickster was at the door greeting people. Once he reached us, he gave my mother the goo-goo smile—I guess a pre–hanky-panky look. She in turn gave him a little schoolgirl smile and began to giggle really funny like one of the characters in a cartoon. Those two had to go. Even if Brother Quincy had been someone other than the Dickster, the thought of those two getting married and cohabitating in the same household with Kevin and me was enough to make me crawl under a rock. Those two sugarplums should never live under the same roof with us.

We were early; the service hadn't started. People were milling around in their Sunday best, talking—or as they say fellowshipping—with one another. And lo and behold, my grandmother was early for a change and was standing in the back with a gang of women around her. Polly looked at me and smirked.

"It must be Armageddon today if Mama's early," said Polly.

"Oh, maybe she's turning over a new leaf," I replied.

When we reached Mama, the women were oohing and aahing over her hat, a new creation of hers that she had whipped up a day ago: it was a pastel tulle with a net that reached just below her nose, and a portion of the hat was decorated with real flowers, red and white carnations. It rested on her head like the crown of some great kingdom, and Mama arched her neck as if she were a great monarch.

The melody from a temple song began playing on the loudspeaker. The Dickster, or if you will Brother Quincy, got on the platform and announced that the meeting was beginning. Mama left and went to the front seat; Polly, Kevin, and I sat in the middle. We sang the temple song, which was "Love Jah." When we finished singing and sat down, Brother Quincy announced the topic for the public talk and who would be giving it.

"Let us all welcome Brother Ronnie Bethany, a newly minted elder from the nearby Bulwark congregation, who will be giving the Bible discourse: 'Why True Christians Should Avoid Porneia.'"

My mother gently nudged my right side with her elbow and whispered, "Why didn't Butch tell me he was appointed an elder?" I just shrugged. But it was like, *Wow, Butch an elder? He has reached the stars.* Nobody gets appointed elder just because he wears trousers, even though only men can be appointed. A person has to be of good character, must be spiritually sound, and has to get approval from the headquarters of the faith after being recommended by the elders at the individual congregation. I was still kind of shocked that they hadn't appointed him a ministerial servant first as they usually did when they promoted people—that he'd just leapfrogged it to the top.

Butch was sitting in the front row with Suki, Mama, and Lisa. He walked the short distance to the platform and stepped up with vigor. He placed his notes and Bible on the lectern and stood like a statue. He was clothed in a tan tweed polyester suit with a surreal white shirt, which seemed to have invented its own gleam, and a bone-colored tie; he was it, and he knew it—a somebody.

"Brothers and sisters, as Christians we should guard against any forms of porneia," said Butch. "Some may ask, 'What is porneia?' Porneia can be anything from fornication to masturbation."

I looked around the hall to see if anyone was moving nervously in their chair. If they were, then in my book they were guilty of porneia. Butch gave the full definition of porneia in his baritone voice with a silkiness that only made you want to listen more.

"*Porneia* is a word found in the Greek Septuagint scriptures, and it means any illicit sexual relations. In our translation, it is called fornication," said Butch. "If we turn to 1 Corinthians 5:9 KJV, we can find that fornication is detestable to God," said Butch.

I watched as he thumbed through his New World Translation Bible, so mesmerized that I didn't even bother to open mine. Just think, the boy whose mother had ignored him for seven years because she was too young to know what to do with a baby, whose father had questioned his paternity when he was getting a divorce from his mother, and who had to wear the same gray pants and orange mohair sweater to school every day for a year after his father left had now gotten the last laugh. He had beaten the odds and won the game of life.

I marveled at this Horatio Alger story until a tinge of fear coursed through my veins like hot vinegar. It seemed Kevin and Butch were making a ring around me. Butch had all of this, and Kevin had his basketball; his coach sounded like he could go pro. If they were to lose all their pluses today, at least they'd be has-beens instead of never-beens. Was I on my way to becoming a never-been, some black sheep of the family, or worse, "poor Toddy"? How was I going to catch up with them, Mr. Everything and the soon-to-be basketball star? Impossible.

By the time Butch finished his lecture and the congregation thanked him by giving him a round of applause, I had gone from being giddy with pride to navigating an emotional roller coaster. Brother and brother seemed to be breathing down my neck and saying, "You can't do this." Well, I had news for them: I was sick of them. I wouldn't let them make a ring around me.

After the meeting, the members of the congregation flocked around Butch like he was a piece of new money, congratulating him on his new spiritual appointment as elder; after all, his appointment had to be prayerfully considered. I tried to weave through the throngs of people to congratulate him and thank him for the wonderful talk he'd given on porneia, but my heart and feet weren't in it because his shine seemed to be making me look bad.

Polly pushed through the throng and whispered in Butch's ear. A look of terror crossed his face; I knew that she was bent out of shape about having been left out of knowing of his appointment as elder and had given him a tongue-lashing. Mama popped up, grinning from ear to ear and acting as if she were his mother by chitchatting about how wonderful he'd been as a boy, definitely taking the role of Polly as mother, as her hat bounced on her head until it looked like a wobbly crown, the two carnations moving every which way as she advertised about this great man.

Of course Polly, hell-bent against this maternal hijacking by Mama, put her mouth to Mama's ear and whispered heaven knows what. Mama, who didn't seem shocked at all, looked as if someone had robbed her of the $500 she had been swindled out of. Polly had a tongue like a whip; it could either lash or massage. Once Polly finished bending Mama's and Butch's ears, she patted both on the back with either hand and said, "I hope you had an earful."

The music started playing again; it was time for the second meeting, the magazine. I had a chance to get a little shine like Butch; the magazine was questions and answers, so I could answer one of the questions. A girl needs a little shine. I know I did, especially with these great men for brothers.

I'd studied *The Magazine* at home for this week's lesson, but as the questions were asked from the podium and members of the congregation raised their hands to be chosen to give the answer, I wimped out. There were just too many stars in this galaxy. If I answered correctly, I'd take the shine off Butch or put the shine on Butch for sounding like a fool. After all, Butch was an A-plus speaker, and he had a good job to prove it.

Finally the last paragraph came. Polly pinched me on my elbow and whispered, "Answer a question." I raised my hand, and the brother called my name, Toddy Bethany, instead of saying "Sister," because I hadn't been baptized yet. I answered the question swiftly. I didn't care if I shined; I just wanted Polly off my back.

Once the service finished, Kevin, Polly, and I headed for this big meal at Mama's house; really it was for Polly to snare the Dickster. We prepared for Mama's palm-sized portions by stocking up on some snack foods at the stores we passed, which we stuffed in our bags: Kevin's briefcase, my tote bag, and my mother's handbag held the stash.

When we entered Mama's house, it smelled like a restaurant. The Dickster came right after my mother, Kevin, and I had settled down and were sitting on the sofa waiting for this meal Mama was cooking and heating up. Once the Dickster entered the living room where we sat, his and Polly's eyes locked; for a second they made goo-goo eyes at one another, but they shut down the stare once they realized Kevin and I were looking at them.

The Dickster gave everybody a quick hello then hustled to the sofa where Polly was to nuzzle in a love nest beside her. But Kevin sat between them before the man could sit his ass down. They looked like three peas in a pod, stuffed on the sofa. As the lovebirds tried to get closer, Kevin stretched his arms and legs to keep them apart. Kevin made such a gap between the two would-be lovebirds that the Dickster appeared to be agitated.

This was a good thing; all he needed to do was say one bad thing to Kevin or me and this love fest was over. My mother ignored or wasn't paying attention to what Kevin was doing; she was smitten with this undercover strangler. She was aglow with the lovebug, looking pie-eyed from love like I probably did when I was with the Gingerbread Man.

From her look, those starstruck and smoky eyes for the Dickster, I could tell that she had failed my test. The last thing that was on her mind was a late night for me. *I'm out of here; I'll never be branded a never-been and remain a slave. I'll be an old woman stuck in the house asking for a late night from Polly. As for the Dickster, Mama and Kevin can take care of him.*

The Dickster seemed to be getting a little edgy, trying to navigate the canyon Kevin had created between him and Polly on the sofa. He looked at the top of Kevin's head like he wanted to chop it off. He must have realized that the last thing he wanted to do was to get his beloved's son hot and bothered about something he'd done, so he shifted his eyes to me and gave me a smile. I could see why my mother would want him; he was tall, dashing, and handsome. If he hadn't tried to hang me, I'd give him a shot at my mother.

"Toddy, that was a good answer you gave during the magazine study," he said.

"You sure did a good job, Toddy," said Polly. "Keep up the good work."

"Thanks," I said.

I blushed at the stroking. I didn't know if the Dickster meant it, but I knew Polly didn't give any fake compliments. The doorbell rang, and Mama, who was in the kitchen getting dinner ready, answered the door. I could tell by the lumberjack footsteps beating against the wood floors in the foyer that it was Butch and Suki. I shook my head.

Oh no. They're eating here too.

Butch and Suki walked into the living room. I didn't care if Butch was an elder; they still looked goofy. The goofy couple exchanged greetings with everyone and parked their behinds on the sectional sofa, squeezing into the little space left next to my mother. The weight was crushing Kevin, so he got up and took his canyon with him, closing the gap he had created between the two lovebirds, so much so that Polly and the Dickster were now snuggled eye to eye.

"Toddy, you really gave a good answer at the meeting today," said Butch.

I thanked him and blushed again. Coming from the big man on campus, this was a double piece of chocolate cake. Mama came into the living room wearing a chef's toque—probably Uncle Philbin's, because he was a chef. She had a smirk on her face like she was up to something. Whatever it was, it'd be a doozy, because when she started stirring the pot, whatever came out was big.

"Chow is ready," she said.

We followed Mama into the kitchen. There was a large oak folding table to accommodate the big brood: Polly, Kevin, Suki, Butch, and Lisa, the last of whom was angling to sit next to Kevin. She motioned for the Dickster to sit at the head of the table.

"You're the guest," said Mama, "so you sit at the head of the table."

"Thank you, Sister Cornwallis-West," said Brother Quincy.

After the Dickster took his place, we all fell into whatever seats that could be found. The table had been set with Mama's finest china and silver; everyone knew, except the Dickster, that if you broke anything, you'd be charged for it. Mama placed a big silver roaster with a lid in front of the Dickster. It smelled like beef, sweet and tangy.

"Please say the prayer, Brother Quincy," said Mama. All of us lowered our heads and closed our eyes in deference to God as Brother Quincy belted out a short prayer thanking God for the meal. I bit my tongue so I wouldn't say something out of place at the nerve of this hypocritical devil saying a prayer to God. My stomach growled in anticipation of the meal. I wondered what was inside the silver roaster that Mama had cooked.

After the prayer, Mama darted to the utensil drawer in the china cabinet, got out a large fork and knife, and laid them next to the silver platter. She removed the lid from the platter. Once everyone got a full view, the air was sucked out of the room. On the platter rested a twenty-pound pink tongue, looking as if it had just been removed from the cow, its tip pointed like a petulant child who was sticking its tongue out in anger.

Butch and Suki, who were sitting across from me, were whispering and giggling in their private love nest that always seemed to be with them. Polly had a flabbergasted look on her face, identical to the one she had had on her face when the nondescript boy came flying out of the closet naked. Kevin and Lisa looked at this thing as if they were scientists and had found a new species. And the Dickster, whom the tongue seemed to be gunning for because the petulant tip was pointing at him, was trying to keep his cool, but his eyes gave him away; they were wild as if he had been shot out of a cannon.

Polly eyed Mama, who was standing over the tongue with a shit-eating grin, and gave her a "How dare you?" look. Everyone seemed to get over the initial shock and began to look at this platter again, only to be shocked once more, for it was garnished with what seemed like hundreds of miniature tongues made from dough with identical petulant tips.

I waited for the Dickster to tell Mama that he didn't eat tongue; that would be the end of the lovebirds' romance because Polly would think he had disrespected Mama. But the Dickster recovered from the initial shock and complimented Mama on her devil's work.

"What kind of meat is this?" asked Kevin.

"Tongue," said Polly.

Kevin placed one finger in each ear and stuck out his tongue, trying, I guessed, to mimic the petulant tongue. Polly told him to stop the nonsense. This scene seemed to further rattle the Dickster, who looked as if he was going to explode. I wanted to help him along, so I took a stab at rattling him by kicking him in the knee. I apologized as he grunted in pain. He looked at me like he wanted to noose me again, but he turned on the charm before he said something that could banish him from Polly's life. Mama lobbed off the petulant tip of the tongue and set it on the Dickster's plate. She then served us. The meal was uneventful after that; in fact, it was quite good.

The sound of the chirping sparrows nested in the brick by my window bent my ear. I got out of the bed quickly, trying to avoid Polly when she came home from her new job. She had failed the test; she had not given me an answer about the late night.

I had $100 saved, and I was going to leave to start a new life, away from Polly and my larger-than-life brothers who were making small fry out of me. It would take me a hundred years to achieve what they had achieved.

Kevin was already dressed when I entered the living room. He gave me a fast look, then leashed Buck and took him out the door for a walk. A tinge of regret filled me about running away, but it was replaced by the thought that I would be free as those birds nested in the brick by my window. By the time Kevin came back with Buck, I was dressed and ready to roll.

"You're up mighty early," said Kevin.

"Yeah, I am trying to do something different," I said.

"I guess it's never too late to do the right thing."

I took that as a cheap shot he was lobbing at me, but I ignored it; he would be history in a couple of minutes. After he left, I glanced at the clock on the wall in the kitchen. It was 8:00 a.m. Polly would be home in half an hour, if not sooner. I didn't want to see her face again—if I did, I'd get cold feet and decide to stay.

I decided to come back that night to get my things after I got situated at the motel and Polly was at work. I was going to the Pelham Ching Ching Motel on the edge of the New England Thruway. I had seen it many times when the family went to Freedom Land Amusement Park, a place with rides and fun. The motel was adjacent to the amusement park, and the latter looked like a ghost town; it was a bunch of ranch buildings sprawled over a couple of acres. The amusement park was eventually torn down, and now they were building some co-ops on it called Co-op City. I opened my chest of drawers and got out the $100 that was in my shoebox. I would call my Gingerbread Man tonight and let him know I had moved and give him the telephone number at the motel.

As I walked down the block to the private cabstand on East 225th Street, down the street from where I lived, I looked for any sign of Polly, who was the last person I wanted to see; if I saw her, perhaps I'd lose heart and scuttle my entire freedom ride. I bumped into Rene Wilkins once I made it to the cabstand and told her I had an errand to attend to for Polly.

I got in the cab, and as it pulled out of the block, headed toward the motel, I felt free for the first time in a long time; the only time I remembered feeling this free was when my father lived at home. I wondered, when Polly and the rest of the family found out I had run away, what would they do? Would they cry or throw a parade? Perhaps the lovey-dovey for me all these years had been just hype; maybe they didn't care for me.

Once we reached the New England Thruway, it began to drizzle, and a couple of rumbles of thunder startled me. I rubbed my brow; it was as wet as a river. I was sweating. I know I was terrified of something, but what? When I caught sight of our destination, it looked eerie; the sprawling buildings on the acreage looked like a town that had been abandoned—or worse, a ghost house. If a gargoyle came out of each cabin with a pickax, I wouldn't have been surprised.

The cab driver dropped me off at the office to get registered and waited for me to open the glass doors to the office. Then he drove off. The front desk looked like it was a mile from the doors. I could see it, but it was a walk. I inched down a dingy red carpet, which reminded me of those movie premieres where they walk on the red carpet. The place smelled of old odors basted with the new odor of fried chicken coming from somewhere. Faded posters of movie stars long gone, from another time, hung on the walls like medals: Humphrey Bogart cool with dangling cigarette, Clark Gable swashbuckling in some costume of the nineteenth century, and Betty Grable looking alive and well in an army uniform from World War II.

The man at the desk had on pilot's glasses, looked to be about forty, had a medium build, and was very muscular and athletic-looking. He peered up from a book and acknowledged me for a second, then shifted his eyes back to the book he was scanning.

"What can I do for you?" he asked.

"I'd like a room for the night."

I really didn't know how long I wanted the room, but saying one night sounded kind of cheesy to me. He looked up from his book again and gave my face the once-over. I pushed out my tits to make myself look older. I'd forgotten to put on makeup; it would have aged me.

"How old are you?" he asked.

"Eighteen."

"You have proof?"

I didn't. The fake birth certificate that I had bought and fought for from Viola was in my drawer at home. I was sure I was turning purple searching for an adequate lie. The phone rang in another room; the sound was loud and shrill as if the bell needed to be adjusted. The man started jogging in the direction of the phone to catch it before it stopped ringing.

"What, you son of a bitch?" he yelled into the phone. "I'm not cooking the books for you!" He slammed the phone down on the receiver and jogged back to the desk. He didn't even look at me but put his eye on the book again.

"What type of room you want? Waterbed or no waterbed?"

"A room for one occupant with waterbed," I said.

"It's seventeen dollars and fifty cents a night with the waterbed," he said. "The only food in here is in the vending machines, and checkout time is noon tomorrow." I wanted to thank God that he had perhaps forgotten that he wanted proof of my age. I gave him the money, and he reached in a drawer behind the desk and handed me the room key.

SPRING 1968

PART III

Huh. So this is the adult world.
—Toddy Bethany

CHAPTER 16

The room was a couple of doors from the office on the first floor; I was glad of this because the motel and the experience was kind of spooky. Besides, I had never been in a motel before, or if I had, it was when I was a baby and with my parents. It wasn't spectacular: it was small, it smelled spicy like a restaurant, and it had an old red Persian rug that looked like it had been there since year one. The spicy smell made my stomach growl.

I went to inspect this waterbed to see how cool it was. It was round and in the middle of the room, covered in sheets and blankets that were clean but that looked as old as the Persian rug. On the headboard was a switch to turn the waterbed on. I flipped the switch, and the bed started gyrating. It exhaled and inhaled like a chest that was breathing, and it had a hissing sound too. I turned it off because it didn't sound too cool, and I really didn't want to fall asleep with its inhaling and exhaling because then I might drown. I heard people had sex on waterbeds, but if this was true, it must have been like having sex on a horse's back.

There was a TV set resting on a cheap dresser that looked like if you sneezed, it would fall apart. I went over to turn it on, to end the soundlessness in the room, which seemed as if it would drive me mad, but it was pay. It had a slot on a cheap antenna with bulging rabbit ears and a sign asking for twenty-five cents for an hour. Mama must have owned the TV; she probably came at the end of the week to collect all the quarters. I laughed. I would sure miss Mama.

I went and lay down on the bed and looked at the ceiling. The entire ceiling had mirrors on it. I knew that this wasn't the temple or the Girl Scouts and that people had the mirrors on the ceiling so they could sexualize.

The room was too dark; it reminded me of a dungeon. The only time I saw anything in its true form was when I was a couple of inches from the object; the other things looked like shadows or facades.

I hustled to the window and pulled back the curtains so I could get some light and life into the room. It was really two long windows side by side. Once I pulled back the curtains and the light blasted into the room, I hopped back in bed. I wondered when the world would know I was a runaway. What would Polly say? What would Mama say? I guess the school would call and ask why I hadn't come to school the second day in a row, because I hadn't gone to school on Friday. But whatever happened, I was now as free as those birds that nested in a brick by my window.

As I lay in the bed contemplating my new life, I looked at the windows, where this brilliant light was coming from. One of the windows was clear, and the other had a painting that looked like a fresco, one of those antiquities that I'd seen at the museum. It was pastel, and there was a man with a long silver beard and a bell hat pointing a pogo stick at, I presume, the audience. I was very proud of this cultured display of the antiquities. The man reminded me of a kindly grandfather, one of the munchkins with a flowing white beard—a true fairy tale.

I glanced again at the hand on the thick pogo stick, and it moved from north to south. I wanted to scream, but it was as if my vocal cords had been glued. This was a live man, and the pogo stick was a penis. I shook my head in disbelief and took a second look. It was big and ugly, not like the small compact one I saw when I used to change Kevin's diaper. It looked like one of the tentacles of an octopus. I hadn't had time to look at the penis of the nondescript boy who had fallen out of the closet. This definitely was porneia as Butch's talk at the temple defined it—illicit sexual involvement.

I tried to scream again, but the only thing that came out was air. I hopped out of bed, grabbed the key, and ran out the door to the office, taking care to avoid Mr. Porneia and his naked behind. I made it to the glass doors of the office, pulled them open, and ran down the long path to the desk. The same man was at the desk, his eyes glued to the same book. My vocal cords finally came out from under anesthesia, and I coughed.

"There's a naked man in front of my window," I said.

"That's Hal, my brother," he said.

"Hal?"

"Yeah, he didn't take his medication," he said. "So now I have to call the guys with the straitjackets."

"I'm checking out," I said. "Can I have a refund?"

He opened the register and handed me a twenty-dollar bill.

"Keep the change," he said.

I asked him to call me a cab so I could fly out of there. I was starving. After he did so, the same green cab with the same driver came barreling down the road in front of the office. I ran down the long path to the car, I guess to avoid Hal. So this was porneia: ceilings with mirrors, a naked man, and his oblong penis, which looked like it belonged to an octopus. I was getting away from this house of horrors.

As we rode down the New England Thruway, I felt like a failure. If I couldn't fit in a motel, where could I fit into? It seemed that I was always the extra finger or foot that didn't belong. I didn't really fit in at school and just showed up because I had to. And really, Kevin and Polly were in perfect harmony. He never really did anything to get on her nerves. He was always on time at school and got out of bed without her begging him. He was neat and accomplished like her. All these folks were shining, Butch, Kevin, and Polly, whereas I was the dull piece of silver that wouldn't shine.

When I got home, I was ready for Polly to give me a tongue-lashing because I knew the school had called and told her I'd missed two days. I really didn't care what she did; I was glad to get home for now. As I opened the door to the apartment, it reeked of fried chicken, and my empty gut growled. The curtain to Kevin's room was open, and he was sitting on the floor, brushing Buck's fur. He looked at me for a second then glanced back at Buck and kept brushing. I looked in the kitchen for Polly.

"Where's Ma?" I asked.

"She went down the block to call Mama because all the telephones in the building are down," he said.

"How long have they been down?"

"Since seven this morning."

Great. I was off the hook because the school couldn't get to her to let her know I had missed two days. I reached into the huge pot on the stove, got a drumstick, and went to my room. When I got to my room, there was a box on the chest; it was giftwrapped in silver paper with white stripes and had a pink satin ribbon on top of it. I smiled and flew to the chest to unwrap it. On the bow of the ribbon was a card which said, "To Toddy, from Mother." I opened the package, and the first thing I saw was a letter on composition paper that read as follows:

> I give you permission to have one late night per week. I do not believe in fornication but have enclosed some items so that you won't be left holding the bag. I've enclosed some birth control pills. And please remember that syphilis and gonorrhea are worse than a cold, so I have enclosed some condoms. Please remember to take care; you are my only daughter.
>
> Always your loving mother.
>
> PS: Your brother was a virgin when he got married to Suki; why don't you follow in his footsteps?

Oh, not this again, this Butch stuff. Butch at the Creation; Butch at the Last Supper, the mysterious thirteenth disciple; Butch at Gettysburg, both a Confederate and Union soldier; Butch at Ford's Theatre seated next to President Lincoln and his wife; and Butch at Valley Forge encouraging General Washington to forge ahead. I was sick of the Butch stuff. My cup had runneth over with the Butch throne. Maybe if he'd gotten some before he was married, he wouldn't be so goofy now. And what was so bad about it was that he walked around like he was very modest when really he was his own publicity agent. Like who told Polly that he was a virgin? The bees?

But wow. I'd finally won something. She didn't have to worry about me getting pregnant or catching VD from the Gingerbread Man; he was attracted to the knucklehead powder. If she knew the Gingerbread Man was dating me, he would be a dead man. I would be worthy of this new privilege—well, most of the time; nobody's perfect. Besides, life would be dull if there weren't a little pepper in it. I'd go off course just a bit by taking an extra late night or several every once in a while until I built up enough stock with Polly to go out every night.

Polly came into the room. I swung around and hugged her.

"Thanks, Ma, for letting me have a late night."

"Don't mention it," she said. "Just come back in one piece."

Her eyes turned dark as midnight as she sat on the bed.

"You're my only daughter; don't be caught up in some stuff," she said. "There's worse things than getting pregnant."

"Ma, don't worry. I'll be careful," I said. "But please stop comparing me to Butch."

"But you should be proud of your brother."

"I am."

She giggled like a little schoolgirl. "Guess what? Kevin stopped speaking to Butch; he's mad at him," she said.

"I want the whole scoop," I said. "Maybe this is a good thing; it'll save some oxygen."

She frowned at the suggestion then giggled again. We went into the kitchen to eat supper. I was tickled pink, and it was hard to tone down my rosy emotions. I had everything now—a late night and my Gingerbread Man.

Kevin was mad at Butch because he'd called him trifling. It seemed Butch had gotten Kevin a part-time paper route to teach him to have a work ethic. It was on Friday and Saturday, and Kevin had to meet Butch at five in the morning to deliver newspapers. Kevin tried it for one week and quit. He said it was too much, between going to school and being on the basketball team. Butch told him that if he could do it, Kevin could do it. Kevin apparently huffed and puffed, and Butch called him trifling. The trouble was that Kevin was not trifling, but Butch thought that if Kevin didn't do life the way Butch wanted him to, then Kevin was wrong. Kevin wasn't lazy. If you looked in his room, you'd see it was as clean as a museum. I agreed with Kevin—how much time in the day does a nine-year-old boy have?

Polly decided to paint the apartment on Wednesday before she went to work; she was doing this because she'd invited the Dickster for dinner on Sunday and she wanted to wipe away the taste of the surprising tongue meal that Mama had fed him. Besides, she felt for the Dickster like I felt for the Gingerbread Man. She asked Kevin and me to help her paint, and we obliged.

I put on an old gym suit—a legless blue one-piece uniform—and helped her. Polly was strong; all that was needed from Kevin and me was to paint the baseboards and keep her company. This was a good thing because I sure didn't want to spend my energy before I went on a date with my Gingerbread Man.

We started in the kitchen, painting it a semigloss peach. Of course Polly yakked it up while we were painting. She was a talker, so much so that years ago a kid had called her Polly Cracker, as in "Polly wants a cracker," the words they say to parrots who talk too much. But my mind could only digest twenty minutes of Polly speak, then it would begin to wander. She could talk and labor at the same time, something I found fascinating because to me it seemed hard to do.

"I'm still young," she said. "I'm looking to get married again."

At that Kevin got up from his knees and dropped the paintbrush in the pan.

"I've got to go," he said.

"Well, keep on trucking, Mr. Man," said Polly.

He went out of the front door, spotted with paint, something he would otherwise never do because he was so neat, and slammed the door. I knew he was angry if he slammed the door, but about what? Of course: fear of another man taking over his mother and the house. Butch lived somewhere else, so Kevin was top dog in the house when it came to being the only male.

"That boy thinks he's my father and husband," said Polly. "If he's a killjoy who's trying to block my happiness, I'll send him to boarding school. Before you know it, I'll be too old for somebody to want me."

"He'll get over it," I said.

But I felt bad for Kevin. Polly was the only thing he had. Our father only met him once and never tried to establish a relationship with him. Butch and I were really just visitors in Kevin's relationship with our mother. I wondered if he would become the Boston Strangler if my mother were to remarry and do the man in.

"Brother Quincy is cute, isn't he?" said Polly.

"Yes, but so are monkeys."

Polly gave me the evil eye at that remark. I'd better be careful; I didn't want to bring any of Polly's ill wind on me. Besides, the Dickster could take my mother anyplace, so long as I was with them. He'd never put his paws on my mother like he did me; if he did, it would be curtains for him.

Kevin finally cooled off, came back, and resumed painting with us. The apartment looked brand new by the time we finished. The rest of the apartment was painted plum, which was really a mixture that looked like light purple, but it seemed to blend with everything. The sturdy secondhand furniture that gave the apartment a hominess, and our lifestyles, which were always on the go, our family always pushing for the next step up in life, seemed to give the furniture an added glow of usefulness.

We finished at 3:00 p.m. and were so hungry that we went to the pizza shop down the block and chowed down. I left a part of my stomach empty for the date with my Gingerbread Man. We were going to the opera tonight, and I was sure he was going to take me to dinner. I didn't care where he took me; I'd eat dirt cakes if they were served. I was happy as a lark, as Mama liked to say. If I died this moment, I'd die with a smile on my face. I had a late night, and I had my Gingerbread Man.

My mother gave me one last warning about the dangers of nightlife, then went to work. I dressed down this night; I didn't want to outdress my Gingerbread Man by wearing a gown like I had done when we went to the concert, so I wore what my Gingerbread Man wore: black Levi's, a black shirt, and of course my virgin pin pinned to my bra, which I might throw away in a minute if my Gingerbread Man gave up the knucklehead powder. (Well, maybe.)

It had warmed considerably for the middle of May, but I brought a light shawl that I had crocheted when I was bored, because the nights were still cool. It was white and went with my black attire; it was a standby just in case I got a chill. But what I really wanted was to snuggle under one of my Gingerbread Man's armpits if he were so inclined.

We had set the date for 7:00 p.m. I went out feeling free as the birds nested in the bricks by my window because now I didn't have to hide and sneak. I had a legitimate late night. I was standing in front of the building when Butch drove up. The first thing he said when he parked the car and got out was, "Where are you going this late at night?"

"Ma gave me permission to have a late night."

He nodded, then went on his way. The problem with Butch, the thing that was probably responsible for his getting under Kevin's and my skin and made him seem goofy, was that he acted like our father sometimes, bossing us around like he was our father. And Kevin's and my attitude was *Who died and made you boss?* From the newspaper route that Butch and Kevin argued about to this encounter with me, he was always rearing his goofy head.

The bottom line was that he was our brother, nothing more and nothing less, and when he assumed the role of our father, he was just—well, goofy. But I wasn't going to let that urinate on my parade; this was my night and my time. I had ascended above it all. I was able to reach Polly's heart and get a late night, and best of all, I had my Gingerbread Man.

My heart pitter-pattered when my Gingerbread Man drove up in his Cadillac. He stopped the car in front of me as if he'd been drawn to me by a magnet. Before I entered the car, my nose began to imagine the smell of the cologne he'd worn on our last date, and I envisioned the soft look of his brown-colored skin. If he didn't kiss me with those candy cane lips tonight, I'd kiss him again.

Once I opened the car door, I was hit by a putrid medicine smell—the kind I smell I sensed when I visited my mother on the job if she was working in the hospital instead of someone's home. It was an odor of unwellness, wellness, and death mixed together to form a beef stew of ambiguousness. A flash of car light gave me a vista of my beloved. He looked like he had not shaved, gotten a haircut, or combed his hair in days, as if he had just gotten out of bed and was going to brush his teeth. To top it off, he had a mean, sleepy look on his face. I hopped in the front seat, hoping that it was just a bad cold he was suffering from, but even though hope springs eternal, the truth will snuff it out.

"Hello," he mumbled.

"What's new by you?" I asked.

He grunted as if he were passing gas then said something that sounded as if it had come from a headache commercial, it was so dour. I was glad when he started driving. When we hit West Side Highway, the car became entombed in silence. The lights from the buildings, which flew by my eyes at the same speed as the car, were like daggers, and my eyes began to water. It was allergies, spring allergies, but in my soul I wanted to cry. I wanted to scream because it seemed the Gingerbread Man was a knucklehead again.

When we reached the garage to park the car, my worst fears came true. Norman was high, and he looked like a bum. His speech was slurred, and his clothes, a dark shirt and Levi's, looked wrinkly. But I still held on to the hope that he just had a cold. "Come on," he slurred. We went out into the night; it was festive with the sound of giggly people tickled with the beauty of the starry night. I, on the other hand, felt lonely and sad.

When we got on the subway and into bright lights, it exposed us for who we were, a knucklehead man and his apprehensive lover, or perhaps his daughter, because now Norman looked as old as Methuselah. I was glad when we were out in the street and his ugliness and my awkwardness were both covered by the darkness. But the sounds of the festive night with its giggling and happy chatter in the darkness made me want to run as far away from this knucklehead I could—and as soon as possible.

Once we got to the opera hall, we sat in the middle in the orchestra section. When we sat down, Norman grabbed me by the hand. It was so lifeless that it felt like a lobster was holding me. I quickly pulled my hand away, and Norman grumbled something that I couldn't understand. Finally the orchestra music burst into the air like a sudden storm. The lights dimmed until it was sightless, and the curtain rose slowly.

I was content now. The show drowned out the very ugly knucklehead, and once the curtains were up, I waited patiently for the proverbial fat lady to sing. This was supposed to be a performance of *Carmen*, which I knew nothing about, but my mentor (now drunk) was supposed to fill me in. The costumed people began singing at the top of their lungs. A woman and a man were locked in a singing embrace, nose to nose, belting a song in a language I had never heard before.

The knucklehead mumbled something then got up. He was going to the bathroom, I guess. I looked at the costumed couple on the stage, definitely lovers, definitely star-crossed, belting out lyrics from their souls to one another. They were arguing, and she seemed to be winning the argument. I wanted to get on the stage and say, "You aced it—you graduated from Argument University, the school of Polly."

After a while, I reached over to touch the knucklehead's hand to make nice. I felt guilty about having pushed his hand away, but all I got was a handful of felt cushion. I was alarmed that he had not returned, so I placed my shawl on my seat and a newspaper on his, then I weaved through the aisle of people and went to the lobby.

There was no concession stand in this ostentatious music hall, which reminded me of the splendor of Carnegie Hall with its Greek and Roman columns and a couple of busts of the greats of antiquity scattered and tucked away. I walked on the thick carpet to the lobby, which silenced my footfalls at every step.

Once I reached the lobby, I saw that a group of people had formed a large circle around what seemed to be an important event that was happening. I gently opened a chain in the circle and saw several police officers standing over an emergency medical technician who was on his knees administering aid to someone on a stretcher. The person on the stretcher raised his head; it was the knucklehead, looking as cheesy as a piece of gum stuck on the bottom of a shoe, with a hypodermic needle in his arm.

"Overdose," whispered one cop to the other. My stomach twisted as if I was going to vomit. What could I do about this situation? My brain wouldn't give me one answer—it was telling me to leave and go home, while at the same time telling me to become an actor on this stage.

My feet seemed to have a mind of their own, because before I knew it, I was smack-dab in the middle of this stage, standing above the stretcher and within earshot of two policemen. The knucklehead was breathing, but his gingerbread color was a sickly gray and he looked as if he had shrunk like one of those mummies of the antiquities display.

"You know this fella?" asked one of the officers.

I looked around, searching to see if there was anyone I knew or, worse yet, if the invisible or visible eye of Polly was watching me. I nodded. One of the emergency medical technicians jimmied the hypodermic needle out of Norman's arm and handed it to one of the officers, who deposited it in an empty glass Coke bottle and sealed the top.

"This is evidence," said the policeman.

The attendants hoisted the stretcher from the floor, and the knucklehead opened his eyes and looked right through me as if I were an object instead of a person. Now I knew: I was Norman's dessert and the knucklehead powder was the main course. I was no more than a handbag to go along with the suit he loved if he were a woman.

I followed the stretcher as the audience to our bit of theater dispersed. Once outside, the officer who had secured the hypodermic needle said to me as Norman was being hoisted into the ambulance, "You seem like a nice kid; don't get involved with this. What would your parents think of you with a criminal?"

"You coming in?" asked the attendant in the ambulance.

"No. What hospital is he going to?" I asked.

"Bellevue."

I watched as the ambulance sped away, until I could no longer hear the siren. The police car followed behind the ambulance. The Gingerbread Man was a complete knucklehead, and now he might be going to jail. Tears streamed down my cheeks as I went back inside the opera hall to get the shawl and newspaper I had left in our chairs. If Polly were to find out what had happened on late night, she would take it back. Jeez, what a late night.

When I went back to my seat to get my shawl, suspicious faces looked me over. I was exposed, naked among strangers; I wanted to hide under a rock, I was so ashamed. The words of my grandmother echoed in my brain: "Always put your best foot forward, and don't let your hair down when you're around folks or anyone who's not a Way person and goes to the temple." I didn't know what she meant, but I could tell by their executioner's eyes that she meant strangers.

My subway ride home was a dark voyage; my head spun with unanswered questions: What if the knucklehead died—what would I do? What if the Knucklehead lived—what would I do? What would Polly do if she found out? After all, she knew everyone, and perhaps someone in that crowd knew her and would go back and tell her about this knucklehead business.

The answers to those questions pounded my head like a toothache because they were not the answers I was looking for. If Norman died, he would leave me; if he lived, I would have to leave him. And if Polly found out, she would hang him by his you-know-what. A fresh stream of tears ran down my face as I mulled over the answers. Then I heard the words of Mama and sometimes Polly: "The Bible says that bad associations spoil useful habits, that a drunkard will go in rags, and that you mustn't bring reproach upon the faith by your bad behavior." What they said seemed to be right, but what could I do? I was in love with him, even if he wasn't in love with me; he was in love with the knucklehead powder.

When I got home, Kevin was asleep and Buck greeted me at the door. As always, I patted him on the head. After my roller-coaster ride of the night, it felt good. Before I got undressed, I got on the phone in the kitchen to call Bellevue to see how Norman was doing. Then it dawned on me that I didn't even know his last name.

After I got the number for Bellevue from the operator, I called the desk. I told the woman that I was looking for a man whose first name was Norman, but I didn't know his last name. She seemed amused by this and told me that there was only one Norman who'd been admitted that night, and his last name was Easter. Norman Easter.

"Mr. Easter is in critical condition."

"Thank you," I said and hung up.

I wasn't too upset; Polly always told me that when you are admitted by an ambulance to a hospital, you are always listed as critical in the beginning, and then you are upgraded or downgraded to your real condition. Polly ought to know; she was a nurse.

Once I finished the phone call, I got dressed for bed. I plopped into bed a physical dynamo but an emotional wreck. A funny, scary question was circling my brain again, more terrifying than the others: what kind of woman was I to be bested by some powder? Usually when something came between lovers, it was another person. I'd heard the whispers about my father, that he left my mother for another woman—that was normal.

"Oh Lord," I whispered, "not only are my brothers running rings around me, but also now it's smack—I'm being beaten by smack." I added some music to my new tears; it was boo-hoo-hoo, the cry song.

When I woke up the next morning, I rushed to get out of the house before Polly came home from work. I was in a sad mood: my face was puffy from crying, and I knew she would read my bad mood and ask about it. I got out of bed and went to my dresser where my mirror rested. I looked a sight, almost as old as Polly: rounded shoulders like I was a beast of burden carrying an overloaded yoke, dark circles under my eyes that gave my eyes a moonish look, and a kind of hound dog expression as if I were searching for something but couldn't find it.

After I got dressed and scarfed down a bowl of oatmeal, I called Bellevue again. My heart was beating in my ears like eternal drums. Was Easter dead or alive? My Gingerbread? My Gingerbread Man, my Knucklehead Man, wherefore art thou? I said his name like an automaton and wanted to scream hallelujah when the clerk said he was in good condition and was being discharged at noon.

My Gingerbread Man had bested death for now. I left the apartment head-over-heels happy, but once the sun hit my face, I knew that I had some questions to answer and that I would have to come down off this cloud and answer them. A bitter taste like rotten eggs came into my mouth; it seemed like what Mama and Polly always said was true: "Life can be a bitter pill sometimes."

CHAPTER 17

By the time I got to school, I had answered all my questions. Really, I had to answer only one to answer all the questions, and that was "Should I go back to the knucklehead and begin anew?" The answer was a firm no. The knucklehead was a no-go. If I could forget my father, who I thought rose and set the sun, then I could forget my Gingerbread Man. Even though my father was my father and the Gingerbread Man was my boyfriend, the latter was a knucklehead now and was in Knucklehead Land, so he had to go.

I walked up the staircase to my class, saying hello to all who greeted me, but I was as far away and disengaged as the moon. Once I reached the landing to the floor where my class was, I began feeling dizzy. I was falling backward. An arm caught me just as I was about to keel over. I looked up and saw it was Hayes who had caught me, the chump who went to the temple, whom I had smacked down a couple of years ago for taunting me about my mother being excommunicated.

He didn't look like the scrawny, quirky kid that I had beaten long ago, but instead he appeared rather manly.

"Are you okay, Toddy?" he asked.

"I'm okay," I said. I still felt kind of wobbly on my feet but was able to get a good look at Hayes's face. He had a smile on his face that seemed to run from ear to ear. It was wide and infectious, and I began to smile too, even though I was completely screwed up. His smile appeared to be genuine, from deep within his soul, and it seemed that his soul was at peace like still waters on a balmy day. Of course he was handsome—his muscles were bulging from the blue suit he wore—but he wasn't my kind of handsome; he was someone else's.

"I'll walk you to the infirmary so you can see the nurse," he said.

"Okay."

Hayes gently grabbed my arm and walked me to the infirmary. His scent, the cleanest of clean, made me forget my knucklehead encounter and problem. I felt safe, like I felt with my mother and especially when my father and mother were together. I thanked Hayes; I was glad I had bumped into him because for a second I'd forgotten about the knucklehead. Norman seemed to be everywhere in my life: my dreams, my brain, my nostrils, and everything that was in existence inside and outside of me.

The diagnosis at the infirmary was dysmenorrhea, or menstrual cramps. Now the knucklehead had even shell-shocked my hormones, my estrogen. I was a week early, which meant that my cycle was changing dates. I guess I had the knucklehead syndrome. It was better than being pregnant. I was given Midol and a sanitary napkin and then was sent to class.

I had seven classes that day in different rooms with different subjects, but my mind was on Knucklehead University with knucklehead subjects. I tried in vain to erase him from my mind, but he just stayed there like an albatross. Even my lunch hour turned into his lunch hour. And these were not happy thoughts with happy pictures; these were bad thoughts, with the picture of him laid out on the stretcher with the hypodermic needle in his arm being the ugliest picture.

The only thing that sparked my interest and made me forget the knucklehead was when I was in Miss Ciotti's class and she started telling us about our assignment in a couple of days—looking at the California presidential primary on June 6. This was an all-night thing. Everyone knew that our state's senator was running in it, and everyone believed that he would win. I bumped into Rene Wilkins coming from her brainiac class. She looked at me like I was the new disease on the block.

"Bethany, you look like death warmed over," she said.

I nodded. We made a date to meet at her house on Friday, because it was a half day. I had to share this with somebody; I didn't care if she ridiculed me or told me, "I told you so." I needed someone to talk to, to let go of this burden, someone who could give me some good advice about the Gingerbread Man. Besides, two heads are better than one.

When I got to Rene Wilkins's house, I spilled my guts about my knucklehead problem and about my overachieving, movie star brothers running rings around me, making me the laughingstock of my mother's three children. We were in Rene's basement drinking lemonade at the pool table.

She looked at me as if I were an alien from another planet. Rene looked like a taskmaster, a demon, and an angel all wrapped into one, and her freckles changed into pockmarks instead of the polka dots they usually looked like. She paced back and forth in front of the pool table as she talked to me.

"Bethany, you are a live fool for messing with that knucklehead grandpa," she said.

"I know, but I love him," I said. "I mean, loved him."

"If you love him, you need your head examined."

I kind of regretted telling her; the tongue-lashing she was giving me was wearing thin, and I was beginning to feel that I should tell her to take a long walk on a short pier and, when she got to the end, to keep on walking, but I didn't have the stomach to act out in her house. After all, she wasn't Viola the funky doll bandit. She finally stopped pacing and sat down beside me at the pool table.

"You're finished with this nut, aren't you?" she asked.

"Sure."

"If you're worried about being a never-been, keep hanging around him," she said. "Besides, Bethany, you should get on the ball, do something like your brothers to make your mark on the world."

"But what?"

"Mrs. Waxman thinks you're another Shakespeare, and she wanted you to join the newspaper at school," she said. "Why didn't you? You're an ace in vocabulary. Didn't you win a contest a while back?"

"I did, but you can't make a living from writing."

"Think big, Bethany, or else you'll stand still."

I had won the city championship in vocabulary but was afraid to compete again because I was scared of losing. Mrs. Waxman, our seventh-grade English teacher, was impressed by my performance on an impromptu writing assignment she had given the class, pitched working at the school newspaper to me. I didn't accept the offer. It was like pouring water on a duck's back as Mama and Polly liked to say when nothing comes of nothing.

"You ought to be glad those Hondos didn't arrest you after finding the hypodermic needle on that knucklehead," she said. "Besides, your mother will string him up when she finds out about you two."

Fear coursed through my veins at the thought of Polly finding me out. I didn't know if it had more to do with shame or reprisal. Since Wilkins was a brainiac, I took her off the subject by asking her if she had been given the assignment for the California primary in her brainiac class.

"Yeah, but if I could vote, I would vote for Eugene McCarthy," she said.

"But why not our senator?" I asked.

"Yeah, I know, but Senator McCarthy is against the war in Vietnam," she said. "Besides, I can't vote until I'm twenty-one."

Someone was coming down the basement steps. Once they made it to the edge, I could see it was Rene's mother.

"It's time for your ballet lesson," she said.

"Bethany, don't give up your virgin pin for that knucklehead," she whispered.

"Rene, you're a brainiac: Why do the girls have to be a virgin and the boys don't?"

"I don't know."

"The adult world is funny. In the Way, they want everyone to be a virgin when they marry," I said, "and outside the Way, they only want the girls to be virgins when they marry."

I took the last sip of lemonade and placed the glass on the tray resting on the pool table. Rene got up and walked as if it were her last mile before she was going to be executed. I trailed behind her, relieved that this cross-examination had ended. I was glad that I had released this burden, this load off my shoulders, even though the haranguing bothered me. Rene gave me one last look when we reached the front door; it was a "Do the right thing or else" look, the same look that Polly gave me when she was being stern. I was through with Norman, my former Gingerbread Man, and it made me feel completely empty inside, the same feeling I had when I knew my father was never coming home again.

It was almost 4:00 p.m. when I left Rene's house. The day looked untouched, clear, and cloudless and was sunny but not humid. It was the poster child for Daylight Savings. The doubts came as I headed in the direction of my home. Rene Wilkins was not a doctor, and she was not a drug addict. How could she know whether Norman was good for me—a good man, a bad man, or whatever?

Sure, she used her cousin as an example because he was a drug abuser, but was that really enough? Kevin was a basketball player, but did I know about basketball? No. Butch tooted his horn on the saxophone, but did I know about tooting? No. So how did this brainiac know-it-all, this honors class program chick, know about drug addiction? She didn't. She didn't know squat. In the game of life, she was just like me: she wore a virgin pin and hadn't gotten her cherry busted. Maybe I needed to talk to someone who was an ex-knucklehead who could give me some pointers about this knuckleheadish way of life. It was worth a try.

I remembered Mr. Jimmy. He was an ex-knucklehead. He was a preacher who fell from grace and began getting high—on alcohol, I guess, but it's still knuckleheadish. He used to get high, stand in the middle of Laconia Avenue, a two-way street, and direct traffic. He was around 6'6" and 400 pounds and looked real odd standing on the yellow line waving his arms to direct the traffic.

His alcoholic pouch would loop over his belt and out of his pants until he looked like he was pregnant. When he directed traffic, it went smoothly. He never asked for money. Once he was finished for the day, people would let him stay in their basements overnight. To make a long story short, he got himself together and now he owned a thrift shop on Laconia Avenue, facing the traffic he used to direct.

I pivoted and started walking in the opposite direction of my home and toward Mr. Jimmy's thrift shop. Once I got in front of the store, I got cold feet; I wanted to pivot again and walk in the direction of my home. But there stood Mr. Jimmy in the door of his store, smaller belly, smaller frame; gone were the days of the kangaroo pouch that used to fall out of his pants. Our eyes locked for a second, and I looked away out of respect. He stuck his head out of the door.

"Come in, child," he said. "Don't be afraid."

"Thank you, sir," I said.

I walked inside, and the smell of mothballs pierced my nose; the same smell was in Mama's closet, where she kept scores of bedsheets probably as old as I was. There were vintage clothes on six long racks, some looking like they had come from a 1940s film: a fox shawl with a real fox head on it (Mama had one), and mink pelts with heads looking like they would lurch at you in a second.

I felt Mr. Jimmy's large, restored body next to me; the hugeness was calming, like the stillness I had felt when Hayes took me to the infirmary. He motioned for me to sit in one of the two wooden rocking chairs facing one another that rested in the middle of the store in an empty space.

"I know your grandmother, Mrs. Cornwallis-West. What's your name?"

"I'm Toddy."

"Pleased to meet you. No young people usually come to thrift shops." He smiled. "What brings you in here?"

My tongue became tied when I realized that what I wanted to ask him was very personal and that he might be offended if I asked it. But I had to know. I had to know what made him get away from the knucklehead juice and perhaps the knucklehead powder.

"Well, sir, I'm doing a school paper on the abuse and use of drugs and alcohol." I was rather surprised and ashamed that I could cook up a lie on such short notice. Then I remembered that I hadn't prayed to the celestials in a long time, that even though I went to the temple, I was not keeping a personal relationship with them by doing daily prayer.

"Go ahead and shoot the questions at me," he said. "I'm used to it."

"Can anybody get off the stuff?" I asked.

"It's like this, child," he said. "A person can't get off it unless they want to get off it."

I wanted to cry; he had answered my question. The Gingerbread Man would never get off drugs until he wanted to, and he didn't want to. Even if I lay down and died for him, he would not get off this stuff. I rubbed my eyes to prevent any tears from falling down my face.

"And remember, child," he said, "God only helps those who help themselves."

"Can anybody help them?" I asked.

"If they want help. If they don't, you should run every time you see them coming, especially if you're a child like you are; they'll ruin your childhood."

"It's so sad," I said.

He smiled and nodded. "Toddy, you want a Coke? I know your grandmama likes it."

I really didn't want any, but I accepted his offer anyway to be neighborly; I didn't want him to think that Mama had a disrespectful granddaughter. He went to the refrigerator to his left and brought back the Coke. We talked until I finished the Coke about how people waste their time getting involved in things that are destructive. When I finished, he walked me to the door then said with a smile on his face, "Tell your grandmama I said hello—and good luck on your assignment."

He acted like he was sweet on Mama. I could tell by his face; he had that moonbeam look as if he'd been struck by the lovebug. Mama's husband, my grandfather, died when I was a couple of months old; my mother had taken me to the funeral swaddled in blankets. My father's father died this year, and he had been brain dead for years because he was gassed in the First World War. It seemed I was in an amazon world run by manless women; even Aunt Helen and her husband had separated the same year my mother and father had.

I guess I was struck by the lovebug with Norman, but no more. I painted him into something I didn't want to date. His skin became the texture of sandpaper. His mouth, the sensual juicy lips that I longed to kiss, became two oversized raw sausages. And the tongue, I imagined, became a dragon tongue that spit fire. I touched up his face in my mind portrait until he changed from man to gargoyle, so that by the time I made it to my block, he was the ugliest thing I could ever think of.

When I got home, Polly was dressed in her nurse's uniform and on her way to work. The house smelled of ham and macaroni pie. She turned to me as she exited the door. "Mama wants you to call her," she said. "And how was your late night?"

"Okay," I replied.

Then I remembered my absentmindedness. I usually called Mama every other day, and I hadn't called her since Tuesday, so not only was the knucklehead messing with my period but my calendar too. He was now a definite no-go with me anyway. I called Mama, and she told me she wanted me to go out and do field service with her. This was part of the ministry for the Way, going out and preaching to warn people about Armageddon, the Day of Judgment by God, and teaching them about the Bible. I enjoyed going out because I met interesting people while doing it. Besides, it would get my mind off the knucklehead mess.

I ate and then played a couple of hands of casino with Kevin until he fell asleep. Then I went to the phone to call the knucklehead to tell him the score. I figured he should be rested from his hospital stay by now and have his feet on the ground, if that was possible. I was determined to keep calm, give him my goodbye song, wish him well, and go on my merry way.

"How do you feel?" I asked.

"Fine, baby, just fine."

"Norman, I can't go out with you anymore," I said, "because you're into some negative stuff."

"I know. I understand."

"No you don't, you goddamn knucklehead."

"Milady, I'm sorry."

"You abandoned me! You deserted me," I yelled. "Among strangers and enemies, you left me flat—just like my father."

Before another ugly word could come from my mouth, I hung up the phone. Buck started barking and Kevin stuck his head out of the curtain that divided his bedroom from the living room, because of my big mouth.

"What's going on in here?" asked Kevin. "You sick?"

"No, I'm fine. I just had to straighten someone out."

"Okay, but you have to remember folks are sleeping in here."

I nodded. He closed the curtain, and Buck followed him. I was outraged. The nerve of that knucklehead having me work so hard to get a late night, and then he showed his true colors like a typical fool. I marched to my room, still steamed. I undressed and put on my pajamas in rhythm with my anger—hot, furious, and fast.

I slipped into the sheets on my bed, sealed them over me, closed my eyes, and gave Norman my Bethany blessing: "Good riddance, Norman; there's too many fish in the sea, as the song goes. I'll fix you, knucklehead; I'll get an older man, forty. I don't care if I must answer one of the personal ads in the girlie magazines with the nudie women hidden in the back of the candy store." Now that was an idea—I bet there were plenty of older men in those magazines. When my anger and disappointment faded at the exciting thought of answering an ad in a girlie magazine, I fell asleep.

The only thing I didn't like about field service on Saturday was that I had to wake up early; you had to be at the temple or an individual's home by 9:30 a.m. or you would have to meet the group at the territory. Sometimes the territory, the area where we would be preaching, was far and the congregants had to drive those who didn't have cars to the area. Today I was going to meet for field service at the temple because Mama had asked me to meet her at that location. She always said that a little spiritual food is good for the blues.

When I reached the temple and opened one of the large wooden doors, peace and calm waved through my body. It was like all was well and the knucklehead was forgotten, left outside with the troubled world. When I opened the second set of doors, which led to the actual hall, I was greeted by the smiling, khaki-suited Hayes, who smelled like he had just stepped out of the shower. His face broke into the same toothy wide grin it had when he saved me from keeling over on the steps at school. Of course his smile was still infectious, so I automatically smiled too.

"Hi, Toddy," he said. "Glad you came."

"Glad to be here," I said.

We began walking in the direction of the seats, our footfalls cushioned by the plush carpet. This Hayes didn't seem like the one who had made fun of my mother being excommunicated and whom I had to fight. This one was nice. We sat in the front near the platform with a group of ten other congregants.

"Are you going to the get-together at Sister Quan's house?" he asked.

"No," I said. "I have something important to do."

"That's too bad. There's going to be games, food, and music, but it's going to be theocratic."

I felt bad that I had disappointed him, when the only thing important I had to do was go home and sleep. The last thing I wanted to do was go to one of these get-togethers, do something off the wall, and put shame on my family—especially now since Butch was an elder and Polly had just been reinstated after a long excommunication. And it would be like child abuse taking advantage of a clean-cut guy like Hayes after dealing with knuckleheaded Norman and the Dickster. Hayes still had a glow on his face, so I was glad I hadn't really hurt his feelings.

While we waited for a brother to instruct us about what we were pitching in field service that day, the brother who was leading us broke from a cluster of people whom he was talking to and stood dead center in the middle of the first row. This was a cue that that the meeting was beginning, and the cluster of people began moving in his direction.

His name was John Leach. He was a tall blond brother with blue eyes who was married to a black woman. There were a lot of interracial marriages in the Way; even though the society did not approve of such matters at the time, these marriages were accepted. I looked around for his wife, but she wasn't there.

"Brothers and sisters, let's begin the ministry for field service," said Brother Leach, "with a prayer from Brother Hayes."

Brother Hayes went next to Brother Leach and said the prayer. It was short and heartfelt. At the end he asked God to bless our endeavors in field service. Brother Leach again took the leadership position as Hayes sat next to me. I felt a little funny when he did that. He wasn't my kind of a guy; he was too young and too clean-cut. I liked my men older and kind of bent—but heavens, not as bent as Norman the knucklehead.

Mama came in with Lisa, late as usual, and sat with me. Brother Leach took out his New World Translation Bible and began thumbing through it. "Brothers and sisters, please turn to Revelation 21:4 KJV." He read the verse with vigor: "'And God will wipe every tear from their eyes and pain, sickness, and death will be no more.' Look, he is making all things new. And for those who don't believe in the New Testament, we have Isaiah 65 in the Old Testament." Brother Leach raised his eyes from the Bible and looked at the pool of the congregants who had swelled to over twenty from the latecomers.

"We are admonished in Matthew 24:14 KJV to preach the good news of the kingdom so that people may be saved. We may offer the literature for study, but we should aim for Bible studies so that people may learn the Bible, serve God, and be saved at Armageddon. The book *God Inspires* is the book we may use for the Bible study, but others may be used in place of it as well.

"Remember, we as Christians are supposed to preach the good news of God's kingdom as it states in Matthew. We do this because we love our neighbors and God, and we desire that they not get destroyed at Armageddon." Brother Leach closed the meeting by saying a prayer.

When I opened my eyes, Jill Moran was standing in front of Hayes—vamping, I guess. Her movements seemed to highlight her body. She had hips that wiggled like Jell-O and lips that were on the verge of a moue and ready for lip gloss. She was of mixed race: whatever and whatever. I had not seen her in years, and unlike me, she had grown tall and added some extra curves that made her more womanly. True, I had gotten some extra curves, but I was vertically challenged and sometimes horizontally challenged as well.

"Tommy," she said, "are you going to the get-together at Sister Quan's house for the newly baptized?"

"It's not only for the newly baptized," said Hayes.

So that was his first name—Tommy. I'd remember that for future reference. I guess that left me out because I wasn't baptized. Maybe this vamp was letting me know to back off Tommy Hayes. Mama and Lisa rose from their seats and were watching the vamp play Jill Moran was acting in, wiggling her hips and sounding sultry as she inched closer to Hayes with her short dress.

"I'd like to congratulate both of you for dedicating your lives to Jehovah," said Mama. "I know Sister Quan. She doesn't mind people who aren't baptized coming over; she just wants them to act theocratic."

The vamp seemed to be bent out of shape from Mama's correction, but she managed to squeeze out a smile from her crestfallen face. She was replenished by the time she focused her eyes on me. She looked me up and down as if I were a student being inspected by a teacher.

"What a nice dress you have on," she said. "It's something my grandmother would wear."

"And yours looks like what the whore of Babylon would wear," said Mama.

Mama could get away with saying a lot of off-the-wall things in the congregation because the congregants looked upon her as the faithful of old who had served Jehovah for over thirty years. Besides, at least she was biblical, as the whore of Babylon was the world empire of false religion according to the Way. The vamp blanched then targeted me again.

"Are you going to the get-together, Toddy?" asked the vamp.

"Yes, I am," I said.

"That's great, Toddy," said Hayes. "You changed your mind."

If it was the last thing I did, I was going to the get-together to save Hayes from being devoured by this vamp. All this witch needed to do was clasp her talons around him and turn him into a good-for-nothing. Well, I had news for this Vamp the Tramp hiding behind the Bible; I was the protector of my dear honest-hearted brother Tommy Hayes, protecting him from a miscreant like her.

"There's transportation to the territory for people who need it," said Brother Leach.

"Toddy, you, your grandmother, and Lisa can come in my father's car," said Hayes.

"Thank you, young Brother Hayes," said Mama.

"What about me?" asked the vamp.

"There's enough room for you in the car, Jill," said Hayes.

I saw the sour look on the vamp's face, definitely sick over the attention that Hayes was giving me. This was a good thing. If I had to marry this brother to keep Missy off his case, I'd just have to bear the burden.

I wanted to laugh. It would be like a giraffe getting in a Volkswagen as far as the vamp fitting in the car, she was so tall. As we left the temple to go to the territory, I erased any negative thoughts I had in my mind and concentrated on field service and how to help my neighbors build a relationship with Jehovah. I wanted to remain theocratic if it was the last thing I did.

The morning was made for field service: the sky was blue and flawless, the birds flew overhead in crazy formations as if they were at an amusement park, and the smell of late spring was waxed with perfumed flowers and seemed to be singing its own song via its odor. Brother Hayes, Tommy Hayes's father—a man taller than his son, with broad shoulders and a slight resemblance to Tommy—ushered us to his blue station wagon to be transported to the territory.

There were twelve of us in the station wagon: Tommy's father, Mama, Lisa, Brother Leach, Tommy Hayes, the vamp, me, Brother and Sister Nixon, Brother Jimmy Lee, and Brother and Sister Haddock, a newlywed couple. The other congregants, twenty or so, either had their own cars or went with congregants who did.

The vamp tried to sit in the front with Tommy and his father, but the elder Hayes waved her away. She sat in the seats behind them with Brother and Sister Dixon. Lisa, Mama, and I were directly behind her row. Sister Dixon turned and looked at Mama with terror in her eyes, then she pointed her nose in the direction of the vamp. I looked over to where the vamp was sitting as Mama dived her eyes to the row in front of us. The vamp's very mini miniskirt had hiked up her legs and was now an extension of her panties; in other words, her butt was taking pictures, as Mama liked to say. Brother Dixon was next to her with his nose turned up at the scene.

The vamp placed the entire car into an untheocratic noose. She was immodest in a modest situation; her dress was too short to be wearing to field service to represent God, as the folks seemed to be saying with a silent rebuke. As Mama said earlier, it was more appropriate for the whore of Babylon. While the others tried to ignore the vamp's immodesty, Mama had had enough and pointed to the exposed butt.

"Why don't you stop taking pictures and shining," said Mama, "and cover up your shortcomings?" The members in the car seemed to breathe a collective sigh of amen once the vamp covered her shortcomings. They started chitchatting about the next convention, which was in August, where people from all over the world would meet, fellowship, and talk about God's kingdom. In the city we would meet at Yankee Stadium.

The vamp redirected this invigorating conversation to focus on her individual adventures: about how she was going to Europe to the convention, about how she went to Fuji last year to the convention, and blah, blah, blah; me, me, and me. Now I knew why my goofy brother Butch didn't promote himself and let others toot his horn by promoting him. Her I-ism was so uncool and untheocratic. Amid the vamp's saleswoman's puff, Tommy Hayes turned around and said out loud: "Toddy, we're going to play Bible charades at the get-together. Do you know how to play?"

"Yes, I do," I said.

The vamp turned around and looked at me with a scowl on her face. Rah-rah-rah; I'd taken her man and limelight—go to Fuji, go to Europe now. Tommy Hayes went on about the different games we'd be playing at the get-together and was definitely honking the horn about what a great cook Sister Quan was. Every once in a while, he'd turn and smile at me; this made the vamp burn, and she would redirect the conversation to herself, talking about any random subject just to bring the focus back to her.

Once we reached the Mount Vernon–Bronx border, we parked on a tree-lined residential street. Four other cars with congregants were already there. We were divided into two groups: Tommy's father was in charge of a group of thirteen, and Brother Leach was in charge of a group of fourteen. Mama, Lisa, and I were in Brother Hayes's group.

We were then broken down into pairs. In Mama's and my case, we were a trio because Lisa was going to preach with us. The vamp, of course, wiggled her way into Brother Hayes's group and was campaigning, like she always did—in this case, to be paired with Tommy Hayes, I guess, to lead him down a bad road and stir up his emotions to commit fornication. The boy's father wanted no part of it, so he assigned her with us.

The vamp twisted her mouth in a moue to let us know she was dissatisfied. Mama had a smirk on her face like she had something up her sleeve. I scrutinized the vamp; her dress was extremely mini, and any movement would have her butt taking pictures again, fanning her shortcomings for all the world to see.

Our group walked up a little hill to the only apartment building on the block among private houses, a red-brick six-story building. Brother Hayes gave us the first two floors to work on. The others were assigned other floors. As soon as the group got on the elevator, Mama reached in her handbag, pulled out a razor, grabbed the hem of the vamp's dress, and plucked a piece of the thread on it and began pulling.

"What are you doing?" protested the vamp. "You're ruining my silk dress."

"Eh, this is the cheapest-quality silk I've ever come across in my life," said Mama. "You were gypped."

The hem of the dress fell to the vamp's knees, and Mama smiled with satisfaction.

"You have no right to tinker with my dress."

"It was too short," said Mama.

"I have a right to wear what I want."

"You do," said Mama, "but not on God's time; besides, you'll scare the sheep away, flashing your shortcomings."

The vamp seemed to get a thrill out of fussing with Mama; if she liked to fuss, she'd met the right person—the Cornwallis-Wests had it in their genes. Mama and I worked the first door, leaving Lisa and the vamp to wait in the shadows. Too many people at the door would give the person opening it the creeps. I rang the bell and was met by a gruff inquiry from behind the door.

"Good morning. We're here to share the good news of the kingdom with you," I said.

The door swung open, and a fat white man with hard blue eyes in a hard face appeared and gave me a scowl. A chill ran down my spine because I knew this man was not a happy camper. All at once I lost my backbone, my spine, and knew that whatever words came out of my mouth would be babble.

"I'm sick and tired of you Ways knocking on my door," he said. "I got my own religion." He reached in his pocket and pulled out a wad of bills and shook it at me. "This is my religion," he said.

I was dumfounded. I didn't know what words I could say to this man. My faith had the strength of a feather against defiance. But Mama came to the rescue and said, "I guess if you lose your money, you'd lose your religion."

The man broke into a smile and began giggling until his big body shook like thunder.

"Touché," he said.

"We're not Ways. We're Wayans," said Mama.

He apologized for being such an ogre and invited us in. Once we were inside, he told us he gave up God when his son died in Vietnam. Mama read him a scripture, Revelation 21:4, to give him hope. Surprisingly he agreed to have a Bible study with Mama.

CHAPTER 18

Thomas Ulysses Hayes Jr. was a big fat liar. I thought he was a clean-cut, righteous, God-fearing young man, but he turned out to be a bigger liar than the devil himself. He was worse than my goofy brother Butch when it came to publicizing his now faux righteousness, but at least Butch was true blue, whereas Hayes was striped wicked. He was the ultimate Beelzebub playing righteous in the house of Jehovah, all the while dancing with Satan.

I'd found this out when we went to the get-together. We ate and played in Sister Quan's spacious backyard, nestled in the rear of her big red house with two Greek columns welcoming visitors in the front. Everything was okay until everyone's true soul colors were bared.

Tommy Hayes grabbed my hand after the charade game and cradled me away from the vamp, who had gone home and changed into something sporty and appropriate: jeans and a nice sleeveless gray blouse. We walked on the edge of the circular crowd, giddy from the good time.

"Toddy," he said, "I want to apologize for picking on you about your mother being excommunicated way back when and for beating you up that time."

"But it was I who beat you up," I said.

"No, Toddy, it was I who beat you up."

Didn't he remember the black eye I'd given him, a shiner that would have made Muhammad Ali proud? I should have won an award. I believed that credit should be given where credit is due, and I wasn't going to let someone cheat me out of something that was justly mine—namely, a win in the win column.

"How could you have won?" I said. "You had a big shiner on your left eye like a prizefighter, and I didn't have a scratch on me."

"Toddy, I beat you up," he said.

It was then that my blood began to boil. I had the urge to place a new shiner on his eye, but instead I yelled, "Stop lying. I'll beat the stew out of you." I felt eyes staring at me. I looked around and saw that the entire party was looking at us; I had alarmed the place. I walked over to Kevin and Polly, who were on the far end of this theater of eyes, and left Hayes to stew in his own juices.

After the scene, I avoided Tommy Hayes at every turn as he followed me around the area to talk to me. It was like we were playing tag: he'd go left, I'd go right; he went west, and I went east—until time and the largeness of the crowd made me disappear. I left the get-together without saying a word to Hayes. I had news for him—I didn't fool with hypocrites who'd just gotten baptized a couple of weeks ago and who lied enough to make a bar of soap.

When we got home and everyone had gotten settled, Polly came into my room. She looked at me gravely with her whiteless eyes as if I were not myself. She plopped into a chair next to my bed, where I was lying down.

"What got into you, screaming at Tommy Hayes like that?" she asked.

I sat in my bed in the lotus position. Wouldn't she'd like to know? She'd be the last person I'd tell, because I knew that no matter what came out of my mouth, she would condemn me. I didn't know of any other words that came out of her mouth most of the time other than, "Don't do that" or "Why didn't you do that?" when she was talking to me.

"I guess I wasn't feeling well," I said.

"Well, please, people will start talking. And remember, Brother Quincy is coming over tomorrow."

Oh, heck, how could I have forgotten that the Dickster was going to grace the scene? That was Polly, always thinking about her standing in other people's minds. Mama wasn't like that; she didn't give a hoot about what other people thought about her.

"Later for people," I said.

"You are a careless child—you really don't care," she said. "Remember—don't care, don't have a home." She sighed. "I'm looking for a husband, so be on your best behavior when Brother Quincy comes over. Don't rock the boat."

"How could I forget?"

"Stop being sarcastic."

"Why don't you leave me the hell alone?"

"I can't. You're my daughter," she said. "And don't curse at me, or else I'll smack you in the face."

"And if you do, I'll smack you back," I said. "You'll never beat me up like you did Butch. I'll bite back."

She looked at me, shocked, then a smug look came over her face like she was a prizefighter content in knowing that she could beat her opponent's ass.

"I'll tend to you later," she said. "I have to go to work."

She had said her piece, so she whizzed out of the room as if she were a hot burst of August air. I was thinking about going to get my earplugs if her fussing got too hot, but she stopped because she had to go to work. She was right—I didn't care, not about the junk she thought about and not about what people thought of me. I got up, dressed, and headed to the candy store to get a girlie magazine so I could answer a personal ad to meet a real person, a man who was forty—heck, maybe even fifty. By the time I started to the candy store, Polly was gone, Kevin was asleep, and Buck was stretched out in front of the door. Polly must have been really bent out of shape about me because she hadn't even said goodbye. I changed my mind about the magazine because the shopkeeper was looking at me and knew my family.

Before I went to bed, I looked out my bedroom window at the dark and starry late spring night; a half-moon blared orange in the darkness, and the streets were filled with happy people in their glory because it was spring. The sound of crickets and the flash from lightning bugs added to the happy carnival atmosphere. I tried to piggyback on this festive mood, but I was in an abyss of darkness. Things that were preying on my mind were spinning in my head as if I was having a concurrent nightmare: the knucklehead Norman; the nooser, the Dickster, the very Brother Quincy; and now the biggest liar on earth, Tommy Hayes. My headache needed more than a simple aspirin—it needed general anesthesia.

When I got to school Monday, I was rather tired because I had stayed up and listened in on the date my mother had with the Dickster. I was in my room lying in my bed with the door slightly open. When things got quiet, I went in the kitchen, on the ruse that I was going to the refrigerator, to see if this fake Christian was strangling my mother. But they were nestled on the secondhand sofa like two lovebirds, I guess whispering sweet nothings in one another's ears.

At the same time, Kevin was doing sentry duty in his room with the curtain closed, drinking in every word of this male usurper. Every once in a while, Kevin opened his curtain and went to the kitchen, I guess to let the lovebirds know that he was watching them. The Dickster left at a respectable hour, midnight, but I didn't get to sleep until 3:00 because my body just wouldn't shut down.

I had to talk to my mama about my problems—well, the Hayes problem: the Dickster and the fading Norman problem were too much for Mama, I believed. But I was glad that the thought of Norman was fading away and was now being replaced with Tommy Hayes. I made sure to avoid him at every turn in school and at the temple on Sunday; I would not talk to him until I talked to Mama. But he almost snared me on the cafeteria line. I was on the line with Rene Wilkins when I smelled the familiar odor of a freshly showered body peppered with the hormonal fragrance of testosterone.

I turned around and it was you-know-who, smiling from ear to ear. For a second, I became infected with this good cheer like I always did, and I almost smiled, but the feeling waned as soon as I remembered the big fat lie he'd told about the fight. Despite my frown, his smile still seemed to be illuminating. The otherwise never-ending smile finally fell off his face until he looked solemn, too solemn for Tommy Hayes.

"Toddy, may I speak with you?" he asked.

"Well, I can't, because Rene Wilkins and I have something important to talk about," I said as I nudged her elbow before she could say something to expose my lie.

He forced a smile on his face. "Okay. I'll talk to you later."

He stood quietly behind us on the line as Rene frowned at me. After we got our tray of food, Rene and I sat at a table as far away from Tommy as possible.

"Bethany, you're a live fool," she said. "You'd better snatch that man up."

"He's not my type."

"Who's your type? That Methuselah, knucklehead man?"

"Look, leave him out of it," I said.

"You'd better get on Tommy Hayes like white on rice," she said. "Half the girls in school want to snatch up that dreamboat, but he's stuck on the Way girls."

"Of course."

"Some of the girls want to convert to the Way religion so they can snatch him up."

The bell rang from the intercom, signaling lunch had ended. I was glad it had muted Rene Wilkins's conversation about my knucklehead and Hayes problems.

She told me that Tommy Hayes had recently moved to the area. So that's why I hadn't seen Tommy Hayes in school till recently, because he'd moved from West Bronx to East Bronx. He was also a brainiac and was in the same program as Rene Wilkins.

After school I went to Mama's house because my heart was heavy and I knew a dose of her funny stories and advice would bring me cheer. Much to my chagrin, the vamp answered Mama's door, dressed down from her whore of Babylon, Vamp the Tramp look and wearing a gray sweat suit. After we exchanged greetings, I looked at her sort of dumfounded and followed her to the living room, where Mama and Lisa were.

Mama was standing over a dress pattern, pinning the fabric to it. It rested on two tables that I guessed she had pulled together for her visit with the vamp. She usually sewed in the bedroom, but it was reserved for relatives, only female. The men avoided it like it was the plague, just as if it were Kitchen University. Lisa was on the floor playing with her dolls and talking to them.

"Sister Cornwallis-West, is that all you want from the store?" asked Vamp the Tramp.

"Yes," Mama said. "If you have any money left over, bring back some vanilla extract; I want to make some sweet bread."

After the vamp left for the store, Mama saw the surprise on my face about the visit from the vamp, but I shouldn't have been surprised, because as Polly always said, "I like to help the downtrodden; Mama likes to hang out with them and help them." Polly was a snob. Mama was more democratic. I liked that about her.

"She needed help with some sewing," Mama said. "It's a good thing—I don't want her scaring the sheep away by exposing her shortcomings unnecessarily. And she's a lonely child ... her parents are too busy making money to pay her any mind."

Mama was hell-bent against materialism. Sure, she liked money, but to pursue it to the ends of the earth seemed stupid to her. I sat down in a chair beside her, watching her pin the pattern for Vamp the Tramp.

"You know your ma called me," she said. "She said you threatened to slap her in the face."

"She started it," I said. "She said she was going to smack me in the face."

"Look, Toddy, I know your ma. Sometimes she's a volcano about to erupt. And what do you do you when a volcano is about to erupt?"

"What?"

"You don't fight it or bite it; you get away from it."

Now I felt like a fool. If I had said nothing to Polly, she would have just burned out like a candle, but she pushed me to the edge. In the end, when a kid bucks up against an adult, it's bad; people always say that the kid is disrespectful.

"I know your mother is mean sometimes, but she loves you children very much. She has a lot of responsibility working and raising you kids by herself," said Mama. "She wants you to make something of yourself, even if she has to do you in—and you know Polly; she'll die trying."

"Yes, I know."

"You know Polly lives in the past, and she cries a lot. You may not see it, but she cries a lot. She feels like you and Kevin should have a father, and she wishes Royal would come back."

Tears welled in my eyes, and I smacked both palms over my cheeks to stop the drops from running down my face. For a second, I wished that my father was back too, that he would drive up in his white and pink Pontiac and take us to the carnival, just like he did when we were at Carnegie Hall.

"Child, you have a heavy heart. A part of life is tears and joy."

"But it's hard to be a kid."

"I know. And remember, the Bible says that a kind word will take away wrath, and blessed is the peacemaker and woe unto the peacebreaker," she said. "So remember, when everybody is hollering and screaming, keep your voice low and sweet."

She patted me on the shoulder and handed me a tissue from a box on the end table. We both laughed. My tears seemed to have returned to where they'd come from, and I felt good, like I always did when I talked to Mama; she always seemed to put everything into perspective. Polly was a volcano, but she meant well, and it was no heaven raising kids without a father, I guessed. "And your ma also says that you and Kevin are preventing her from having a second chance at getting married."

I smirked and said, "She should date someone else, not"—the name Dickster almost slipped out—"Brother Quincy. I think she can do better than that."

"I agree. But there's no law against choosing the wrong man; if there were, your ma would have gone to jail for marrying your father. So, you and that half of the cousin brothers Kevin ought to buck up and bite the bullet."

Okay, I'll do that, but Brother Quincy is not taking my mother to some far-off place and noosing her like he noosed me. He puts his hands on my mother and he'll be among the missing, as Polly likes to say.

"Child, what's on your mind?" Mama asked. "Are you holding back from me?"

"No," I lied. The last thing I wanted her to know was my dealings with the Dickster and my bar night escapades. Even though I knew she wouldn't condemn me for it like Polly, I still didn't want her to have those visions in her head about me pretending to be a grown floozy.

"Remember what the Bible says—what is hidden won't remain hidden for long."

She finished pinning the pattern and went and sat on the sofa across from me.

"How do you like the young Brother Hayes?"

"Well, he's okay, I guess," I said, "but I did catch him in a lie. He just got baptized, and it doesn't seem right for him to be mocking God by being such a liar."

"Before seeing the beam in your brother's eye, get the mote out of yours," said Mama. "Haven't you ever lied before?"

"Of course," I said.

"What did Brother Hayes lie about?"

I told her about the fight. She laughed and said, "Toddy, you're expecting too much from the brother—no man will ever admit that he was whipped by a woman. Did he hit you?"

"No," I said. "Tommy Hayes didn't put a hand on me, but he held my hands down when the going got rough. Like, when I socked him in the eye, he didn't hit me back."

"He's like Butch, a gentleman who never hits a woman. The only reason he didn't knock your mother down that time when she beat him was that he is a gentleman, like young Brother Hayes."

But pray tell, I hoped Tommy Hayes wouldn't end up goofy like Butch.

"Toddy, you need a Bible study. You've forgotten everything in the Bible about forgiveness and mild temperament. You've gotten lax. Have a Bible study with me."

I nodded. Anything for Mama; she was my girl.

The bell rung. It was the vamp. All of us chatted for a while, and then I left with a big head full of wisdom.

Polly was home for the evening. When I came in, she acted as if we'd never had an argument. She had on a Horace Silver record with my favorite song, "Song for My Father," playing moderately in the background. She was cooking her favorite southern dish, fried porgies and collard greens, perfuming the house with the smells of collard greens and grease. The house had a happy tempo to it, both a silent and an audible beat that seemed to flow in our bodies as if we had been dosed with adrenaline. Even I had a spark of energy flowing through my veins, which was unusual for a Monday after school.

Once Kevin came in, we ate and went our separate ways, I to the bedroom, he to his bedroom behind the curtain, and Polly to the convertible sofa in the living room, which had she opened. When everyone was in bed and Polly's snores seemed to be directing every sound in the house, my mind began to work overtime. I tried to flip the switch in my brain to stop the thoughts, but they just kept coming.

Perhaps I had been acting too self-righteous—or as Mama put it, looking at the mote in someone else's eye instead of the big beam in my own eye. She was paraphrasing Matthew 7:1–7 KJV, which tells us to stop judging other people, because if we judge ourselves, we see that our sins are larger. Perhaps I was a bigger liar than Tommy Hayes, and perhaps I should stop judging the knucklehead. Maybe the needle in Norman's arm at the opera wasn't for illicit drugs but for diabetes; yeah, ha-ha-ha.

I muffled my giggle so I wouldn't wake up the house. The diabetes drug was wishful thinking. Now I was acting like a live fool as Rene Wilkins would say. Whatever the case, I couldn't be going around the world judging people. I was not perfect; only a perfect person could judge someone—either Jehovah or Jesus Christ—and I wasn't in that category. Finally my mind was at rest with this wisdom; it shut down, and I went to sleep.

The next day as I was walking up the steps to class, I smelled the familiar scent of a freshly showered body, followed by a cheerful "Hello, Toddy." It was Tommy Hayes, carrying a long-stemmed rose. We stopped at a landing. He handed me the rose, lowered his eyes, and then said, "I apologize for arguing with you at Sister Quan's get-together."

"Apology accepted," I said, biting my tongue to prevent any garbage from coming out of my mouth that would stoke any fires left over from the last argument.

The second bell rang over the loudspeaker, and we went down the hallway to our separate classes. He was in the SP class, the special program class—or what the hip called "special pussies' class"—with Rene Wilkins. It was for brainiacs, but I wasn't far from being a brainiac; I was in a one class, the class just below the bighead brainiac people. Wilkins said that he was smarter than anyone in the class. That was good—it showed the Wayans weren't dumb.

Tommy came and sat with Rene and me at lunch, and he brought his just-showered smell with him, still fresh even though it had been hours since I'd seen him. Rene looked like she was vamping at him as they discussed what they were going to do when they left junior high school. Her freckled face flushed just as mine had when I used to think of the Gingerbread Man before he became a complete knucklehead.

"I'm going to the Bronx High School of Science," said Rene. "If I'm not accepted, my mother is going to send me to boarding school."

"I'm going to Stuyvesant," said Tommy. "If I'm not accepted, I'll try the Bronx High School of Science or go to a regular school."

I felt kind of small around these bighead brainiacs; they were headed to special schools, and where was I going? Here we go again, back to those feelings, those Kevin and Butch feelings that made me feel that I was rotten meat between two pieces of Wonder Bread: Kevin, current and future basketball star, and Butch, Mr. Elder Deluxe with a good job and a good wife, all at an early age.

"What school are you going to, Toddy?" asked Tommy Hayes.

"Oh, my feet are headed somewhere," I said, feeling like a complete fool for my stupid answer.

"She better be headed someplace soon," said Rene. "We're not getting any younger."

"I guess it's good that she's deliberating," said Tommy.

Tommy Hayes, old good-hearted Tommy Hayes, defending me like this before this vamp. He was as sweet and good as sugar—on the sugar lane, he was my Lollipop, like the knucklehead used to be my Gingerbread Man. Rene was staring at my rose, which I was fingering like a vital vein, with that green-eyed-monster look of envy. I had told her my Tommy, my new Lollipop (I didn't say this name), had given it to me. Her face literally turned green after that. She turned to Tommy and smirked.

"Her grades have never been that good," said Rene.

"They've been good enough. I'm in a one class," I said, "just a rung below the bigheads."

The bell rang; we gathered up our books, and I went to class. All the while Rene was edging closer and closer like static cling to Tommy, vamping to the nth degree. I had news for her: if I wasn't going to let the Wayan vamp take advantage of dear Tommy and corrupt him, I wasn't going to let her corrupt him either. After all, he was my Lollipop now, a candy so innocent that it was like a virgin pin standing proudly without reproach on a stick.

Polly and I were at a truce, and there was peace in the house. I thought it was safe until I came home from school. When I opened the door, the voice of Johnny Mathis filled the air with the ending of the song "The Twelfth of Never": "You ask how much I love you. Must I explain? I need you, oh my darling, like roses need rain. Until the twelfth of never, and that's a long, long, long time."

My mother was sitting in the dining area, her faced flushed, looking younger than her thirty-six years and with a silly lovestruck look on her face. She greeted me cordially but with a distracted look. I sat next to her at the table, grabbed a grape resting in the fruit bowl, and waited for the latest on whatever. As I looked at her lovestruck face, I thought my father had decided to return to the fold. The scratching sound of the needle against the album signaled that Johnny Mathis was long gone. Polly took a deep breath.

"Guess what?" she asked.

"What?"

"Brother Quincy and I," she said, "I mean Richard and I, are going to Whitestone."

"Really?" I said.

Whitestone. Damn Whitestone. A drive-in movie on the Whitestone Bridge. The Dickster could noose and kill a city full of people, and they would never be found. The last thing Polly needed to do was be alone with that dude. This damn Dickster, this pretender defender of the faith and deluxe hypocrite, wouldn't be alone with Polly as long as I was alive.

"Yes, that sounds good. Kevin and I should really enjoy it," I said. "What's playing that night?"

"You and Kevin won't be going on my date," she said. "I'm not running a nursery school."

That was a good try. I guessed I'd better try again. Polly had a slight indignant look on her face, her nose in the air, and an inch rise in her high cheekbones. She got up, went to the record player, and played the flip side of the Johnny Mathis record, adjusting the volume so that we could hear the music and hear each other at the same time. Once she came back to the dining area, I had a new plot.

"Look, Ma, people talk at the temple," I said. "They'll say, 'She just came back to the fold after being excommunicated, and here she goes dating an elder before her feet have a chance to get warm.'"

Polly sucked her teeth. "I don't give a hoot what people think." She looked at me like I were a piece of dust, the equivalent of a powerless kid, then her eyes blazed like an active volcano, much worse than they had when she

195

caught Karen's naked nondescript boy in the closet. Her eyes were whiteless and the lashes were gone, giving her the look of a snake ready to strike, to kill.

I knew then that her attitude was going someplace, and it was not a good one. I remembered what my grandmother had said: "Run from Polly's volcanoes." Polly chewed the last piece of the grape in her mouth and then spit out the pit in a cup.

"I don't care what you kids think. I want a husband, and I aim to get one," she said.

"Okay, Ma. I hope you enjoy the movie," I said.

"Don't worry, sweetie. You and Kevin can go to the drive-in the next time."

Johnny Mathis belted his last word to the ballad, and the needle began rubbing against the album again. Polly got up to change the record, and I went into my room to brainstorm. I plopped on the bed, and my mind began racing wildly: if I were to tell my mother that I was at bar night and had picked up a man, she'd call me a strumpet; if I did not tell her, then the Dickster would noose her as he had tried to strangle me. This was a no-brainer; I wouldn't let my mother get noosed just to save face. Finally an idea came into my head: if Kevin was sick, my mother wouldn't go to the drive-in. At least it would postpone the date.

Waiting until after my mother had left for work, I went to Kevin's room. The curtain to his makeshift room was open. I pressed my face against it, and he waved me in. He was on the bed with Buck, brushing the dog's hair. The dog raised his ears and looked at me as if I were a burglar who had come into man and dog's lair to disturb the peace.

Kevin waved his hand in the direction of the ottoman at the foot of his bed. When I sat, I looked into the face of my father, Royal Bethany; Kevin looked like a statue of him, as if he were cursing the man who had deserted him when he was six weeks old. True, the pencil-thin lips—stingy, as Polly called his and Mama's lips—were Mama's, but the face, from the bogey eyes to the round, flat checks, and the cowlicks were Royal Bethany's.

He stopped brushing Buck's hair and looked at me as Buck had, as if I had invaded his lair even though he had invited me in. He gave me a minute smile with Mama's lips, then parted them in a smirk as he began to speak.

"What's up?" he asked.

"You know Ma has this man, this Brother Quincy, on her mind," I said, "and I don't think it's a good fit."

"I don't know why she's thinking about getting married," he said. "She's too old to be thinking these things."

He sighed in a way that was too old for a young boy but too young for an old man. This selfish little tart, he wanted Polly all to himself. It was him and Polly against the world; all he had to do was get rid of me, and he'd be on cloud nine. I didn't want to disagree with him because he was an ally, and I didn't care why he wanted to get rid of the Dickster—I just wanted to get rid of him. Wars make strange bedfellows. Just look at World War II and the alliance of the United States and the Soviet Union, opposites in the universe.

"First let's get rid of the"—I bit my tongue before the word came out—"dear old Brother Quincy."

The face of Kevin, Polly's crestfallen, sexless, faux beau, glowed as if he had discovered the wisdom of the ages and some great light shone beneath his skin. I pitched my ruse to Kevin: get sick so Polly would have to postpone her date with the Dickster. After I finished my salesman's puff about how good the ruse would be, he reached over and gave me a high five. Our palms met—probably the only and last time we would be in sync about anything.

"To make it a cinch, I won't even take a bath on Friday and Saturday," said Kevin. "Then Ma really will think I'm sick."

"Yeah, if you don't take a bath and start stinking," I said, "Ma will know it's Armageddon, because usually you're so clean."

We called it a night, and I went into my room thinking how creative the little devil was. Perhaps he would become a mama's boy and remain with his mother till the end of time. Who knew? But it was sad that Polly's life was wrapped around her children. Really she had no life despite all the work she did, and I couldn't remember her ever taking a vacation; she went to work and came straight home to us. What would happen if she did find someone nice enough to marry? What would Kevin do? What bully pulpit would he hop on to stop the marriage?

I turned the television on when I got to my room, and there was an advertisement about *Romeo and Juliet* playing at the opera house; the last place I wanted to see was the opera house, on television or in person. The memory of the knucklehead's escapades at the opera was still like a piece of overripe fruit in my mind.

The two young lovers on the screen were in one another's faces, holding hands and singing the laments of their doomed love. I turned away quickly; it brought back bad memories. And the story line of two lovers killing themselves over love was too much to bear. In my logic they just should have run away from their bickering parents.

In my mind, I transposed the two faces of the lovers with the faces of knucklehead and me, only this time we were singing and lamenting over his knuckleheadedness. Tears fell down my cheeks. I felt like a complete idiot for screaming at him when I broke off our—whatever it was. I wondered if he was as sad as I was about the ending of our whatever.

Suddenly the sad feeling was replaced when the taste of chocolate ice cream entered my mouth. I wanted some Carvel. I slipped on some dungarees and headed for Carvel Ice Cream Store. I peeked in as I passed Kevin's curtain to confirm that he and Buck were sleeping, and then I eased out the door.

CHAPTER 19

I was walking in the direction of the Carvel store for ice cream on 225th Street and White Plains Road, a small shop compared to the humongous ones on Laconia and Webster Avenues, when I pivoted in the opposite direction to go to the one on Laconia Avenue farther north. It was right across the street from where the knucklehead worked at the cabstand. I just wanted to see how he was doing, not speak to him; I really didn't know what to say. The orange moon pasted in the sky and the stars scattered about gave the vista a spooky, sneaky Halloween look.

Even though I had one late night a week and hadn't used it this week, I looked from side to side as I crept up the semidark block of single-family houses with shingled porches and ample front yards, watching for any relatives straying in the night, like Mama and Lisa coming from shopping on Fordham Road, or Butch and Suki coming from or going to whatever, or their friends who might say, "I saw Toddy on so-and-so street at so-and-so hour." Sure, I had a late night, but who wanted a bunch of nosy adults knowing what you were up to 24-7? Besides, being sneaky was more exciting; it was like being a spy and having an aura of mystery around you, which made you look cool. It was better to be cool than look like a fool.

The Carvel on Laconia was so huge that it lit up the entire block and the two-way street of the avenue. I shadowed my eyes from the glare of its brightness with my hand once I'd stepped from the sheath of darkness on the last block. The Carvel sat in the middle of a large parking lot for cars as if it were a ride at a carnival. There was a line in front of the counter. I scanned it for any sign of the knucklehead and any relatives.

I looked across the street at the cabstand where my ex–Gingerbread

Man, now Knucklehead Man, worked. The black Chevys with the telephone number FA-111-1111, stamped in white on the front doors, drove in and out of the storefront cabstand. Some of the cars were parked in front of the stand, waiting for a call for a fare. I searched for any sign of him, looking at the silhouettes of drivers for some semblance of the knucklehead, because the illuminating Carvel light did not extend to the outline of the faces of the people across the street.

My eyes and heart bled for any sign of him; my blood raced through my veins like balls of fire. Where was he? In jail? Dead? If only I hadn't yelled at him. No matter what he'd done, my last words to him shouldn't have been, "You deserted me. You left me flat just like my father."

I walked to the curb to get a better view, when someone tapped me on my shoulder. I spun around, and it was you-know-who: no goatee, freshly cut hair, and a smell to go with it. "Toddy!" he said. I didn't answer. For a second I stood there dumbstruck, but then I pivoted and ran in the direction of my home. The knucklehead yelled my name as I ran and ran down 225th. I ran and ran until I reached my apartment. Then I locked myself in the apartment as if I were being chased by a boogeyman.

The last question on my mind as I fell asleep was *Why did I run from him?* Then I remembered what Mr. Jimmy had told me: if you see someone like him coming, start running in the opposite direction.

Lollipop, the very good-hearted Tommy Hayes, had now started eating lunch in the cafeteria with Rene Wilkins and me on a regular basis. She was the ultimate vamp, trying to seduce Lollipop, it seemed, at the drop of a hat. I was sure she would give up her virgin pin for him if Tommy Hayes was inclined to have her. She had even managed to put on makeup for her vamping, despite opposition from the adults. And to make matters worse, she did her best to shut me out of any conversation between the two of them, by always referring to their brainiac classes that they took together. I, on the other hand, sat there feeling like I didn't belong and like an oaf. But I was glad to be with these kids even though I really didn't like to hang with people my own age, because it kept me off my knucklehead mess.

We had just finished downing the day's lunch, sloppy joes and french fries, when this ultimate vamp started on a new campaign to ensnare Tommy.

Rene Wilkins was batting her eyes on her polka-dot face and speaking so sensually and velvety that it sounded like a whisper.

"I'm so impressed with how you Wayans are so skilled with the Bible," she said.

"Thank you. We study the scriptures a lot," said my Lollipop Tommy Hayes.

"I don't know any parts of the Bible past the Garden of Eden in Genesis," she said.

I had had enough of this cafeteria Mata Hari trying to corrupt the morals of Lollipop Hayes and using the name of God to do it. It made me want to puke. But instead of puking, I belched to let out some of the gas this Vamp the Tramp was causing in my stomach.

"Why don't you have a Bible study, if you want to ride past Genesis?" I asked.

"That's a good idea," Rene said, turning to me and giving me a shitty grin, and then turning back to Tommy and giving him a look as if she had stumbled upon the Holy Grail, "Will you have a Bible study with me?" she asked Lollipop.

"Of course," he said earnestly.

This vamp was something else. I could imagine them getting married and having a bunch of polka-dot children, all freckles like Rene's and Brainiac's. To be Negro was horrible enough in this society, but to be a polka-dot Negro was another story. I felt I must prevent Lollipop from being ensnared in a relationship with polka dots. I would watch over him like I watched over my family, with heart and soul.

"But when do you have time to study?" I asked.

"I can make time if Tommy is willing to do it."

"I can." Tommy turned to me and said, "Toddy, will you come to the Bible study with me?"

"Yes, of course," I said.

Rene Wilkins's face became very cloudy once she learned that I was coming to the Bible study—or was it perhaps that Lollipop favored me? Well, it was a waste of favor because he wasn't my type: young, inexperienced, and unbent. If the Gingerbread Man weren't such a knucklehead, I wouldn't have had time to prevent Lollipop from being sucked in (no pun intended) by this Vamp the Tramp.

"Bethany, why are you so quiet?" Rene Wilkins asked.

"I'm not into physics and gravity like you two are; I'm just interested in the fact that they work, not how they work."

"Don't feel left out, Toddy," Lollipop said. "A person only knows some things, not everything. You know something we don't."

"But what?" Rene Wilkins asked.

I wanted to manually remove every freckle from her face with a spoon.

"Like why I don't have freckles," I said.

The bell rang. Lunch was over. We got up from the table and went to class. I felt bad that I couldn't go with these brainiacs to save Lollipop from this new vamp, but I wasn't in the brainiacs' classes.

Kevin Bethany was a great basketball player, according to his coach, Mr. Bell, and was going places. But Kevin also proved to be a great actor, if not having a bit of overkill. He feigned illness so well on Friday to prevent the Dickster date that even I thought he was ill. He didn't take a bath and his skin looked gray, a wan look that tore at my mother's heartstrings.

Polly had a soft spot for Kevin because he was the youngest. If Polly had any favorites among the three of us, it was unknown. She seemed to treat us according to our individual needs: Kevin needed her to be his number one, I needed her to be my number one, and Butch seemed to need her as an adversarial sister always vying for Mama's approval. Mama really raised Butch the first seven years of his life because my mother was too young.

Kevin waited until Polly came home before he got dressed for school. My mother saw that he wasn't ready to go, definitely unusual for him, and went into the room to find out if there was something wrong.

"Kevin, are you okay?" she asked. "You're not dressed for school."

"Well," he said, "I'm kind of under the weather. I have a headache and a stomachache."

"Do you want to stay home from school?"

"No. I'll miss my gold star for attendance."

I was in the kitchen drinking coffee and bit my lip, trying to stop from giggling at this great actor. He wouldn't stay home from school if he had died in his bed. He had a shiny medal from school for perfect attendance, and nature couldn't stop him from getting another, unlike his sister, who preferred the softness of the sheets and bed to the hard wooden chairs of academia. It was a challenge for me to get out of bed in the morning; sometimes I won, sometimes I lost.

Kevin dragged himself out of bed and took a bird bath instead of a shower to emphasize to my mother how under the weather he was. Anything, Lord, anything to dedick my mother's life of the Dickster. My mother took his temperature before he left. She was somewhat reassured when it was normal; if it hadn't been, she would have pulled rank and kept him home. Kevin finally left the house half washed with ashy skin and a hangdog look on his face.

Kevin's and my ruse didn't work. When he continued his ruse on Saturday, the day of the Dickster date, my mother called Mama over to watch him so she could go to the drive-in with this quick dick Dickster guy. Once I knew that I couldn't stop this date, I spilled my guts about what had happened on bar night: going to the bar and ensnaring the Dickster, the ride to Mount Vernon, the rope around my neck, etc.

We were all in the living room as I became Toddy the confessor to Mama, Lisa, Kevin, and Polly. After I'd told the truth and nothing but the truth, my mother looked at me incredulously and then frowned until the ends of her lips were pointing south, a signal of her disgust.

"You are nothing but a strumpet," said Polly. "I go to work at night to take care of you, and your ass is running the streets while I'm burning the candle at work."

"Polly, stop low-rating the child," said Mama. "The Bible says no stream gets above its source. She's doing no more than you did when you were a child."

"I want my daughter to do better than me," Polly yelled. "I don't want her to get pregnant at fifteen and have to stop school. I don't want that for her."

"Did he put his hands on you, baby?" Polly asked.

I nodded yes.

"His ass is mine," said Polly.

The look of disgust on her face turned to rage. Her eyes turned lashless, and the dark irises took over the whites of her eyes. From a distance they looked like the eyes of a snake. Kevin began giggling. Polly went to the car when the Dickster arrived and confronted him; he denied everything, so she sent him on his merry way.

My mother believed me, but my backstory about what had happened at the bar, the flirting and everything else that had to do with loose living, made me worth two cents in her eyes—and after this I felt like two cents.

As I was sitting in the cafeteria with Lollipop and Rene Wilkins, I mirrored the disappointing look on my mother's face over the entire incident, which was really about me: about my sneaky, untrustworthy behind. But Polly just didn't understand; I just had to have fun.

"Toddy, cheer up—things will get better," said Lollipop.

"Yeah, take that sourpuss look off your face," said Rene Wilkins. "You'll get old before your time."

I glanced at Lollipop's face; he had that wise look, the look that said, *I know what happened to you.* Apparently the Dickster was looking for blood, and he spread rumors around the congregation that I was a crazy kid who was telling lies about him. When we went to the temple on Sunday, I felt those condemning eyes of the congregation rip through my skin like razors.

Polly was a proud woman, a woman who needed a good reputation, but when it came to her kids, she wasn't about to save face. Thus she returned the condemning eyes to those people, and they knew that if they stepped too far, they'd get a tongue-lashing; if theirs were razors, hers was the largest sword in the world. And no one in the congregation wanted to tangle with Polly. She had a mouth like a whip, and it was unpredictable—her tongue was like a surgeon's knife. I raised my head from my self-imposed pity, smiled, and reminded myself that it wasn't the end of the world.

"This is going to be so boring," said Rene Wilkins. "We have to look at this convention stuff tonight."

"At least we can come in an hour later tomorrow," I said.

"Yeah, that's a good deal," said Lollipop.

Our homework was to find out who'd won the presidential primary in California—really the only thing that seemed exciting in it was that there was a senator from New York, our state, who was running and in the lead.

"It won't be so boring," she said, "because the senator from the great state of New York will be there."

We giggled at Rene's mimicking of congressional lingo when they were on the floor of the House with the words the "great state of New York." The bell rang, and we left for class.

I began looking at the convention around 7:00 p.m. Polly was not working that night, so we had a sumptuous meal of steak, potatoes, and collard greens. Once the food saturated my stomach, I was feeling a little woozy. I fell asleep once the senator had made his speech after winning.

My mother came in later and whispered, or what sounded like a whisper, "He's been shot." My brain awakened as if I had been shot out of a cannon. I raised my head from my pillow and adjusted my eyes until I saw her housedress.

"Who?" I asked.

"The senator from New York."

I thought I was dreaming. I dropped my head on the pillow and fell asleep again, sure that it was just a dream. But when I woke up, I found out it wasn't a dream. My mother and the news on television filled me in. My mother stuck her head in the room and said, "The devil is a busy man. Just when we think he is through with us, he pops up with more devilish tricks."

"Amen. But maybe the senator will pull through."

"Hopefully. But this is too much. First King, and now this."

She came all the way into the room and gave me a hug. "Do you want to stay home from school? With this man being shot, it might not be a good idea to be on the streets."

"I'm fine, Ma."

"I'm not staying home either," Kevin yelled from the other room.

But who really wanted to stay home at a time like this? I wanted to go out and move, move, move—sitting still and being miserable was a bad idea. Kevin's school was down the block. He didn't want to miss his gold star for perfect attendance at the end of the year. Besides, what did a nine-year-old boy really know about this? If he knew, he sure wasn't talking. You never really knew what was going on in Kevin's mind until he got mad.

The next morning as I walked up Barnes Avenue, the buzz about town was the shooting. When I passed the newsstand, all the dailies had a picture of the senator. I darted my eyes away from the horrible scene. In fact, it all seemed like a dream, unreal—first Martin Luther King and now the senator. Maybe Armageddon was coming soon.

The school corridors were quiet, too quiet, and people moved in the hallways as if they were old, slow, unsteady, and stiff. Suddenly the world seemed old, and I felt old. The morning classes seemed more like a funeral procession, silent and—yes—old. When the adults spoke, namely, the teachers, they seemed to be acting, as if they were saying something they didn't mean. It was like that for all the classes I went to that morning. In English, it seemed like the teacher was speaking the words of a farce. During home economics, while the class was working at baking biscuits, there seemed to be some subliminal message in everything the adults said—and the students too.

I was glad when lunch came. I was sure things would get lively with Lollipop and Rene Wilkins on the scene. They were already at the table, Rene Wilkins with a sourpuss look on her face and Lollipop with his Bible beside him. They barely noticed me when I sat down beside them at the table with my tray full of lunch. Both gave me a nanosecond's glance then started talking.

"But why? Why did God let this happen?" asked Rene Wilkins. "First Martin Luther King, and now the senator's been shot."

"God didn't let this happen," said Lollipop calmly. He opened the Bible to Revelation 12:12 KJV and began reading slowly, deliberately, as if he were speaking to a toddler, teaching him his first words.

"On account of this be glad, you heavens and you who reside in them. Woe to the inhabiters of the earth and of the sea for the Devil is come unto you, having great wrath, because he knoweth that he hath but a short time."

"It's not Jehovah that's doing this; it's the devil stirring the pot," I said, helping Lollipop defend the faith.

A shadow came over Rene Wilkins's face as though she were looking at something terrible behind me. I turned to see what it was—it was the flag in the front yard. It was being lowered to half-staff on the flag pole, to the mourning position; the senator was dead. Everyone was looking at the window where Old Glory, the flag that had waved proudly, arrogantly, and devil-may-care in the warm spring breeze, turned within seconds into a shroud, limp like a spent rag, as it went ceremoniously down the flagpole.

The cooks and the dietitians left their stations, from the serve line to the cook line, and came to observe the passing of the senator. It was so silent that I couldn't even hear myself breathe; it was as if the air had been sucked out of everything moving. I could tell by the expressions on people's faces that we were living history, an ugly history.

Then the PA system made its scratching song. The man who had taken Mr. Lieberman's place, Mr. Baker, far removed from the nineteenth century, which had birthed the former, told us in a squeaky voice that the senator was dead. "Go to your homerooms to sign out and go home."

Lollipop, Rene Wilkins, and I glanced at one another as if we were looking for an answer to some impossible brainiac question. Lollipop broke through this torture chamber of silence. "Toddy, Rene and I will wait for you on the steps in front. I'll call my father to pick us up from the pay phone in front of the sandwich shop across the street." I nodded like an automaton. But as the crowd drifted out of the cafeteria back to our respective homerooms, Rene and Lollipop to the brainiacs' class, I to the almost-brainiac class, a silent cloak of death smothered the air. It was like my brother Butch said: you could see sound, and this sound of silence was eerie and infinite.

Once we went down the corridor to our classes and we made it to the turn where Lollipop and Rene went to the brainiac class, Lollipop tapped me on the shoulder and said, "Don't forget—meet us on the steps."

His calming and self-assured voice took me from my automaton, sleepwalking state, and for a second I felt spry, young, not like some old-minded person who had witnessed two assassinations in two months. But once he left, I walked as if I had been chloroformed: hesitant, old, and unsure.

Once I signed out, I went to the front of the building. There were many students out there, but Lollipop towered above them all. He waved to me to come to where he and Rene Wilkins stood, but then a new crowd of students came into the crowd who had been milling on the steps and stymied me from moving. A voice barked from the crowd: "See, what did I tell you, Corinth? You cried for the senator, but you didn't cry for Martin Luther King." That voice, I knew, was Viola, reminding Corinth of what had happened when

MLK was assassinated. Corinth ignored her. I had known her since grade school; maybe she had pretended to like us, when inside we were just a bunch of coloreds to her, an irritant itch. But maybe that wasn't the case.

The crowd of students had grown to a tight-knit sea, and I seemed to be at the mercy of this towering wave. At five feet tall, I found that everything in this crowd was taller than me, and this colossal wave of humanity, which was in disarray above my head, was sucking the air and moving like waves in the sea during a storm: spastic, angry, and unpredictable. I was at the mercy of this sea. But Lollipop's voice reigned above the colossus: "Toddy, Toddy, where are you?" he asked.

I was breathless, searching for a way to escape this colossus, and I knew that Lollipop couldn't save me. I looked for an opening, a hand in this colossus, which was now home to groups of people pushing, shoving, and fighting, that would rescue me from this raging sea. The people were faceless and undistinguishable to me, until one face looked directly at me: Viola. She wafted through the crowd like a spirit walking on air—calm, serene. I smiled at her; she was rescuing me. Once she made it up to where I was, she socked me in the eye then drifted back into the sea. This was payback at the wrong time. My knees buckled and I began to fall. Lollipop's voice sounded muffled as if he were in another state. "Toddy, Toddy." He yelled.

I was going down like an aged prizefighter on his last day. As I fell, I knew that if I reached the bottom, I would be trampled to death by this sea of feet. But a white hand grabbed my hand and hoisted me firmly on my feet. It was Corinth, my savior. Once she let go of my hand, she started flailing at whatever was in her way and disappeared into the crowd like a ghost. I was still in trouble; the crowd was kneading me like I was a piece a dough being rolled by a pin. Blood streamed down my face, oozing into my mouth until I tasted its metallic goo.

I prayed to Jehovah to get me out of this mess, but I felt guilty because I was becoming a bad-weather friend, calling on him only when I was in a jam. The crowd expelled me like I was a piece of counterfeit money, and I ended up on 213th Street. A police car with full siren was blaring toward the school as I made it to White Plains Road.

On White Plains Road, traffic was at a standstill; cars were lined up in either direction under the el train. People were honking like mad, and patrol officers on foot were trying to do something with the traffic and the people. "Toddy, Toddy," someone yelled from the convoy of cars. It was the Gingerbread Man or the knucklehead—hopefully my Gingerbread Man. He was in his car, and I raced to him. I struggled into the car, sore from the banging I had gotten. He touched my hand, and my heart melted.

"Poor baby," he said as he reached into his pocket, got a handkerchief, and dabbed at the river of blood streaming down my face. I looked at him from the corner of my eye to see if I was dealing with Norman the knucklehead or Norman the Gingerbread Man. The smell of cocoa butter soap peppered with cologne seeped from his pores. His skin was as smooth as a dark piece of silk, and those lips, those full lips, looked as inviting as a piece of candy.

He smiled and he glowed as if he had found some inner peace. No, this wasn't a knucklehead before me; this was a clean machine, as clean as Lollipop—impossible, but on the road there anyway. Yes, sir, my Gingerbread Man was back. And this clean picture of gingerbread almost obliterated the picture of him sprawled out, knuckleheaded, in the lobby of the opera house with a needle of dope in his arm.

"What happened?" he asked.

"Some kid gave me a sucker punch at school when they let us out early."

I had to bite my tongue not to let it slip out that I was still in junior high school, which meant I wasn't sixteen, which was what I'd told him. Either he would know I lied to him about being that age, or he would think I was real dumb to be three grades below my age group in junior high school.

"You're going to need some ice or a steak on that eye soon, so it won't swell," he said.

The convoy of cars started moving; whatever was going on had been fixed. I swooned over his velvety skin and the fresh smell that oozed from his pores. It was like old times, the times I wanted to remember—the Gingerbread Man and not the knucklehead at the steering wheel, driving his lady love.

"I've got a surprise for you," he said.

"Surprise?"

"Yes. Come with me Saturday to the carnival at the state park in Mount Vernon, and I'll tell you about it."

"Okay, but what is it?"

He turned for a second and pointed his index finger at me. "No, no, no. This is a real surprise—no telling."

We were in front of my apartment building in no time. He took another look at my eye. The cut underneath it had stopped bleeding, but I could feel the heat from the swelling.

"Like I said, a raw steak or an ice pack is what that eye needs."

"I'll do it when I get into the house." I opened the car door to leave, but I looked back for a second and marveled at my clean-cut Gingerbread Man, who seemed to have given up knuckleheadedness.

I was in daze, flying on cloud nine in the universe. My Gingerbread Man was back. As I walked into the courtyard of my building, I bumped right into someone whom I didn't want to see—my brother Ronnie Bethany. He had one of these shocked, concerned, and condemning looks on his face that was standard fare for adults, but it made my stomach churn.

"What happened to you? Who was that man in the car?" he asked.

"Please mind your business; you're not my father."

"It is my business; you're my sister," said Butch. "Did he put his hands on you?"

"Mind your damn business, you black spasm, you," I said. "That's why Kevin isn't speaking to you—you've always got your nose where it doesn't belong."

I wanted to snatch the words back, but it was too late, so I rushed up the walkway, leaving the words and Butch behind. He was the one who'd started this, but I would be blamed. I could just hear Polly's tongue-lashing ringing in my ears, loud enough to penetrate the earplugs.

Once I got inside the apartment, Polly didn't like the looks of my eye. She asked me what had happened, and I told her there was rioting in front of the school and I fell, omitting the fact that I'd gotten sucker-punched by Viola. I just didn't want to worry her. She decided to take me to the hospital for a head x-ray then go to work late if everything was all right and have Mama come over to the house and watch me to see if anything went wrong—or else she'd stay home from work.

We went by cab to Mercy Hospital on East 233rd Street. The x-ray read that I had no concussion. My mother sped to work in a cab we had hailed and dropped me off at the house before her shift. It was around 10:00 p.m. when I got home. Kevin and Buck were in the room asleep, the curtain divider to the room closed. Mama was in the dining area eating walnuts, and Lisa was asleep in the living room on the convertible sofa.

"How are you, baby girl?" asked Mama. "I heard about your misfortune."

"Fine."

I went and sat at the table with her and grabbed a shelled walnut from the bowl. My eye burned, and as it did, the condition of the world felt more painful than my pain: Martin Luther King assassinated, Senator Robert Kennedy assassinated, riots, and racism.

"Mama, why is there so much hate in the world?"

"Toddy, hate is of the devil. We all were made in the image of God, and God is love. So we have that capacity to love," Mama said as she spooned a walnut from its shell. "So remember that all people love and want to be loved; God put that in our system. It's the devil that promotes hate, and you know he's in earth's vicinity stirring up trouble."

"This is hard to understand."

"Don't worry; you'll get it one day."

"But, Mama, what if you had a fight and you won? Can you make peace with that person?"

"Yes. But you must be the peacemaker. You must help them heal their wounds. It's like the Good Book says." Mama reached into the bowl and got another walnut. "Blessed is the peacemaker. You have to take the lead, Toddy, to patch this up. You won, right?" I nodded, still unsure about how I was going to work on repairing my relationship with Viola. The thought of how I was going to make it right with Viola made my head spin; I had no answers and no ruse I wanted to play. What about Viola? Did she have the capacity to love me after I'd thrown her in the Bronx River? I guess the sucker punch that she gave me that knocked me out for a second had answered the question. Mama went into the kitchen and came back with a large piece of uncooked sirloin steak, which she slapped on my eye. I winced.

"That ought to do the trick," she said. "After it plays doctor, it should make a nice dinner with baked potatoes and gravy."

I yawned. The day had been long, like a thousand years. I dragged myself, holding the steak over my eye, to bed, thankful that Corinth had saved me and tickled pink that my Gingerbread Man was back—I hoped permanently. But maybe I'd been too hard on the Gingerbread Man; maybe I expected too much of him. After all, he was human. Maybe if I did like 1 Corinthians 13 said about love—"Love believes all things and hopes all things"—I could stomach the Gingerbread Man's and everyone else's imperfections.

True, Mr. Jimmy had told me that if Norman was still using drugs, I should run when I saw him coming, and the Bible did say that bad associations spoil useful habits, but maybe I should try 1 Corinthians 13; maybe that would work. I closed my eyes, exhausted; the last thing I remembered was the bloody smell of the steak on top of my skin.

When I awoke the next morning, the steak had vanished, and its cooked carcass smell was all over the apartment. Mama had cooked the doctor. Kevin and I had steak and potatoes for breakfast. "Your eye looks better," said Mama as she served us the steak and potatoes. It did look better. The blue discoloration on my eye was still there, but the swelling had disappeared.

CHAPTER 20

By the time I got to school, I had removed the assassination, the riot, and Viola from my mind and thought only about the Gingerbread Man. I daydreamed in class about how we would meet on Saturday and how we would eventually marry and then I'd be Mrs. Gingerbread Man. I was still on cloud nine when I went to lunch with Lollipop and Rene Wilkins. I heard during a commercial break in my daydream about the Gingerbread Man, which consisted of a yawn that brought me back to the here and now, that Corinth and Viola were on detention—I assumed till the end of the school year, which would be in a little more than two weeks, so I guessed the two were getting a bargain; after all, Viola and I had been on detention for six weeks.

When I got home, I heard Polly playing "Slaughter on Tenth Avenue," and I knew someone was in trouble—and that someone was probably me. The tune, all instrumental, was her battle cry, her Battle Hymn of the Republic, and I knew when I opened the door that the feces was about to hit the fan.

Of course, she was in full battle regalia. She was sitting at the kitchen table, her hair pulled back in a bun on top of her head with a mother-of-pearl barrette holding it together. She shot her eyes at me then looked away; I was the target or whatever. I passed her, gave her a whispered hello, and went into the kitchen to get a cold soda. When I came out, she was ready. She poked that snobby keen nose in the air, as if she were smelling something rancid, and began her battle cry.

"Butch said you cussed him out," she said.

"That's a possibility," I said.

"Don't get coy with me. Either you did or you didn't," said Polly. "You should apologize for calling him a black spasm."

I've got news for you, Polly. I'm not apologizing to His Lordship the eldership. I'll never apologize to anybody, even if I'm wrong; it's a chump's walk. I sat with Polly at the dining room table but kept enough distance that I had a path to my room if I had to go mayday like they did in the army when there was an emergency and run.

"Ma, he's always poking his nose in Kevin's and my business—after all, he's not our father."

"Father? What father? Royal was your father once; now he's just someone who sired you," said Polly. "If Butch wants to pick up the slack of this sire and give you some good advice, jump on it. I can't be with you all the time."

I looked up at the ceiling as if I were looking for an escape hatch from this conversation.

"Yeah, yeah, yeah," I sang.

"Some answer. And remember, the Bible says don't be disrespectful to your parents."

"Yeah, and Colossians 3:21 KJV says parents, 'provoke not your children to anger, lest they be discouraged.'"

"Girl, don't you ever call your brother a black spasm," said Polly. "You know how they tried to railroad him at that school on Long Island when we lived on the air force base."

I had to end this story before she told it again: about how Butch was the only black kid in the class when he was in second grade and his teacher told Polly that he was so lamebrained that she was surprised he could hold up his head; that he was hopelessly, not remotely, retarded; and that there was nothing the world could do but let him vegetate. If only this academic guru could see Butch now.

"Look, how come everyone is always on my back?" I asked earnestly.

"Missy, you're on your own back. Maybe it's time to look in the mirror," said Polly. "You shouldn't be low-rating your brother. You should be proud of him. You sound like you're envious of him."

"I'm not!"

"You are! Why don't you get off your duff and get started with your life?"

I shook my head in disgust. "I can't. Kevin and Butch are running such a ring around me that their stardust is blinding my eyes."

We both giggled. Then Polly turned serious. "You want to be grown. So stop copping out and take responsibility for your actions—the first sign of growing up is admitting your mistakes and apologizing."

I couldn't take it anymore. I bolted out of the kitchen chair and announced, "I have to go to the bathroom." My bladder had no inclination, but I slipped out and ran in the direction of my bedroom.

"Cop-out. I'm going to see you make something of yourself, Toddy Bethany. Then you're out of my house, woe be gone, and heaven help the man who marries you," said Polly. "But have something to fall back on before you get married, like a good education."

I sat on my bed and looked at the black-and-white television on the stand. I sure wasn't going to turn it on; there was too much of that funeral stuff for the senator on it. I remembered the funeral for Martin Luther King. That was enough for me. Instead, I put on a cheap flowered housedress, lay on the bed, closed my eyes, and got into my daydream mode about the Gingerbread Man. I dreamt of the first adult kiss that hadn't come yet but definitely would, tongue and all; our marriage; our house with a backyard and a dog, bigger than old Rene Wilkins's house; and the pitter-patter of little Bethany-Easter feet after a visit from the stork.

Then a lightning strike of excitement raced through my body, and my eyes flitted open. A surprise? What type of surprise did he have for me, I wondered? I'd find out on Saturday. There was a furious knock at my bedroom door.

"Toddy, are you looking at television, the news?" asked Polly.

"No," I said.

"Come in the living room—boy, have I got something to show you on the TV."

When I went into the living room, I saw she had rolled the color TV from Kevin's room into there. I looked at the TV, and lo and behold, there was a headshot of the pretender defender of the faith, the very pronounced Dickster, Brother Richard Quincy. He looked as if he had been shot out of a cannon—eyes bulging, and a creepy look that seemed to spell *I am guilty*. The anchor then broadcasted: "This social worker was arrested for allegedly stealing his client's underwear and attempting to strangle her with ropes." My mother and I looked at one another. Then, in shock, we held our breaths.

"I guess what doesn't come out in the wash comes out in the rinsing," said Polly.

"Yeah, Mama said Jehovah has a way of cleaning out his organization," I said.

"Maybe he's innocent. They say innocent till proven guilty," she said. "But he did something. I know he tried to strangle you."

At this, Polly raced to the phone. She called Mama, and they exchanged I guess what you could call congratulations about the dedicking of the Dickster. They only talked for a nanosecond, and then Polly burned the telephone lines to tell other people. She called Aunt Helen downtown at Kitchen University and told her what had happened.

I slipped into my room while she was on the phone, happy that I had been vindicated, that those condemning looks at the temple that followed me after my mother confronted the Dickster would change to "I'm sorry this happened" or "Perhaps we were wrong." But whatever; the icing on the cake was that I was vindicated.

I slid back into bed and returned to my daydream about the Gingerbread Man, letting the tingly feeling about the mysterious surprise intrigue me again. What could it be? An engagement ring? A million dollars? A partridge in a pear tree? I giggled and then turned on my side and went to sleep. I dreamed about the Gingerbread Man and the knucklehead: the former pure candy, the latter a nightmare from hell. As I dreamed about the knucklehead Norman, a nightmare where he was a bad character who shot up half a Midwestern town, I was awakened by Kevin's and Polly's voices.

"Ma, this thing about Brother Quincy—ah, the Panty Strangler Bandit," said Kevin, "should let you know that dating is not for you. Plus, my father wasn't too hot either."

"What?" said Polly.

"Like I said, Ma, your dating is bad. Besides, you too old to date."

"Look, boy, I'm dating, and if you give me any trouble, I'll work two jobs and send you to boarding school."

I snickered through my grogginess, kind of surprised that Kevin had mentioned his father. I couldn't remember a time when he acknowledged him without being questioned about him. You could never tell what was in this soon-to-be great man's mind.

The world is a bad place. These words buzzed in my thoughts like a melody, like one of those solo jazz sessions that Butch used to have in the basement of a house we rented; he'd blow and blow into his saxophone until he was breathless, then he'd walk up the basement steps into the kitchen and go look in the refrigerator for something to drink.

That's what the world had done to me in the last couple of days, months—left me breathless and searching for a cure. First MLK, then the senator, and some comic relief from the pretender defender of the faith Brother Quincy or, on a raunchier note, the Dickster. It was sort of like slapstick how he was arrested as a panty thief and strangler. The only gold star in this life was my upcoming date with the Gingerbread Man. I prayed and waited with bated breath for Saturday, and it came, sending my heart into overdrive as I wondered what surprise the Gingerbread Man or perhaps the knucklehead had in store for me.

At my request, he picked me up at 225th Street and White Plains Road, far away from the prying eyes of my do-good relatives and the goofy one, my brother Butch. My blackened eye had turned pink, and I dabbed some makeup on it so I could look like a dreamboat for the Gingerbread Man. It was warm, though early June, so I slipped on some Levi's and a blue short-sleeved psychedelic shirt—the off-orange and other colors appeared as if they were new hues introduced to the world, the prominent ones being yellow and pink. I debated whether to wear sandals or Converse sneakers. I choose the latter because if we were going to an amusement park, sneakers might be safer.

As I walked to my beloved down 225th, my giddiness had me singing that stupid song the cousin brothers had made up about Converse sneakers: "If your shoes slip and slide, get the one with the stars on the side—Cons, baby, Cons." I was Aladdin flying on a carpet cloud. The street was full of giddy people hugging the summer weather. I checked as I made my way to White Plains Road to see if any of my nosy relatives were perhaps following or watching me: my mother, Butch, Mama, or maybe my uncles Carey and Philbin.

The Gingerbread Man's car was parked under the elevated train, across the street from the Blue Moon Bar, which had become an emblem of the Dickster in my mind. He was sitting on the hood. Once he saw me, his mouth crooked into a smile. He bowed once I made it up to him and said in a faux British accent: "Milady, your faithful serf at your service."

"Where's the surprise, faithful serf?" I said.

"Well, milady, you'll have to wait until we get to the carnival."

I giggled and hopped into the front seat of the car. I was disappointed. I wanted the surprise now—front and center. But as he drove off, I studied him to see if he was the knucklehead or Gingerbread Man: his skin was smooth like black velvet, his voice sounded energetic, not the melancholy voice of a loser, and his smile seemed to come from something that glowed inside his soul. He turned for a second from the road, and our eyes locked. I knew then that he was pure Gingerbread Man.

"What're you looking at, good-looking?" he asked.

"You tell me," I said.

We both laughed. The car clanked up White Plains Road until we reached 241st, and then he turned left to enter the hilly Mount Vernon. He whipped the deep slopes of Mount Vernon—which could make you nauseous from its steep slopes—like a mountain climber, skillfully.

Strangely enough, our destination was where he'd found me that fateful night when the Dickster was strangling and shooting me—in front of McLean State Park. This time it wasn't cold and barren like late winter or early spring as it had been; everything was abloom: the oak trees, foot-long daffodils, and grass, which looked blue from a distance, made a great picture.

And there was a carnival smack-dab in the middle of this. The Ferris wheel, the roller coaster, and the carousel jutted above the crowds and the other structures of the small carnival. Their colors were pink, yellow, and red—all the boldest pastels. I was sorry I hadn't brought my camera. The Gingerbread Man parked in a lot for the patrons across from the entrance of the carnival. He shut off the engine and took the key out of the ignition.

"Is this the surprise?" I asked.

"No," he said.

"Well, what is it?"

"I'm off of drugs and alcohol. I'm clean and dry," he said. "After that night at the opera, I did it; you helped by letting me have it about leaving you flat like your father."

"Wow, Norman, you're not a knucklehead anymore."

"Whoa, what's this knucklehead business?"

"It doesn't matter; now you're my Gingerbread Man."

"I guess I'm as sweet as sugar now and remind you of your father."

"Of course not."

"Of course I do. My brother, who is a psychiatrist," he said, "says a woman really marries a man like her father, and a man marries a woman like his mother."

"Really?"

"And this is the other surprise—two tickets to the opera I messed up for you. You said I left you flat with your enemies." He reached into his pocket and produced two green ticket stubs. "So we'll go back to the opera and stick it to your enemies. I will redeem myself with you, milady." He did a half bow and handed me the tickets.

We left the car and went to the carnival. He coaxed me to get on the roller coaster, which I was terrified of, and once I did, I felt right at home in the carnival. He won me a three-foot teddy bear by shooting balloons with an air rifle. I felt like a little girl again when we went on the carousel, getting nauseous like I had when my father took me.

By then it felt like late August—hot, humid, and gooey, as if I needed to take another shower. It wasn't even officially summer yet, but the heat was stifling. Norman bought me a drink of root beer soda and a hot dog, and it seemed to reinvigorate me. Then we went to the Ferris wheel. I thought it looked tame compared to the carousel and roller coaster.

We hopped on like a bunch of schoolchildren. Once the circular movement of the ride started, the engineer who worked the ride begin blaring the music. As the lyrics being sung by Johnny Mathis blared from the record player, the Gingerbread Man put his arm around me and pulled me closer to him. The singer belted out the ballad.

"I'll be seeing you in all those all familiar places that this heart of mine embraces all day through …"

"My mother has that record," I said.

"Mine does too."

The sun blazed on the side of his face, giving him a silhouette aura, and his profile reminded me of my father. I was embarrassed about what he'd said about people marrying or loving someone like their mother or father. I wanted to love the Gingerbread Man for who he was, not for who I wanted him to be. Sure, I wished my father was at home being my mother's husband

and our father; this way my mother wouldn't have to work twelve hours a day, and we'd have a bigger apartment—maybe even a home like Rene Wilkins's. Sometimes I dreamed about having an at-home father, and it made me sad because it was just a dream.

"A penny for your thoughts," said the Gingerbread Man.

"Thanks a million," I said.

Suddenly the record began speeding out of control, making the singer sound like Alvin and the Chipmunks; the Ferris wheel stopped as if someone had stepped on the brakes, and the wheel started going counterclockwise. It was moving real fast, seemingly fifty miles an hour, while the record continued in its chipmunk sound. My teddy bear went sailing out of my arms. As things went haywire, I was afraid that I was going to fall out of my seat because I was sliding back and forth and side to side.

Norman held me close to his chest to steady us. "Hold tight, baby, this is a bumpy ride," he said.

Then the sun disappeared beneath a big cloud and the sky turned gray. It began thundering, and I remembered everything in the book about the dangers of lightning and thunder. Buckets of rain came down like cats and dogs. The Ferris wheel sped on until it stopped, leaving the Gingerbread Man's and my seat at the top near the bolts of lightning and the rumble of thunder. Then Johnny Mathis's voice returned to normal. No longer the chipmunk-sounding bard, he resumed singing, "I'll Be Seeing You."

A couple of bolts of lightning shot over our heads. I screamed, "Norman, we'll die up here from a lightning strike—we're unprotected."

"Don't worry, milady," he said. "Your faithful serf will take any lightning bolt that comes this way, and if this poor serf survives, I will marry you."

A tingly feeling came over me, like the time I was at the recital at Carnegie Hall and curtsied and curtsied on stage, holding onto the moment and not wanting to let go, until I was led off the stage by Professor Mills. But the sounds of sirens interrupted this rush I had from the marriage proposal. It was the fire and police departments coming to rescue us.

As I clutched onto my Gingerbread Man's water-soaked body, I felt safe like I'd felt when my father was around, like my mother did too. When he first left and we rented a new apartment, Polly was so frightened of being alone that when we went out, she poured flour in front of the door and in front of the windows just in case someone broke in, so she could capture their footfalls. Somehow, even now, but not as much so, we lived in a state of perpetual fear, even with the hand of God on us.

By the time Norman and I were lifted from the Ferris wheel, the machine was completely broken and our rescuers had to go seat to seat to take us off the ride. Once we were brought to safety, I got the big teddy bear; it had fallen where the engineer worked, and he handed it to me. When we got to the car, Norman went into the trunk and got two woolen blankets for us to keep warm.

"Can you come to my house tomorrow?" he asked. "I want you to meet my mother."

"Sure. But what should I wear? Is it formal or informal?"

"Just wear you—" he said. "Wear whatever you want—just don't come in the buff."

We both giggled. Then he began belting out the song that Johnny Mathis had sung while we were on the Ferris wheel, a beautiful song until everything went haywire and the voice went to chipmunk. I joined in too. It was my business to make this song my own, to make it the Gingerbread Man's and my signature song, as my mother and father had made the song "The Very Thought of You" their personal love song.

We ignored the uneven and steep slopes of the roads of Mount Vernon, which could bounce the sturdiest of drivers and passengers, and sang our love song with perfect tempo.

> I'll be seeing you
> In all the old familiar places
> That this heart of mine embraces.

I looked at the Gingerbread Man, and he had a satisfied look on his face. We had made it to the Bronx and were under the elevated train on White Plains Road; we had whipped the treacherous hills of Mount Vernon and finished *our* love song even though we had swiped it from my mother's generation. This love song was written for parting lovers during World War II, but it was ours now.

I was still wet, but the chill from the water was gone; my body was invigorated with warmth as if my veins were full of hot chocolate. I moved a matted, rain-soaked piece of my hair from my face.

"We sounded better than Johnny Mathis ever did with that song," I said.

"Milady," said the Gingerbread Man, "it is you who has the voice, not your faithful serf."

The Gingerbread Man was like Lollipop and my father—always propping me up, cheerleading me to great heights. When he dropped me off in front of my house, he gave me a slip of paper with his address on it. "Dinner is at 6:00 p.m. I won't be in until 5:00 p.m.," he said. "My mom is kind of sick, so she might have to go rest if she starts feeling weak."

"I'll help out if you need me, Norman."

He smiled then got out of the car and went to the passenger's side to open the door for me. He gave me one of his faithful serf bows and handed me the three-foot dark-brown teddy bear that he had won at the carnival. It was still soaking wet. I wanted to kiss him, but I didn't.

CHAPTER 21

Polly saw me coming into the house soaking wet and had her usual whiteless-eye expression on her face. The house smelled of lamb spiced with parsley. I still had my love-infected smile on my face from my encounter with the Gingerbread Man. I had news for her: I wasn't going to let anyone urinate on my parade—not even Polly.

"Huh. You need to take that simp look off your face and take those clothes off before you get pneumonia." She pointed at the wet teddy bear I had draped in my arms. "What've you got there?"

"A teddy bear."

"What's its name?"

"Gingerbread Man Jr."

"Sounds serious to me."

"Yeah, it's as serious as cancer."

"I hope you're using that birth control I gave you," said Polly. "Do you need a refill?"

"No," I mumbled.

I clicked my teeth and sucked my tongue. Oh, how repulsive. It was all about getting pregnant and not about love. She'd be as happy as a lark to know the Gingerbread Man hadn't laid a hand on me and that I could still wear my virgin pin honestly and proudly, if she even knew that the girls wore it to show they still had their cherry. I bid her good night and went into my room.

I took off my wet clothes, placed the teddy bear on a chair, and covered it with a beach towel, taking care to leave its face exposed because it reminded me of the Gingerbread Man. The tickets he had given me for the opera on

Thursday were a little damp, so I placed them on the radiator, even though it was too warm for steam to come up.

I dropped into bed exhausted—being in love was tiring. If I was tied to the Gingerbread Man, I had to leave Lollipop and his vamp problems alone. If Rene Wilkins and the vamps at the temple were putting a noose around his life, the boy had better come out swinging. He'd learn. Let him learn on his own; I was too tied up to teach him. It's like they say: "Experience is a good teacher, though not the best."

I awoke giddy with anticipation about eating dinner at the Gingerbread Man's house and meeting his mother. I got out of bed and looked at the address he had written on an index card to find out where I was going. It was on the radiator with the tickets, which were now dry. The index card had become fragile, and some of the ink had run down the card. I fingered it gingerly, looking for the address.

I looked at the address and gasped, and then I felt completely out of my league. He lived at 969 East 231st Street, a big building that looked like a mansion with eight Greek columns and a porch so big that it looked like it could hold the entire Roman senate. There had even been an article about the building in *Better Homes and Gardens*.

My Gingerbread Man was a somebody. Polly would be tickled pink to know I knew someone of this stature. She thought people who accomplished things were great people, maybe too much so. Just because you were accomplished didn't make you a good and decent person, or as Mama said, "There hasn't been a good man since Jesus Christ." Of course he was perfect.

What could I possibly wear to make a good impression among these swells? Oh yes, Norman said I could wear anything except my naked behind—maybe the lime gown that I'd worn when we went to Lincoln Center. I think it would be fitting and proper to get spruced up for a spruced-up place; ostentatiousness had its place amid ostentatiousness. Polly came into the room as I became more intoxicated with delight. She had her nose rolled to her top lip, signaling that something was stinking, either literally or figuratively.

"Guess what?" she asked.

"What?"

"According to the grapevine, Brother Quincy has just pleaded guilty to burglary," said Polly. "Mama says the women in the congregation were complaining that their panties were missing." They say he had over ten thousand pairs of women's underwear in his house."

"Well, I guess I've been vindicated," I said.

"Yeah, I can't wait to get to the temple," she said. "I know the hens in the grapevine are clucking like pregnant chickens."

I was tingling with delight that the Dickster, the pretender defender of the faith and my strangler, had had his comeuppance and would be off the streets for a while. I prayed that he would repent and change his ways. Now that the Dickster nightmare was over, it seemed like life was beginning to add up for me: the Dickster had been defrocked, and my sweet, lovely Gingerbread Man was no longer a knucklehead, which meant that he loved me more than he loved that white powder, enough to want to marry me.

Was I too young to marry? What would happen to Polly? Maybe the Gingerbread Man and I were racing to eternity; I was on a roller coaster or that Ferris wheel that had gone haywire, and I might want to get off. I finally got a grip on myself and calmed down. If he asked, I had the option of yes or no—no one could force you to marry. But still I got a tingly feeling in my sex when I thought about the prospect.

CHAPTER 22

At the temple, the hens were in corners talking in muffled tones about the Dickster. On any other occasion, I would have bent my ear to listen to some juicy gossip, but I was too hyped up about eating dinner at the Gingerbread Man's house and meeting his mother. After service, I separated from my mother and Kevin, who were going to Mama's house to oil the gossip and scandal machine about the Dickster, and went home to get dressed for my Gingerbread Man encounter.

It was late June, a couple of days before my birthday, even though I didn't celebrate, and the end of the school year, yet it was as hot and humid as August. Walking home, I was boiled from the heat: my curls wilted, I was wet under the arms, and my clothes clung to my body as if they had been glued.

I quickly reshowered when I got home. I put on the lime gown that had dazzled the Gingerbread Man at the concert and my father at Carnegie Hall, and I profiled and styled in front of the mirror until I was satisfied that I was the belle of the ball. Then I called a cab to take me to the Gingerbread Man's house. When I got into the cab, not only were there butterflies in my stomach, but also they were circulating in my veins. It was like the night of the Carnegie Hall recital; I was exhilarated and scared, but raring to go.

When the cab pulled into the rich-looking block with trees, front lawns, and stately houses that looked like they belonged on a magazine cover, I felt big and small at the same time. I belonged there because I belonged to the Gingerbread Man and he to me, and I was small because these were the things that Polly wanted for us: the house, the front lawn—things she dreamed about but whose reach was too far to grab.

After I paid the cab driver, I pranced up to the front door. It was white, the same color as the eight ostentatious columns that jutted from the front and were undoubtedly more than ornaments to brag that you had something; their purpose was to support the house.

There were crickets singing in the background by the time I rang the doorbell; even they sounded rich. The doorbell sang the forever gongs that seemed to be in every 1940s movie where the protagonist is standing in front of a mansion and rings the bell, and gongs go on and on until the maid with the uniform swings the door open.

When the door opened, I was so bedazzled by the richness of the environment that I expected a maid to pop out in a black uniform and white apron. It was the Gingerbread Man. He looked at me like he was surprised to see me. His eyes were red and swollen as if he had fallen asleep on something that had mashed his face. Damn, was he a knucklehead again?

"Hi," I said.

"I should've called you," he said. "My mother died this morning."

"Wow. I'm sorry. Is there anything I can do?"

"No. But I'll be busy for a couple of days."

I gave him a big hug. He placed his hands on each side of my face. "You take care of yourself." He kissed me—really kissed me. His tongue darted into my mouth and then just as quickly darted back out. My sex twitched, and I became ashamed that it had done this at such a sacred moment as the death of his mother. I knew it was time to go. I gave him another hug and gently pushed him into the open door, and we ended up at the beginning of a long foyer.

I unzipped my gown. It fell to the floor. I pressed my body to his. He bent down, snatched the dress off the floor, and handed it back to me. "Don't ever throw your life away like that. This is your life; don't throw it away."

I threw the dress back on the floor and pressed my body against his again, and we slowly dropped to the carpeted floor. I felt the pain of my cherry being ripped, and I knew it was over. I put my dress back on, and he broke into a smile.

"I'll get back to you after things calm down," he said softly.

We gave one another one final kiss and a big bear hug, and then I left. I was so hyped that I decided to walk home, even though my torn cherry hurt and I was obviously bleeding. The sky turned and it began to drizzle. At that moment I heard the word my mother had called me when I told her about the Dickster and bar night—*strumpet*, a common whore. I seemed to remember every scripture in the Bible about fornication, and at that second I felt worthless—as Polly liked to say, like two cents. But I had given my cherry, which I could never get back, to my Gingerbread Man, who wanted to marry me, so it was worthwhile. It seemed like a good deal.

When I got home, Polly was in the dining area talking with Kevin, I guess discussing his upcoming trip to basketball camp. I waved at her like I was in a trance, but I tried to cover up my feelings because losing my cherry was the last thing I wanted her to know.

"You look like death warmed over in that beautiful dress," Polly said. "You look like a melancholy baby, as the song says."

"I'm on my period."

"Amen," said Polly.

I wasn't, but I knew that this would get her off my back, and she'd be happy to know I wasn't pregnant—or left holding the bag as she liked to say. I hurried to my room to avoid any inquiries about my state of mind. I eventually took a bath and washed the paste of maleness and blood between my legs that was in the place of my cherry.

After I put on my pajamas, I went to the chair where the three-foot teddy bear rested. I pulled him into my arms and gave him a full-tongue kiss on his sewn-on brown lips as I had done with the Gingerbread Man. I placed him back on the chair and said, "I guess we're both orphans now. I'm a half orphan because my father left us flat, and I guess you're one too because your mother died." I had never met Gingerbread Man's father, nor had I ever heard him speak of him. Perhaps he was a full orphan now, I didn't know. But we were kindred spirits. At least I had Polly. A chill came over me just thinking of Polly dying.

The first thing I thought about when I woke up to go to school was the Gingerbread Man. I felt doubly sad because I couldn't help him; all I could do was wait. I dressed and left the house before Kevin, and once I made it to the front of the building, I bumped into people coming from and going to work. Polly was one of them. She smiled. "You're really growing up. I didn't even have to get you out of bed."

I smiled back. "I do my best." The only reason I'd left early was to use the pay phone in front of the school to talk to the Gingerbread Man privately. When I called, the line was busy. I slammed the phone on the receiver, disappointed I couldn't get him. I went through the motions during school, wishing for the day to end so I could call Norman again. When I did phone him, it just rang and rang. I became scared and disappointed at the same time.

When I got home, Kevin was in his room with the curtain open. He glanced at me briefly then turned away as if he were hiding something. My mother was in the dining area looking scared and frightened, the same way she had looked when she found out that my father had deserted us and he was nowhere to be found. She must have seen the concern on my face because she broke out in a smile as if she were trying to cover her real emotions. As I headed in the direction of the kitchen, she handed me a stack of *Ebony* and *Jet* magazines and said, "Take these to Mama."

"I just came from school," I said. "I'm tired."

"But Mama wants to see you."

"Okay, Ma."

Polly knew how to make me feel guilty. I just couldn't say no to Mama—not my mama. Besides, in the laws of the universe, she didn't have many years left on earth, like the Gingerbread Man's mother. I figured I should make every minute like gold for her while she was still alive. I took the stack of magazines, went into the kitchen, got a large paper shopping bag, and placed the magazines in it. I poured a glass of lemonade and gulped it down my dry throat. I glanced at Polly as I left the kitchen.

Kevin and Polly seemed strange; it was as if they were on another planet. The house was eerily silent, no music or anything, not even the fabulous jazz and crooners Polly loved so well. I didn't understand the mood in the house—they were either sad or too tired.

"Ma, what's going on?" I asked.

"Nothing. Just go over to Mama's house," she said. "She wants to see you."

I walked up East 225th Street, hot from the humidity and confused. There was a pay phone on the corner of Bronxwood Avenue. I rushed to it and called Norman again. It rang and rang until it sounded like church bells. "Oh boy, where could he be?" I asked myself when I placed the phone on the receiver. A smile crossed my lips as I remembered how we'd made love on the foyer floor and how now I was finally his. He wanted to marry me, and now I couldn't say no because we belonged to one another. Of course I would eventually tell him I was really going to be fourteen in a couple of weeks.

I crossed the long Paulding Avenue to Mama's house. The building looked like a dreary silhouette; the sun was behind the building instead of in front, making it look like a haunted house. I knew when I walked up the steps that Mama's house would be kind of dark, because as she'd said, "Why shouldn't I cut down on the electricity before sunset to stop making Con Edison rich?"

When I reached the door, before I could ring the doorbell, Lisa popped out holding her jump rope, heading downstairs to play with the children in front of the building. She gave me a sorrowful look, then called over her shoulder, "Mama, Toddy's here," and went about her business. The house was dark as if a cloud was in the apartment. Mama was in the living room, sitting at the sewing machine. We greeted one another.

"Where do you want me to put the bag of magazines?" I asked.

"Put it anywhere," she said. "Don't rush out; sit a spell and talk with me."

I placed the bag of magazines on the floor next to the chair where I sat. I was only able to see the side of her face. I looked at what she was working on at the machine. It was a black dress. The room grew quiet; it was unusual for her not to be singing or chitchatting in the chair. It seemed the world had gone crazy. My family was acting kind of nutty.

"I'm fixing this dress," she said. "I'm going to my friend Norma Easter's funeral."

"Really?" I asked.

I was surprised but not shocked to know that she knew the Gingerbread Man's mother; after all, she knew everyone in the neighborhood. But I wondered if she knew that I knew the Easters, specifically, if she knew Norman's and my business. I looked up to see if she had one of those "I've got your number" looks that she always had on her face when she knew your secret. Our eyes locked; hers were completely dark like Polly's when something was going wrong. "It's going to be a double funeral. Her son Norman shot himself in the head."

I turned my face away from her and pulled my chin to my chest as if I were hiding. This was not so. I just saw him yesterday. It must be a dream. If I pinched myself or heard Polly calling me to get out of bed to go to school, I'd wake up. I looked around the darkened room; everything appeared surreal and gloomy. This undertaker's-looking house couldn't be Mama's house; it must be part of the dream. A flicker of sun came through the blinds and shocked my eyes closed for a second. When I opened them again, the room was alive with sun.

I looked at my grandmother again, who sat waiting for an answer from me about her statement. This was when I knew this was real, as real as cancer. Tears fell down my cheeks like rain from a storm. I stiffened my neck and spine and sat as straight as a board. I splayed my arms and shook them as if I were a rag doll. "I don't know any fucking Easters."

All at once, I bolted from the sofa and ran from the apartment. Mama yelled for me to come back, but the sound of her voice just made me run faster. I ran down the street fast, so fast that all objects were blurred. I was riding on a roller coaster of emotions, confused about Norman and ashamed that I had cursed Mama. I ran until I was breathless.

When I got home, the house was empty. I found out later that Mama had called and said that I had flipped out and that they were looking for me. I grabbed my teddy bear, Mr. Gingerbread Man Jr., and headed for Bronx Park.

CHAPTER 23

When I got to Bronx Park, I sat on one of the cold wooden benches until it got dark. I pinned my virgin pin on the teddy bear, Mr. Gingerbread Man Jr., and threw it in the Bronx River. I watched in the moonlight as it went somewhere in the Bronx, taking my childhood with it. My childhood was over, and I knew it was a possibility that I might be pregnant. If I was going to give up my cherry, it would have made sense to give it up to the Dickster—at least he was alive—or else wait to get married to Hayes, my Lollipop.

Whatever I had for Norman turned to pity. I didn't go to his funeral. I don't know why. Mama went to the funeral, and afterward when she came to pick Lisa up, who'd been left with us because she was too young to go, she discussed the details as if it were a social event and not the passing of someone dear. I blanked my mind completely and ignored the details.

Days later, Polly came into my room, sat at the head of the bed where I was sitting, and patted me on the shoulder, as if I needed it. I had been moping around for days like I was the only one in the universe. She said something about Kevin and Butch patching things up, which I knew, but it seemed she had said it to break the ice for the important things.

"I knew all about Norman, but what could I do?" she whispered. "My friends told me that I should put you in reform school because you don't listen, but I can't throw my baby away like that. You're a troublemaker, not a bad kid like a murderer." We both giggled at that. She touched my stomach and then whispered, "If you're pregnant, you can have it, or I can have it fixed. It's not legal, and God doesn't approve of it, but I can have it fixed." Tears fell down her cheeks. "You're not thinking of hurting yourself like that boy?"

"No!" I said.

My insides felt like two cents as Polly liked to say. She was willing to go to jail for me and lose her religion. I looked in her eyes and saw the hope in them. For all her life, I had been this woman's dream. I fell into her arms, and we began to cry. The next day, my period came.

Acknowledgments

I would like to extend my thanks to the iUniverse Editorial Department for their excellent editing of this novel.

Printed in the United States
By Bookmasters